The biggest secret in London is about to be . . . revealed.

Every gentleman is wondering: Who is the beauty in the scandalous nude portrait hanging in one of London's most fashionable clubs? Is it true that she's a member of the *ton*? Who would be so daring. So reckless?

Julian Delane, Earl of Parkhurst, has a good idea. So good, in fact, that he's willing to make a wager on it. If only the bet were all that's at stake . . .

Determined to clear the family name from a scandal that claimed his father's life, Julian believes the ravishing model will lead him to answers. Rebecca Leland—spirited, adventurous, with a bit of a wild streak—is just as determined to evade his questions. But when Julian finally corners his quarry, he may find Rebecca well worth the pursuit.

In Pursuit of a Scandalous Lady

Gayle Callen

AVON

An Imprint of HarperCollinsPublishers

This is a work of fiction. Names, characters, places, and incidents are products of the author's imagination or are used fictitiously and are not to be construed as real. Any resemblance to actual events, locales, organizations, or persons, living or dead, is entirely coincidental.

AVON BOOKS
An Imprint of HarperCollins*Publishers*
10 East 53rd Street
New York, New York 10022-5299

Copyright © 2010 by Gayle Kloecker Callen
ISBN 978-0-06-178341-8
www.avonromance.com

First Avon Books paperback printing: May 2010

Avon Trademark Reg. U.S. Pat. Off. and in Other Countries, Marca Registrada, Hecho en U.S.A.
HarperCollins® is a registered trademark of HarperCollins Publishers.

Printed in the U.S.A.

10 9 8 7 6 5 4 3 2 1

*To my sister-in-law, Rosemary Kloecker:
Thanks so much for becoming my sister when
you married my brother. You bring such joy
and laughter to our family, but especially to
my mother, whom you love as if she were your
own. Words can't express my gratitude.*

In Pursuit of
A Scandalous Lady

Chapter 1

London, 1846

Julian Delane, Earl of Parkhurst, stared at the painting of the nude woman displayed in the saloon of the gentlemen's club, transfixed. Behind him, the last of the evening's gamblers called loudly to each other at the faro tables. He stood shoulder to shoulder with his friends, Leo Wade and Peter Derby, admiring the way the model's body glowed in candlelit darkness, swathed in a long scarf that enticed rather than hid. She reclined on her side, body arched, head completely hidden in shadows. Though she was the perfection of the female form, his mind was already thinking beyond the obvious titillation to the realization that had swept over him the moment he saw the painting: regardless of her obscured features, he knew the woman's identity by the red heart-shaped diamond resting between the lovely curves of her breasts.

A gift from a maharajah to his father, the rare jewel,

called the Scandalous Lady, had been stolen from his family more than ten years before. Its loss had caused cruel gossip . . . and his father's death. He'd thought it gone forever—until yesterday when Miss Rebecca Leland had appeared at a ball brazenly displaying it for all the world to see. He'd been stunned, nearly overcome by the urge to make a spectacle of himself by confronting her before all of the *ton*.

Since then he'd been making plans for how best to approach Miss Leland with his questions, and had only allowed himself to be dragged out this night in hopes that Leo, who knew everyone, could tell him something about the woman. As he had not considered Rebecca in his meticulous research for a proper bride, he realized he knew very little about her other than that an alliance with her scandal-plagued family would not meet his requirements.

Yet . . . how could the model in this painting be her, a sensual image, a man's desperate dream, the supposedly innocent young cousin of the Duke of Madingley?

"Isn't the painting magnificent?" Leo drawled, his cheroot clenched between his teeth.

Leo grinned, his dimples winking, his blond curls disheveled, as if a woman had recently run her hands through his hair. And one probably had. On Julian's other side, Peter Derby, quieter, tall and sandy-haired, tilted his head and narrowed his eyes, as if he could will to life the secrets of the painting. Both men were younger sons, with competent elder brothers. Julian almost envied them.

Leo had been trying to lure him away from his work for several days, raving about the new painting. Now Julian regretted the lost time.

"Who is she?" he found himself asking, though he already knew the truth.

"That's the interesting part," Leo said. He raised his brows and gave a devilish smile. "She's one of us."

Peter choked on a cough. "What did you say?"

Leo laughed. "She's of Society, my boy."

Julian exhaled slowly. What more proof did he need of Miss Leland's identity as the model? "Surely you're mistaken," he said in a mild voice, hoping for information.

"Not according to the artist," Leo continued. "His name is Roger Eastfield."

"I've heard of him," Peter said, surprise in his voice. "My brother collects his work."

"I can see why," Julian said dryly. It was not so easy to concentrate on the jewel, the source of so much family trauma, when the woman's golden assets were larger than life, glowing as if with the luster of a pearl.

"Eastfield approached the managers of the club with a sad story about the painting," Leo continued. "Apparently he's a rather reclusive young man and not wise in the way of the world. He said it had been meant for a private collection in France until the money fell through. There was something about an ill mother, and needing money to visit her, but in the end, the beauty of the painting persuaded the managers to purchase it."

"But a woman of Society?" Peter asked doubtfully.

"All of us have secrets," Julian mused.

"Let me finish," Leo said with exasperation. "He wanted more money than the managers would offer, so he sweetened the deal, swearing that the model is a woman from a prominent family of the *ton*."

A ducal family, Julian knew. One could not be more prominent unless a member of the royal family. But he somehow couldn't see young Queen Victoria acting so foolhardily.

"And they believed him?" Peter threw his hands wide.

"They did. He has a reputation for honesty. The diamond helps, of course. Exquisite, don't you think?"

Julian said nothing. Cursed was what it was.

Leo threw his arms around each of their shoulders. "I was looking forward to seeing your face, Julian. You're settled now, man, your family at peace at last. Can you not enjoy life?"

Julian had hoped for that, of course, had begun to put into place his plan to find the perfect wife. But the reappearance of the diamond changed everything. He had to see what else Leo might know about Rebecca Leland—without appearing *too* interested. "I'll enjoy taking your money," he said, forcing a smile. "Shall we play?"

Laughing, the three of them left the saloon and found the private card room empty. For several more hours, they played and talked and drank, until the other members were gone, and they'd sent the last waiter to bed in the servants' quarters on the top floor. Julian learned little else about Rebecca except a tidbit from Peter that she had spent much of her childhood closeted away due to numerous illnesses. Julian thought about the woman he'd seen at the ball, the bold way she'd strode across the gleaming floor, the way men had eyed her—she looked too alive to be sickly.

The club was quiet as they concentrated on their cards, eyeing each other with friendly competitiveness, smoke from Leo's cheroot drifting around them. Suddenly, they heard a sound, muffled even as it echoed up the grand staircase in the main hall.

The three men exchanged curious glances.

"I thought the staff had gone to bed," Julian said.

"So they told us." Peter scratched his head and yawned. "Think they're coming to kick us out."

"They wouldn't do that to an earl," Leo said, nodding toward Julian.

"Or the brother of a viscount," Julian shot back, thinking he'd had a bit too much to drink. He put up a hand, frowning, and spoke in a softer voice. "I heard nothing else. Someone is deliberately trying to be quiet." He tilted his head toward the closed door and waited.

At the next creak of the stair, someone hushed someone else out in the hall. The gazes of the three men met and held, even as their smiles died.

Julian reached and turned down the lamp until they could barely see. "So they won't notice us when we open the door," he whispered, then got to his feet.

When the two men crowded drunkenly behind him, he had to push them back, the gloom too great for them to see his warning frown. Very slowly, he opened the door, grateful that the hinges were well oiled. He could see little at first, his eyes yet unaccustomed to the gloom, except for the tiny bobbing flame from a single candle. But the cavernous hall, with the staircase rising up through the center, was lit from below by a single lamp.

It illuminated the cautious steps of three figures just reaching the first floor. They wore dark trousers, coats and hats, but were slight enough that Julian whispered over his shoulder, "They're boys."

He turned back to peer out, feeling his friends crowding behind him. They all watched the youths creep toward the main saloon and disappear within.

Julian gestured and emerged from the card room, the other two trailing behind him. They made no sound, which was amazing for three men well into their cups. Large hunting portraits covering all the way to the ceiling of the hall were silhouetted in the gloom, a spark of light occasionally catching a golden frame.

Julian, Leo, and Peter reached the doorway to the saloon and cautiously peered in. The three young intruders stood with their backs to the door, facing the nude portrait.

"Boys will be boys," Leo whispered.

Julian glared at him and Leo rolled his eyes.

The boys whispered among themselves, then separated along the length of the painting, put their hands on the frame, and attempted to lift.

Those were not the rough hands of boys, but were slim and delicate.

Julian stepped into the room, knowing that the meager light of a single candle would barely illuminate him. "Caught in the act," he said, his deep voice cutting into the silence.

He heard several gasps. The painting frame banged against the wall, but hadn't been dislodged. The three figures seemed frozen.

"You can't run," Julian continued. "We are between you and escape. Now why don't you turn around, so we can see the thieves who dare attempt to steal the club's painting?"

They seemed to share an unspoken communication, then slowly turned around, heads lowered, their faces shadowed beneath the brims of their caps. The single candle wavered on a table beside them. The "boys" slumped, shoulders rounded, hands in pockets, scuffing booted toes on the floor.

"We were just looking," one said in a low, husky voice.

"As you lifted the painting?" Leo asked in amusement. As he used their candle to light a lamp, they all backed up against the wall, shoulders brushing the painting. "I didn't know I was so threatening," he added dryly.

"They should feel threatened," Julian said. "We're witnesses to their crime. It's a shame they can't induce us to forget that this happened."

There was a pregnant pause.

Peter sighed loudly. "Shall I awaken the proprietor?"

"Wait!" one of the thieves called, voice desperate—and an octave higher.

"Take off your hat," Julian commanded.

Again the thieves seemed to commune as they glanced at each other. The one who'd spoken stepped forward, shoulders back, and removed the cap. Dark brown hair gleamed where it wound about her head. One lustrous curl slid slowly to her shoulder. Julian inhaled swiftly.

Rebecca Leland, the woman who'd revealed herself without qualm for a public painting, taking the chance that she would forever ruin her reputation.

In the low light, her eyes glittered, full of pride and

defiance. Her complexion glowed in her heart-shaped face, her lips taut but full. She didn't betray her nerves by licking them, but something dark inside Julian wished she would. He mentally shook himself, irritated that he was distracted by a pretty face. And he never usually overindulged in drink either. The latter was surely why he noticed that the open collar of her shirt showed the delicate lines of her throat. The loose fit of her coat could not hide the roundness of her breasts. He well remembered the way such lushness had framed the heart-shaped diamond.

But the diamond and her indiscretion were all on display, bold as life, filling the wall behind her head like an invitation to sin. What did she think of her erotic exhibit? Was she embarrassed? Did her companions even know the truth?

As the tension in the room escalated, filling the air with the heaviness that usually preceded a thunderstorm, the other two women bravely followed their leader, removing their hats.

"Ladies, we have not been formally introduced," Julian said, feeling as if he were speaking only to Rebecca.

"Susanna—" Peter began, but stopped himself.

The women all glanced at Peter with a trace of chagrin. He was evidently on more familiar terms with the young ladies.

Leo chuckled. "Lord Parkhurst, you are making the

acquaintance of the Leland sisters, Susanna and Rebecca, and their cousin Lady Elizabeth Cabot, sister of
the duke."

Julian knew that the duke was half Spanish, so he
deduced that the black-haired woman was his sister.
That left the redhead for Rebecca's sister. He thought
he saw a resemblance to Rebecca beneath the spectacles
Susanna wore. They had the same delicate nose and
bold cheekbones. But Rebecca by far had the lushest
mouth.

"I can think of only one reason that three ladies of
Society would dare to invade a gentlemen's club," Julian
said slowly.

Crimson splashed across Rebecca's cheeks—but then
he could not imagine that she was innocent.

"We dared each other," she said.

He arched a brow and sauntered closer. He knew he
was too big, too broad-shouldered for a Society gentleman. He had the body of a boxer, and he saw the flicker
of apprehension in Susanna's eyes as he approached.

But Rebecca only glared up at him, obviously unim-
pressed by his intimidation.

"You dared each other to steal this particular painting?" he countered.

She didn't look to her compatriots for confirmation.
"Of course not. We could hardly expect to steal such a
thing. We wanted to play a prank and hide it."

"So you knew about this painting?"

"No! But how could we not choose it, once we arrived? I dare say, men as a species are rather vulgar."

Said the woman who'd posed nude, Julian thought with a trace of amusement. "I think there is another reason you targeted this painting," he said. "The artist, Roger Eastfield, claims the model is a young lady of Society. So which of you is it?"

He pointed to the painting, saw all three women look that way. Color rose in their faces, and he imagined they must feel embarrassed. Rebecca lifted her chin, determination flattening her mouth.

But before she could say anything, both Elizabeth and Susanna spoke in perfect harmony. "I'm the model."

Julian heard Leo chuckle, but he didn't take his gaze from Rebecca's face. She grinned up at him, her changeable hazel eyes suddenly twinkling.

"*I'm* the model," she said.

He crossed his arms over his chest, saw the way her gaze darted—nervously?—down his body. He could not help his reluctant feeling of admiration at their bravery. They were all protecting Rebecca.

"Now, isn't this a puzzle," Leo murmured, amusement lacing his words.

"Oh, come now, ladies," Peter said. "I would not have expected this from any of you. If your brothers knew of this—"

"They aren't in town," Elizabeth interrupted boldly.

"During the height of the Season?" Julian asked.

Now he knew why the women had felt so free to make mischief.

"They're hunting in—" Susanna broke off at Rebecca's warning frown.

"Hunting," Leo said, openly rubbing his hands together. "Hunting in . . . the country? Another country? I happen to know the duke has extensive property in Scotland."

Elizabeth said nothing, but her dark eyes were full of chagrin.

Julian's focus was more intense than any he'd experienced in the ten years since he'd begun to resurrect the earldom. He wanted to demand answers, to shake Rebecca until she told him about the stolen diamond called the Scandalous Lady, and how she'd come to wear it to a ball.

"You have to let us leave," Rebecca said.

He hoped his direct stare was making her nervous. "No, we don't. We could report this."

"Or perhaps we won't," Leo said, sauntering forward. "I don't know you ladies well—"

"But we know of *you*," Susanna said with the disapproval of a stern governess to her charge. Her spectacles glittered in the lamplight as if with their aid she dissected him.

Leo put a hand on his chest and bowed. "Then my reputation precedes me. Allow me to prove that I can live up to your beliefs. Gentlemen, I propose a wager."

Julian didn't want to be distracted by such drunken foolery, but he forced himself to be patient, an ability that had aided him well over the years. He'd spent his childhood patiently waiting to rescue his family, then his adulthood patiently guiding his investments and businesses, even while patiently seeking the proper bride. Leo's wager might work out to Julian's benefit.

"What is it?" Peter asked warily.

Leo smiled. "I propose that we each try to determine the real identity of the model—any way we can."

A momentary silence grew and held, thick with possibilities and promise.

"This is preposterous," Rebecca said coolly.

"You do not have much of a choice," Julian said, thinking how such a wager could lead him to unravel the truth of his family's tragedy. "You are at our mercy. If you don't wish to participate, then you'll have to live with the consequences of your . . . unveiling. There are many men who've seen this painting. I wonder what they would think if they knew . . ."

"That is blackmail," Susanna said tightly.

"Why, Miss Leland, that is such an ugly word," Leo said. "You have put yourself in this situation, and I think you're getting a decent return for such a daring stunt. We'll let you go free, and you'll have to accept our attempts to discover the truth."

"So you think by ganging up on us," Rebecca said, "you'll somehow wear down our resistance? Gentlemen, that will never happen."

"Your voice is full of challenge," Julian said. "I like that."

Her focus came back to him immediately. She betrayed her nerves by licking her dry lips.

And after everything he'd gone through, his single-minded devotion to his family and businesses, his obsession with the Scandalous Lady—one flick of this woman's tongue had him suddenly thinking dark thoughts. He glanced up at the painting, at the upthrust breasts and the dark shadows between her thighs. Clenching his jaw, he focused his thoughts on the lost diamond and his father's downfall.

"I think the model is you," he said to Rebecca in a low, husky voice.

Tension crackled between them like heat lightning on a sultry summer evening.

She tossed her head. "And I've already told you it is. What challenge is that?"

"Two of you are lying. But I think you're not. Leo, what say you?"

Leo rubbed his chin thoughtfully, even as he walked a circle about the women, examining them. They twitched uneasily like fillies up for auction at Tattersall's. "I can see you are all related, at least by the shapes of your bodies. With so many garments on—and male garments at that—it is difficult to see a true difference. So we cannot go by that."

"You are being vulgar," Elizabeth said, her voice haughty with generations of noble blood.

"And you are being scandalous, Elizabeth," Peter said in a low voice. "All of you. I cannot believe—"

"You cannot believe that one of these women would dare so much?" Julian said softly. "Ladies of Society have so little to do before they're married." He saw their looks of outrage but ignored them. He'd been doing meticulous research on ladies this past year. "A certain type of woman might become . . . bored."

"Don't pretend you understand any of us," Rebecca snapped.

"Perhaps I don't now, but I intend to know you very well."

The alcohol was making him lose his vaunted control. He could see her jaw clench. Damn, but she was beginning to intrigue him almost as much as the diamond.

Leo stopped before Susanna, the spectacled Leland sister. She met his gaze, hers full of a withering disdain.

"Peter," Leo said, "tell me you believe Elizabeth is the model, because I want this one."

Peter frowned.

Susanna's brave front faltered as she stiffened. "How dare you, sir! I should not think you capable of discerning the truth. Your reputation speaks of a poor intellect."

"I haven't seen you out and about much, have I?" Leo said slowly. His eyes lit. "You're the bluestocking, aren't you? You dabble in art, I believe?"

"Dabble?" she echoed in a frosty voice.

"I do believe that makes you more likely to pose for a fellow artist. What fun! Peter, what say you?" Leo didn't take his eyes off the woman, as if she might escape if he didn't pin her into place with his gaze.

Peter sighed. "Rebecca, Susanna, your brother is my friend. He has helped me in so many ways I cannot recount them all. I cannot believe you guilty of such a thing, regardless of what you say." He studied Elizabeth. "Then it has to be you."

She smiled cheerfully. "I told you it was."

Peter leaned toward her, smiling back. "And I'll enjoy proving it."

Her smile faltered.

"There we have it, gentlemen," Leo said, his voice full of good-natured ease. "This wager will be enjoyable as is, but I think a monetary reward might give us further incentive."

"My, what big words you use," Susanna challenged.

Julian gave a tight smile.

Leo laughed, then glanced with speculation at Julian and Peter. "Shall we say . . . five hundred pounds?"

Nodding, Julian knew the sum was no problem for

him, but Peter was only the youngest son of a squire.

Peter gave a brusque nod. "Done."

Julian said nothing about his knowledge of the jewel. A wager was a wager, and every man had to use his own advantages.

For a moment, he couldn't believe his search for the truth of the lost diamond could be so close to fruition. He'd spent his adult life resurrecting the respect his title deserved, saving his property and his people. He'd never set one foot outside the bounds of propriety, approaching even the smallest investment with caution and forethought, including even his search for a bride.

Now here he was, dazzled by Rebecca Leland's nudity, lured by the diamond that had contributed to his father's downfall—challenged by the woman herself, who faced him down as if what she'd done were a grand adventure instead of the terrible risk it really was. He didn't understand her at all. But he would learn.

"This is useless," Rebecca said, hands on her hips.

She should not draw attention to her feminine roundness, not when it was so boldly painted behind her.

"We could settle this right now," Leo responded. "You could each remove your clothing and let us see the truth."

The women blushed, their gazes boring into Leo disdainfully.

But Julian didn't really want the truth revealed so

easily. He needed the cover of the wager under which to make his inquiries.

"I'm looking forward to the challenge of discovering the truth—and your motives," Leo said. "That intrigues me most of all."

Rebecca pulled her cap back on her head, hiding the rich sable of her hair. "Now that you've had your amusement, step out of our way."

The cap shadowed her face, leaving her full lips highlighted in a slash of light. Julian found himself far too aroused. Before he could do something foolish— like claim her with a kiss before everyone—he stepped aside.

But instead of marching past him, she led her sister and cousin back to the painting.

"What do you think you're doing?" Julian demanded in disbelief as they put their hands on the frame.

"Taking what is ours," she answered without looking at him.

"The club purchased the painting from the artist quite legally," he pointed out.

"It wasn't meant to be here at all," Elizabeth said, frustration evident in her frown.

"You meant it to be in a private collection," Peter said slowly. "That makes sense, Elizabeth, with your brother being who he is. But you miscalculated."

"You all miscalculated," Julian amended.

"Susanna, spell that for me," Leo called.

She ignored his drunken teasing.

"Surely you do not want every man to see this during your wager," Rebecca said. "What if others hatch similar ideas?"

"You should have thought of that before you posed." Julian wondered if anyone else had recognized the diamond from the portrait—or when it was around her exquisite neck one night at a ball. Or perhaps no one cared any longer about a maharajah's gift, he thought bitterly. It gleamed above both of them now in the lamplight. Why had she been so foolish as to wear it in public?

Because she'd thought her secret well hidden in France.

With a toss of her head, Rebecca demanded, "And what do we get if none of you can determine the truth?"

"So you're going to play an active part in our wager?" Julian asked, intrigued by the possibilities. Why was he so eager to see this young woman—and she was surely several years younger than he—openly participate in something that could ruin her?

But of course, she'd already risked all of that, posing nude for endless hours. He found himself envying the artist and wondering at their relationship. Tamping down his interest, he reminded himself to focus on the diamond.

"Why, you'll win the painting, of course," Leo responded before Julian could.

Julian couldn't imagine surrendering it, but it was too late.

"Let me understand this," Rebecca said, eyes narrowed. "The three of you are wagering with each other over who the model is. If you cannot discover the truth, then we win the painting."

"Correct," Julian said, his mind continuing to calculate the best way to use this ridiculous wager to his advantage.

"Surely we must include the element of time." Rebecca glanced with speculation at her friends, and then at the men. "You have a week to name the true model, gentlemen, presenting substantial proof and not just a guess."

"Ridiculous," Leo scoffed. "A week is not nearly enough time. We need until the end of the Season."

"No," she said. "I'll counter with one month, but nothing more."

Julian exchanged a look with his two friends, and then bowed his agreement. It would give him enough time to follow the clues to the Scandalous Lady and clear his father's name. But it couldn't bring his father back from the dead, Julian thought grimly.

The three women marched past them. Sharing a glance, the three men followed, then leaned over the balustrade as the women descended to the ground floor and out the door.

Leo grinned. "Now, that was an enjoyable evening."

He glanced at Julian. "You surprise me, old friend."

And they were friends, Julian thought, even as he shrugged. Julian had been forced to leave Eton at ten years of age, when his father could no longer pay the tuition. Though he was a future earl, his poverty had many boys—and then men—ignoring him, until he'd made himself into a man who couldn't be ignored.

But Leo hadn't cared about money. He'd still invited Julian home with him at holidays and had still visited him, putting up with the chaos of Julian's too-large family. Peter's friendship had come later, when Julian had sensed that the man needed help finding a place for himself as a younger son with little to recommend him. Peter had taken giant strides in learning to invest, and had become a partner in several of Julian's railways.

They had felt connected, and now they were so again by the risky challenge of three women who seemed determined to skirt the boundaries of ruination.

Leo clapped them both on the back. "May the best man win."

Julian felt as if a spring breeze had blown through his life, awakening him from a dark winter, challenging him in a way he'd thought long in his past.

Thanks to Rebecca Leland, he would solve a family mystery, clear his father's name—and spend time seducing the secrets from a beautiful woman.

Chapter 2

The next afternoon, when the luncheon ended, Rebecca Leland was sincerely glad that Lady Fogge suggested that her guests retire to the conservatory. If Rebecca had to spend one more minute looking across the table at the knowing, amused expression on the Earl of Parkhurst's face, she would betray her upbringing and—laugh. She would laugh and laugh at the ludicrous situation she'd gotten herself into. In her sheltered life, it was the most exciting thing she'd ever done. Her sister and her cousin had been shocked at her attitude when they'd all finally piled into the hackney after leaving the gentlemen's club. Their faces had showed horror and fear, but Rebecca could only feel amusement and intrigue and a certain thrilling excitement—especially when she thought again of the earl, who'd haunted his way through her dreams.

As it was, her sister Susanna kept sending her veiled looks of sympathy across Lady Fogge's table, not yet realizing that Rebecca didn't need such sentiment. She knew that her sister did not see their dilemma the same way, that Susanna thought herself lucky, since her tormentor hadn't made an appearance. It was probably too early for Mr. Leo Wade, ne'er-do-well scoundrel, to rise from his bed, Rebecca thought, hiding a smirk.

But not the earl. He was a man of business, or so she'd been told. As the party of twenty casually strolled down the gallery of the Fogge home, Lord Parkhurst was conversing with their hostess, and she showed her delight by impulsively touching his arm. Lady Fogge was a kind woman with a plump face, both traits she shared with her unmarried daughter. She had to be thrilled that the notoriously reclusive, unattached earl had accepted her invitation.

Rebecca had only seen him a handful of times these last few years, across a dinner table or a crowded ballroom. She'd heard talk of him, of course, and not all of it was complimentary. There seemed to be a sordid scandal attached to the family's wealth, but she'd never heard what it was. Her mother, Lady Rosa, believed that if they didn't want people to discuss the Leland scandals, they shouldn't gossip about others. Lady Rosa did say that Lord Parkhurst didn't behave as an earl should. He spent far too much time with his investments—with his *businesses,* her mother said in disapproval, as if Rebecca should flee at the sight of a man who dared to work for a living, as no gentleman should do.

It would have been very easy for an innocent debutante to flee at the sight of him, she thought, glancing at him again as the party descended several stairs into a small, but lush, conservatory, where paths of crushed shells wound between ferns, trees, blooming camellias, and a gurgling fountain in the shape of a fish. The Earl of Parkhurst did not look like a typical nobleman with elegant bodylines beneath his garments and a patrician handsomeness. No, Lord Parkhurst looked—as her cousin the duke once teasingly told her—like a street thug. He was . . . immense, towering over all the guests, even the men. With his oversized body, his finely tailored clothing looked as if it should be straining to hold all of him in.

But his form was purely muscle, not gone to fat. Once she'd seen him racing his horse, a monstrous black beast, through Hyde Park, unlike the other men who'd casually trotted by the ladies' carriages to chat. No, Lord Parkhurst had no time for ladies. She remembered his coat flapping open, the narrowness of his waist, the power of his thighs, the way he'd effortlessly controlled every movement of the horse, using shoulders almost as broad as the animal's. Rebecca's mouth had gaped open as if she'd never seen a man before.

She could not call him truly handsome. Below his unruly black hair, his nose seemed as if it had been broken once, and the bones of his face were harsh and intimidating. He had a wide mouth that she'd thought incapable of smiling, but had seen otherwise last night, when she could tell he'd gotten foxed while playing cards with his friends. In the gentlemen's club, she'd felt deliciously . . . overpowered as he'd stalked toward her like a man who'd conquered at the head of an army to win his earldom, rather than simply inheriting it.

She remembered his eyes most of all. They were pewter gray, barren as winter, but last night they'd seemed to almost glow, smoldering as he'd looked at the painting and then looked at her, judging her. She had not imagined before then what it would feel like to be in the presence of men viewing the artwork—of Lord Parkhurst, looking down her body as if he could see through her clothing. It had been exhilarating and frightening and powerful all at once.

She banished a momentary unease. It was too late to worry about the painting and who else might connect her to it. And what could an earl possibly do to the cousin of a duke? The wager was surely a drunken lark, something to amuse him and his friends.

But he was watching her now from the far side of the fountain, his dark gaze assessing what he saw. She was standing with Susanna, who tried to tug her until their backs were turned. Rebecca wouldn't play the coward.

"Oh, I do wish he would stop looking at you," Susanna grumbled.

"Take off your spectacles and you won't be able to tell."

Susanna frowned.

"I thought you weren't going to wear those to parties," Rebecca said. "You only need them for reading or painting."

"After last night, I fear to miss too much if we encountered one of *them*."

Rebecca smiled. "You shouldn't worry. Lord Parkhurst, Mr. Wade, and Mr. Derby can play all the silly games they want; they can't harm us. Perhaps they've even forgotten about the wager already as they deal with pounding headaches after a night of imbibing."

"Can't harm us?" Susanna gaped at her. "They *know*. Of course they can harm us. Good heavens, he's speaking to Mama!"

Rebecca sent a sharp gaze across the conservatory. Lord Parkhurst was indeed at their mother's side, bending over to speak to her, making the indomitable woman appear almost slight. Lady Rosa Leland, the daughter of a duke, once had high aspirations for her daughters' marriages. For ten years, she'd been thwarted by Susanna's disinterest in marriage and her unnatural interest in their father's anatomy studies. Their father was a professor at Cambridge, and Susanna had used her artistic talents to sketch his dissections. Naturally, Lady Rosa was appalled, and had gradually given up on Susanna. But since their brother's miraculous return to England, after all thought him dead, Susanna seemed to be trying to please their mother once again, gracing

London Society with her presence. That took some of the pressure off Rebecca, who, since emerging from both the schoolroom and her sickroom, had become their mother's sole focus.

Rebecca remembered wanting to please her mother even as she now tried to pretend she wasn't watching Lady Rosa and the earl. Rebecca had been thrilled to be healthy again, to be out in Society like other young ladies. Men were a foreign species to her, and she immersed herself in their study.

But then, when her family learned of her brother's supposed death, there passed the saddest year of her life. Everything seemed changed, including her. When they emerged from mourning, Lady Rosa was even more determined to make a happy match for Rebecca— but Rebecca had lost interest. She found herself longing to see the world, to travel and experience life. But now she was expected to marry, and be just like everyone else. It was . . . unthinkable.

She felt almost guilty for her secret mistrust of marriage. Surely Lady Rosa would blame her own strained marriage for Rebecca's disinterest. Rebecca didn't want to hurt her mother so openly by acknowledging the truth. Lady Rosa and Professor Leland had mistrusted each other for much of their marriage, and everyone had suffered for it. The lure of adventure seemed preferable to Rebecca, for then no one would be hurt, especially herself, she thought adamantly. All of her male acquaintances seemed too staid and predictable and refined, only strengthening her resistance to marriage. How could she trust such men to grant her an unlady-like freedom?

But the Earl of Parkhurst did not seem refined. She inhaled in surprise as he watched her over her mother's head. He wore that smile again, barely civilized, and his eyes raked her as if he wanted to know her every secret. Good lord, how much more did he think there was, after he'd viewed the painting?

"What do you think they're saying?" Susanna asked.

Rebecca smiled. "She's praising our merits. Remember, never will anyone love us as our mother does."

Susanna glanced at her sister sharply, and they both relaxed into easy amusement. "Yes, I know. But sometimes she is simply so . . . persistent."

"I think she's met her match," Rebecca said ruefully. She looked back across the fountain, but Lady Rosa and Lord Parkhurst were not where they'd last been. Her eyes widened as she saw them on the path leading toward the two sisters. "Brace yourself."

"No, brace *your*self, Rebecca. He is after you! Surely Mr. Wade is not nearly so dangerous."

Rebecca felt a secret little thrill. She saw the way both women and men stepped out of Lord Parkhurst's way. He ignored them all, his every focus on her. Awareness was a prickling flush that started at the nape of her neck and spread along her body. She barely felt Susanna's fingers clasping hard on her arm, as she had to look up and up as the earl came closer and closer. Good lord, he made her feel positively dainty.

She'd been longing for something different to happen to her—and now here he was, large and bold and threatening beneath a veil of civility.

Lady Rosa beamed at her daughters. She had the same shade of dark brown hair as Rebecca, with only a little gray to betray her age. Susanna had inherited her warm brown eyes. She was a striking woman, displaying the easy elegance of her birth, yet at the same time showing her compassion and strength. She'd endured the fear of losing Rebecca to countless childhood illnesses and suffered through a year believing her son dead. Her marriage had almost foundered under the weight of a lifetime of scandal, but Lady Rosa had emerged victorious. Now the only triumph she seemed to truly want was to see her daughters well—and happily—married. And Rebecca almost regretted that she could not appease her mother in such a way.

"My dear girls, how pleased I am to find you together," Lady Rosa said, beaming. "Lord Parkhurst, allow me to introduce my daughters, Miss Leland and Miss Rebecca Leland. Oh dear, I've already gone on so long about them, you probably feel as if you know everything there is to know!"

Rebecca's smile stiffened. Everything there was to know, indeed. Lord Parkhurst probably *did* think such a thing, especially after the way he'd studied the painting for what seemed like forever.

And then it was as if she were in the dark, candlelit saloon again, standing too close to this giant of a man, meeting his intelligent, assessing gaze. He should seem out of place in this false garden, where people talked with little substance. Instead, she could imagine him one with the forest, hunting a beast of prey.

And she realized that she was the prey.

A flush of heat had her wondering if he could see her blush.

"It is a pleasure to meet you, ladies," the earl said, bowing his head politely. His voice was mild rather than challenging, though still deep and rumbling.

She and her sister curtsied. Rebecca could feel some of Susanna's tension subside. Up close and by the light of day, he seemed a bit . . . different. There were lines of strain across his forehead, as if he regularly frowned. His eyes were hooded, almost tired.

Had he spent much of the night thinking about her, as she'd thought about him?

No, she wasn't worth that to him. He was a bored aristocrat who'd found something to amuse himself for a few days—a month at most, she reminded herself. Though he might *look* different, he was surely the same as every other man of her acquaintance.

"Is this truly the first time we've spoken, Lord

Parkhurst?" Rebecca asked politely. "I feel like I've seen you at several events."

"And I have seen you, Miss Leland."

He spoke with all politeness, but she heard another meaning in his words, and barely withheld a shiver.

"I wish to congratulate you all on the miraculous return of Captain Leland," he continued.

"Thank you, my lord," Lady Rosa said with a happy sigh. "I was . . . quite devastated by the loss of my son. With his return, my husband and I are restored in spirit and in our hearts. The captain is spending time with his cousins this month."

"Ah, so I heard," he said, glancing at the Leland sisters. "The captain himself told me. We have had several shared investments recently."

Why hadn't he said that he knew her brother last night? Rebecca wondered with annoyance. She was feeling more and more deflated. The earl was not so removed from Society. She only wanted him to be.

"Did you meet my son at university?" Lady Rosa asked.

Lord Parkhurst linked his hands behind his back, his appearance casual—far too casual. Rebecca sensed . . . something beneath the surface.

"No, I did not, my lady."

"Ah, then you must have gone to Oxford. My husband lectures at Cambridge."

"I came into my title at eighteen," Lord Parkhurst said. "I did not have time for much else."

Lady Rosa's expression turned momentarily pained. "Do forgive me, my lord. I had forgotten that your father died so many years ago."

Rebecca looked between them, curious at what wasn't being said. But if she asked her mother for details later, Lady Rosa would think her interested, and never let her hear the end of it.

To cover the vague unease she sensed in her mother, Rebecca said, "Our cousin, Madingley, did not attend university either, for exactly the same reason."

He nodded. "I remember that."

"Even though you are without an advanced education, my lord," Lady Rosa said, "I hear men talking with much admiration of your knowledge and skill."

"Admiration is it now?" His wide mouth quirked in a faint smile. "That is putting it kindly. But yes, there is education to be had, even if it is self-motivated. Yet formal education is something that should be taken advantage of—as I keep telling my brothers."

"How many brothers do you have, my lord?" Rebecca asked.

He glanced at her, those gray eyes impassive. "Two, Miss Leland, eighteen-year-old twins."

"Young then," Susanna said, nodding. "I feel like my eighteenth birthday was so long ago."

Lady Rosa flashed her a mortified frown, as if Susanna should never allude to her advanced, unmarried age of twenty-seven.

"Youth does not excuse common sense," Lord Parkhurst said.

"Perhaps they see that you do not have a university education, my lord," Rebecca said, "and yet you seem to have survived."

They looked at each other for a moment—a moment too long, for Lady Rosa's brows rose.

"Susanna, do escort me to the dessert table," Lady Rosa said. "I am suddenly quite famished. Enjoy your afternoon, my lord."

Wearing an apologetic look, Susanna was led away.

Julian watched the gaze exchanged between the two sisters and withheld his amusement. Susanna thought she was leaving Rebecca with the devil himself—and who could blame her, after their evening together?

But Rebecca . . . he did not quite understand her mood. Last night, she'd been bold, in command, even fearless, though three men held her and her relatives practically captive. Today she was a subdued lady of the *ton*, patiently allowing her mother the lead, as any daughter who expected to be led to the altar would.

"Lady Rosa did that quite neatly," Julian remarked.

"She has had much practice," Rebecca said dryly.

"Then I suggest we reward her." He held out his arm. "Would you care to walk?"

She eyed him, her eyes faintly devilish, her lips

curved in a lovely smile. Then she placed her hand lightly on his arm. "I imagine I cannot come to harm in a conservatory."

"You could always scream," he countered.

"And find myself married before the week is out? I think not."

"Ah, you are crushing my self-esteem. Would not many young ladies wish to be married to an earl?"

"Perhaps not many, for you are not married."

"By choice. And neither are you."

"Stating the obvious, my lord."

They walked quietly for several minutes, weaving their way out of sight of the other guests, although the murmur of voices never quite went away. At the rear of the conservatory, the glass separated them from the walled garden outside. They paused as if to admire it, but Julian knew she must not be thinking of the view.

He was thinking of *his* view . . . of her. Her lovely rose-colored gown hugged her torso, revealing herself to be shaped much as she'd been painted. She was slender but not fragile, small, yet rounded. Her hair was styled artfully, curled, with carefully placed ribbons. Her bodice was high enough that he found himself wondering if she hid the Scandalous Lady beneath her garments.

Patience, he reminded himself. He'd spent the morning speaking with people about her family. Though he'd heard of several of the family scandals, the Lelands and the Cabots certainly did not seem like thieves. And Rebecca was far too young to have stolen the diamond herself almost ten years before. So how had she come by it?

He'd realized during the long night that the best way to discover answers to his questions was to earn her trust. He had diligently tried to be unassuming at the luncheon, wanting her to believe that his intensity of the previous evening was more about his overindulgence. And to some degree, that was true. He shouldn't have intimidated her, standing too close, looking so menacing, which was always rather easy for him to do.

She didn't seem intimidated. She inhaled the scents of the flowers all around them, then exhaled almost on a sigh—but not a sigh of resignation. There was something very . . . unusual about her nonplussed reaction to the wager.

But then again, only an unusual woman would pose for a nude portrait. He wondered how unfettered her morals truly were.

And that aroused him far too much, he realized. He could not let himself dwell on her nudity, her lack of inhibitions. He had to focus on the Scandalous Lady, and bringing it back to its rightful owner—him.

He began the hunt for information. "You and Miss Susanna Leland seem close to your cousin Lady Elizabeth."

She eyed him, a smile touching her full lips. "We are

of an age, and we were raised together at Madingley Court."

"Your families all lived together?"

"Have you seen Madingley Court?" she asked, amused.

He nodded. "Ah, I see. The palace of a duke, of course. So you were not too crowded living together."

"Not at all," she answered, searching his face with the faintest confusion.

He knew she wondered at his motives, why he didn't bring up the wager. And his talk of crowded living conditions revealed too much of his own childhood issues.

"So the three of you were like sisters," he said.

"We still are," she answered, her voice firm. "We would support each other through anything."

"Obviously," he said. "They risked much for you with their declaration last night."

"We would risk anything for each other."

"You'd risk exposure and humiliation?"

He thought she'd drop her hand from his arm, but she didn't, only looked up at him coolly.

"Are you threatening such a thing?" she asked. "I would have thought you a gentleman."

"I am a gentleman, Miss Leland. But that painting does not make a gentleman remember the civilized part of his brain."

He felt her stiffen.

"But then you knew that would happen when you posed," he continued mildly. "Or did you not think beyond a momentary thrill? Why would you do such a thing?"

"Are you *lecturing* me, my lord? A true gentleman would protect a lady's sensibilities, would forget the things he'd seen."

"You have not displayed a lady's sensibilities, have you?"

She dropped her hand and faced him now, speaking in a low voice, her hazel eyes flashing. "Now you're offending me. You know nothing about me."

"I would like to."

"No, you wouldn't. You want to win a wager with your silly friends."

"Which you and your silly female relatives made possible by your behavior last night."

"How disapproving you sound, my lord."

"No, I am simply stating a fact. Your guilt makes you believe that everyone is censorious."

"Guilt?" she cried, then looked down the path and lowered her voice. "I feel no guilt whatsoever."

"Then why else would you attempt to steal the painting?"

"For the simple reason that it was supposed to be in France, not here where people who know me will see it."

"Then why pose, Miss Leland? Why risk it?"

She paused, and in her mercurial eyes, he could see her weighing what to reveal. He waited almost impatiently—and he was never an impatient man. Then to his surprise, she stepped closer. He could feel the heat from her body, imagined how it would feel with just another step, as she pressed against him. His logical brain threatened to shut down, and that had never happened to him.

"Did you ever just want to be adventurous, my lord?" she asked softly.

He blinked at her, and revealed the truth without questioning if he should. "No, Miss Leland. I've never wanted such a thing in all my life."

She gave him a pitying look. "Then I guess you can't understand my motives." She spun on her toes and began to walk back the way they'd come. Pausing, she spoke over her shoulder. "It would look suspicious if we did not return to the luncheon guests together."

He approached her and held up his arm for her hand. "For someone who wants adventure, you care very much what people think."

"Just because I do not wish to hurt my mother's feelings, does not change my inner longings, my lord."

The pang of lust was sudden and swift, taking him by surprise, darkening his soul.

"You display deep, sensual longings by posing nude, Miss Leland," he said, his voice hoarse.

She didn't look at him. "It is none of your business who or what I might be longing for."

"Not just adventure?"

She didn't answer.

They reached the rest of the party too swiftly, and she left him with a perfunctory smile. He'd been hoping to gradually win her trust, but knew their clash had not helped his cause. He was a meticulous planner, and always held to his plans. Until Rebecca Leland. Somehow, she'd goaded him to a place where his brain couldn't seem to catch up with his mouth.

Other guests glanced at them with interest, and heads came together for whispers. Susanna gave Rebecca a wide-eyed look; Lady Rosa preened with satisfaction.

And Rebecca did not look at him again.

Chapter 3

Rebecca marched boldly into the overheated ballroom that night, and was grateful that her sister
and cousin did not hang back. They were announced,
along with her mother, and the crowd barely glanced
their way as the conversations whirled around them.

"See, no one cares or knows," Rebecca hissed between smiling lips.

She'd spent the early evening insisting to Susanna
and Elizabeth that they could not cancel their engage-
ments and hide at the Madingley town house forever.
She would not have thought them so tentative; she was
learning much these past two days.

Elizabeth took her arm, leading her away from the
crowd to skirt about the edges. Lady Rosa disappeared
within, but Susanna followed them.

Elizabeth ducked behind a potted fern and pulled the
sisters with her. "I know what you're thinking, Rebecca,
but *he* visited me today!"

"So you said." Rebecca put her hands on her hips. "You have spent your entire life around Peter Derby. He grew up as your brother's friend. He is not a bad sort."

Susanna gave a soft snort.

After a warning glance at her sister, Rebecca reminded them, "He has matured, as have we all. You can handle him, Elizabeth. Of all three men, he seems the one who would treat you the gentlest."

"What does that mean?" Elizabeth demanded, eyes going wide. "How did Lord Parkhurst treat you?"

Susanna pushed her way between them and lowered her voice. "He was alone with her for a quarter of an hour. Mama was practically swooning with excitement."

"I hope you told her not to," Rebecca said crossly. "It means nothing. He may be an earl, but he is the most staid, dull—"

"Dull?" Susanna pulled her spectacles out of her reticule, donned them, and examined Rebecca as if she were on a dissection table in the professor's laboratory.

Rebecca tried to will away her blush without success. "You heard me."

"I don't need my ears, because I have eyes!" Susanna said with force. "I saw the way he looked at you last night. And today he was in a hurry to have you alone."

"He is trying to see into my mind, to discover the truth—to win his silly wager."

"It's true, men will do much to prove themselves to other men," Susanna said.

Rebecca rolled her eyes and said to Elizabeth, "Now she wants us to remember how much older she is than we are. That she has so much more experience. I have been out of the schoolroom and in Society for some years now. I may have been sick, but that was several years ago—"

"No, it wasn't," Susanna said softly. "You had a fever only a few months past."

Rebecca dismissed it, though inside herself she knew the unwelcome reoccurrence had . . . changed her. "A cold, nothing more. You all simply overreacted."

Susanna and Elizabeth exchanged a worried glance.

"Stop this!" Rebecca said, throwing her hands wide. "Why can you not enjoy yourselves? There is nothing those three men can do to us!"

"Except reveal it all," Elizabeth said softly. "If my brother finds out—"

Rebecca groaned. "He won't, and neither will ours, if we play this carefully."

"But they plan to stalk us!" Susanna said. "I . . . I didn't say so earlier, but I saw Mr. Wade."

Elizabeth gasped. "Really? He has quite the reputation, and I know ladies have been ruined associating with him!"

"That is an exaggeration," Rebecca said, even as she saw Susanna straighten in self-defense. Her sister liked to pretend she was worldly, but she'd withdrawn from men for many years, had pursued her studies and her interests, insisting she was happy. Rebecca hadn't believed it. And somehow, with their brother's return and his satisfying marriage, Susanna had realized she might be able to find her own happiness.

Much as Rebecca didn't believe in marriage for herself, she suspected that Susanna did. Would this wager turn her away from Society again? Rebecca wouldn't have it! "Where did you see Mr. Wade?"

"In the park. I went for a ride after the luncheon." Susanna hesitated. "I wish you could have gone with me. You know it is not too late to learn to ride."

"Please, we've had this discussion," Rebecca said impatiently. "What about Mr. Wade?"

"Oh . . . nothing much. I had my sketchbook with me, and he saw it, and insisted he would sit in the park with me."

"Did you allow it?" Elizabeth asked, her voice breathless.

"He was . . . insistent. But we remained in a very public place," she added with haste. "I sketched the flowers, and he lay in the grass at my feet. It was . . . peculiar."

"It sounds exciting," Rebecca said firmly. "He is an eligible man with good family connections. His brother is Viscount Wade."

"The viscount is blind," Elizabeth said, as if imparting important gossip none of them had heard. "He's a friend of our cousin Daniel, who says he's so completely normal that—"

"We're getting off the subject," Rebecca said with exasperation.

"Oh, sorry." Elizabeth shrugged. "I feel like I can't even keep my thoughts in order!"

"I understand the feeling," Rebecca said heatedly, even as she turned back to Susanna. "Did anything else happen? Did Mr. Wade press you for details about the painting?"

"Not really. He seemed . . . enthralled by it all." Even as she blushed, her gaze focused over Rebecca's shoulder. "Well, this wager has certainly made the Earl of Parkhurst come out of his cocoon."

Rebecca whirled around, peering through the palm fronds. She saw the earl immediately—how could she miss him? Tall and so solid, with evening clothes that only gave him the veneer of civilization, though tailored well to his muscular body. She shivered, almost wishing she weren't so intrigued.

But he was even easier to spot because at his side were two equally tall, identical young men, both dark-haired. They moved with coltish strides, all arms and legs and eager eyes.

"Are those his brothers?" Elizabeth asked.

"He mentioned them," Susanna said. "They look as if they've never been to a ball before."

"Perhaps not," Rebecca mused. "They're only eighteen."

"Mere infants." Susanna shook her head on a sigh. "This afternoon, Lord Parkhurst seemed quite exasperated with them. And that attitude seems to have continued."

Rebecca watched eagerly as the earl spoke to his brothers, a frown lowering his heavy brows. They weren't even looking at him, glancing everywhere else—at the women dressed as flamboyantly as peacocks, at the dancers already performing a quadrille in the center of the ballroom.

"I wonder where their mother is?" Rebecca asked.

"I do not remember seeing much of her recently, since two of Lord Parkhurst's sisters have married," Susanna answered.

"How many siblings does he have?" Rebecca tried not to sound too eager for information.

"Just one more sister, not yet out of the schoolroom."

"And he's the eldest, in charge of them all." Elizabeth shook her head.

"Overbearing, I imagine," Rebecca said. "I could tell that last night."

"He seemed rather commanding to me." Susanna eyed her too closely. "And you met him toe to toe."

Rebecca shrugged.

"And enjoyed it," Susanna continued, her voice mildly accusing.

"I did, and I don't regret it. If we are to be stuck in this situation, we must have fun. I am glad you sketched with Mr. Wade and, Elizabeth, I'm happy that Mr. Derby called on you. How many more shopping expeditions can we go on, after all?"

Both women sighed, and together they all looked back at the main floor.

"Do you think the other two men will appear?" Susanna asked softly.

Rebecca grinned. "Of course. They want to win, too. We have to make sure *we* win."

"I have a thought for how we might do that," Susanna began.

"Tell us later," Rebecca said, catching a glimpse of the earl alone, now that his brothers had deserted him.

"But—"

Rebecca started to sail out into the crowd, only to have her arm grabbed from behind.

"Wait!" Elizabeth hissed in her ear.

Rebecca realized she'd almost run right into Lord Parkhurst's brothers. They had met up with several other young friends on the edge of the dance floor, too close to their hiding place.

"I didn't want you bowling them over," Elizabeth said in a softer voice.

"I'll head toward the musicians on the right," Rebecca said. "You two go left, as if you've just emerged from the hallway beyond. If either of our mothers see us, they won't think we're up to something."

"They always used to know when we were up to something," Elizabeth said, smiling at the memories.

"We may not be girls anymore, but we can still have fun," Rebecca said with feeling.

Before them, the group of young men all suddenly guffawed loudly, clapping each other on the back. In their midst, the tall Delane boys, the earl's brothers, seemed to be holding court. Rebecca didn't know their names, but that would be useless, because she couldn't tell them apart.

"*We* saw the painting," one twin said, elbowing his brother, who snickered.

There was a gasp from their admiring friends—and from Elizabeth at Rebecca's back.

"We cannot be surprised," Susanna whispered. "Overhearing a discussion between men was how I first heard where the painting was hung. That's why my plan is necessary. I could tell you about it—"

"Shh!" Rebecca said.

One of the young men grumbled, "You're both only members of the club because your brother is an earl. And who is going to go against his sponsorship?"

"Stop being so jealous," one of the Delane brothers said, "or we won't sponsor you when it's time."

"Can't it be time soon?" a freckled redhead asked

plaintively. "How else will we see the painting?"

"It's stunning," said a Delane twin. "Totally nude—"

"There is a scarf," the other said.

Rebecca was indignantly thinking the same thing—as if the scarf made it somehow more acceptable, she realized, holding back a laugh.

"She might even be here!" the first twin said. "My brother heard she's one of the *ton*. Can you believe that?"

They all craned their necks, as if a naked woman was about to appear performing the steps of the quadrille.

The second twin groaned. "She has the pinkest—"

Susanna clutched her arm and yanked, pulling Rebecca against the wall. "That is enough," Susanna said. "You know it was never supposed to go this far."

"Now don't panic," Rebecca said in a soothing voice.

"Panic?" Elizabeth squeaked. "Did Lord Parkhurst talk about the painting to his brothers?"

Rebecca inexplicably found herself defending the man. "They're members, and the painting has been on display for almost a week, or so Susanna overheard. I can't believe he would have told his brothers about our adventures last night. He is far too staid for that."

Elizabeth rolled her eyes. "I don't think you know enough about him to form an opinion."

"He told me himself that he's never once wanted to

be adventurous. How much more dull can one be?"

Ignoring her, Elizabeth turned to Susanna. "You will tell us your idea later tonight?"

"Of course," Susanna said smoothly. "Everything will be all right."

Rebecca used their commiseration to slip away. Much as she'd defended the earl, she felt angry and uneasy. After all, she didn't know him, beyond his possession of a title and wealth, and what the gossipmongers had said about him. He could be a lying rogue.

But the lying rogue was in the middle of a group of older ladies, talking to just one. Though she was far smaller than he, she stood before him and wrung her hands, looking out over the crowd.

Could this be Lord Parkhurst's mother, looking for her twin sons? She pitied the poor woman, even as Rebecca eyed the eldest son.

Perhaps it was time for her to turn the tables on him, she thought, feeling wicked. She marched straight toward the earl, and he saw her coming as he looked over his mother's head. If she hoped for a warning, or signs of unease, she was disappointed. He seemed unflappable.

"Lord Parkhurst, how wonderful to see you here!" she called, waving and giggling as she approached.

She saw his mother's look of recognition, even as the woman glanced up at her son.

Lord Parkhurst took Rebecca's proffered hand in his

massive palm and bowed over it. Thank goodness they were both wearing gloves, for the way he held her hand a bit too long made her feel breathless.

"How pleasant to see you again, Miss Leland." He turned to the older woman. "Lady Parkhurst, may I present Miss Rebecca Leland? Miss Leland, my mother."

Rebecca swept into a deep curtsy, and noticed with satisfaction that the earl's gaze dipped to her cleavage. She would use every feminine wile she possessed to defeat him, hoping that her sister and cousin would do the same. She would have to remind them of the goal.

Lady Parkhurst bowed her head briefly, even as she smiled. "Miss Leland, I believe we have met before. I know your mother."

"Of course, my lady. But we cannot expect a man to realize that." She smiled innocently up at the earl.

The dowager countess sighed. "Forgive Parkhurst. He does not socialize as much as he should, which leads to ignorance."

Rebecca imagined it had been some time since anyone called this man ignorant. He only arched a dark brow and made no reply.

He must have received his size from his father, for his mother was not much taller than Rebecca. Her hair was silver gray—how could it not be, after raising six children!—but it caused a striking loveliness when matched with her gray eyes.

"Ignorance?" Rebecca echoed, putting a hand to her

chest in shock. "Only a mother could accuse his lord-ship of such."

Lady Parkhurst smiled. "I like you, Miss Leland." She glanced at her son. "Cheeky, isn't she?"

He only grunted.

His mother gave a dramatic sigh. "Hardly an appro-priate response, Parkhurst. I was giving you a chance to compliment a young lady."

Rebecca hid a smile, although she knew her eyes must be alight with it.

"I believe I am old enough to know how to do so," he answered dryly.

To Rebecca she said, "Forgive him. He has decided his brothers need his careful tending, and is not tending to himself."

"It sounds like he's a caring brother," Rebecca said.

"But he has a duty to the earldom, as well."

Lord Parkhurst let out a breath. "Enough," he said mildly. "Miss Leland well understands a peer's duty. Madingley is her cousin."

"What a fine family you have," Lady Parkhurst said.

She spoke a little too loudly, as if emphasizing that fact for her son. Rebecca had to bite her lip to keep from laughing at him. But she'd drawn his attention to her mouth, and now it felt decidedly strange to continue talking to his mother.

"Lady Parkhurst, allow me to boldly offer my assis-tance. I assume you'd like your son to dance?"

The earl narrowed his eyes, but his mother looked delighted.

"Miss Leland, you are a smart girl. Do take good care of him."

She left them alone as the orchestra struck up a waltz.

Lord Parkhurst stared down at her, heavy brows lowered.

She stared back, smiling, so immensely pleased with herself. "I chased your mother away. Surely that makes you happy."

"No, you made *her* happy, by encouraging her interest in my relationships with marriageable women."

"You're an earl; that won't go away, not with any mama in Society. And we both know you are not interested in marrying someone like me," she challenged. "I have too few morals—or so you've implied."

Then he surprised her by taking her hand, and sliding his other around her ribs. "Let's see how a scandalous woman dances."

And he swept her off.

Her breath left her; her very will was overpowered. He was so big, so powerful, that he guided her about like a doll, dipping and swaying, steering her between other, slower couples. She knew too many people were watching, including all of her family, and his. She should have been angry at not being in control—

But she wasn't. She felt giddy and breathless, yet

could hardly let him see how he affected her. Teasing him was her only defense.

"Lord Parkhurst, you'd best be careful. You may not be interested in marrying me, but we've both been seen talking to each other's mother. To the *ton,* we're practically engaged."

He only gave another grunt, and took her through a particularly tight turn. To her surprise, his thigh dipped between hers, so gracefully she thought she'd imagined it. Her face was flushed, and she found herself looking into his chest rather than up at his face. Then he did it again, deliberately, provocatively.

Her gaze flew to his. His smile was slow in forming, his eyes hooded, full of amusement and awareness. He knew what he did to her. It was unfair that gentlemen were allowed so much more experience than ladies. It put her at a distinct disadvantage. All she had to counter him were her wits.

Chapter 4

Julian knew that everything he did to Rebecca, every touch, would rebound back on himself. He accepted the risk since it would help him toward the eventual goal. She simply made it so easy to taunt her, to tease a response. She had a tart tongue and a witty, intelligent mind.

Not to mention the lovely body he held so near to his. She was wearing blue silk, and it seemed to shimmer over her skin like sunlit water. He enjoyed watching her face when he crossed the proper boundaries, allowing his legs to glide between hers, everything hidden within the flowing fabric of her skirts.

He'd had to do *something* to counter her affect on him, or find himself gaping down her bodice mindlessly, like a boy who'd never been to a ball—like his brothers, he thought with distaste.

As if she read his mind, she said, "I overheard your brothers talking with their friends about the painting."

Her tone had cooled noticeably.

"They are rather young for you to be showing them such a thing," she continued.

"Not proud of yourself?"

"You know that is not what I'm saying. That painting wasn't meant to be there."

"I did not personally display the painting for them, but they are members of the club. You cannot expect that they would miss such a thing. And yes, they're young, but I thought they would make more appropriate friendships there, perhaps hear about the benefits of an education. I have the tuition money; they need to go." He frowned down at her. "But instead of making friends, they've seen you—your painting anyway. Or one of your female relatives."

"Disbelieving me already?" she replied.

"No," he said, looking down at her intensely as he whirled her about the floor. "You're my choice, after all, and how can I dispute my instincts?" He let his hand slide lower down her back, feeling the faint bumps of her spine, then the curve of her lower back, strangely erotic in such a public place. He splayed his hand, pulling her even closer, so that her breasts brushed his ribs. "My instincts have never failed me. You feel like the painting looks," he said, his voice husky.

Her eyes widened, and she missed a step, but he easily held her up. She didn't even try to escape, as if she knew that he wouldn't release her.

"Do your sister and cousin dance as well you do?" he

asked, leaning down to speak into her ear.

He felt her stiffen and knew she understood his threat. She would not be the only one he talked to in his quest to discover the truth.

If only he could directly ask about the diamond. But she wasn't wearing it, and if he brought it up, he might alert her that something more was going on than a drunken wager. He couldn't risk her speaking to someone in her family who might know more about the history of the jewel—or might have been involved in the theft.

The waltz ended much too quickly, and after a brief curtsy, she left him without allowing him to escort her off the ballroom floor. He watched her go, knowing that others had seen her rudeness. He didn't care—although their mothers might. He almost smiled.

She was more than capable of sparring with him, but it was obvious she didn't like the thought of him doing the same with her sister and cousin.

Late that night while her maid helped her undress, Rebecca thought again of the earl's threat to go after her sister and cousin. She loved Susanna and Elizabeth dearly, but they had not weathered the same childhood storms she had, and she worried that their strength would easily wear down.

At the ball, both Peter and Leo had requested a dance of their chosen targets. Elizabeth acquiesced, while Susanna preferred not to dance. So Leo had doted on her, even though she'd put on her spectacles like a shield.

Lord Parkhurst had watched them all, not bothering to hide his amusement as he stared with open challenge at Rebecca.

He thought he would win. And this was only the first evening!

After the maid had gone, Susanna dragged in a yawning Elizabeth, who promptly sank down on the four-poster bed and curled up among the pillows.

"You'll both hear my plan now," Susanna said firmly.

Rebecca picked up her brush and started on her hair. "Of course. Tell us everything."

"We cannot stay in London and let those three men pick us apart one by one, looking for weaknesses, combining their information."

Elizabeth sat back up, her brow furrowed. "But they're trying to best each other."

"And us. And I'm beginning to think that defeating us is more appealing than defeating each other."

Rebecca smiled at Elizabeth. "She assumes that because she knows what's beneath a man's skin, she knows how he thinks."

Susanna smiled at their age-old debate. "I didn't say that. But I think the best way we can protect this secret is to go our separate ways, not make it so easy for them to question us one by one."

"Separate ways?" Rebecca echoed, frowning.

"Eventually one of us will make a mistake. I think we reduce the risk of that if we don't give them access to all of us."

"But it's like . . . leaving the game," Rebecca finished, disappointment washing through her.

But although she protested, inside she knew that her sister was right, that the men would somehow use them against each other. Lord Parkhurst had openly claimed his intent to do so.

"No, it's like taking the game elsewhere," Susanna said, smiling slowly. "If they choose not to follow, then we win, don't you see?"

"I can't leave," Elizabeth said slowly. "My mother has not been feeling well, and I need to be with her."

"That's fine," Susanna insisted. "We mustn't go together anyway. I've been invited to a house party. I'll attend."

"Mother mentioned it," Rebecca said doubtfully. "She'll insist I attend, too."

"Not if you're going to visit Great-aunt Rianette."

The brush froze in Rebecca's hair as she frowned at her sister. "I beg your pardon?"

"She's been asking for one of us to visit, and Mama has been feeling guilty that we've been too busy. Now she won't have to feel guilty anymore," she concluded in triumph.

Wide-eyed, Elizabeth hugged a pillow to her lower face, as if hiding a grin.

Rebecca rounded on her sister. "You get to attend a party, and I visit an elderly relative—in the remote *Lake District,* of all places?"

Susanna winced and shrugged. "Can you think of a better way to separate? You saw how the men were. If you stay in London, they'll use you and Elizabeth against each other. Don't you see—Lord Parkhurst will most likely follow you. Isn't that what you want, the chance to do something different?"

Rebecca opened her mouth . . . then slowly closed it. "Perhaps he wouldn't," she began slowly.

"Oh, he will," Elizabeth insisted. "I saw him watching you." Her eyes scrunched as she tried not to laugh. "And you were watching him."

"I—I had to!" Rebecca blustered. "It's not what you think. It's part of the challenge, the adventure."

Susanna took her hand and gave a slow smile, saying softly, "Then let us change the rules and surprise them."

"But Great-aunt Rianette?"

"She'll be quite the challenge for Lord Parkhurst."

They stared at each other and then burst out laughing.

"I'll buy you and your maid a train ticket in the morning, and you can leave in the late afternoon," Susanna said, wiping her eyes. "I'll leave it on your dressing table. You'll still have time to attend Lady Thurlow's reception with me. Have Beatrice pack your trunk and send it to the railway station. If you'd like, I'll even speak to Mama for you."

"You really want this," Rebecca said, eyeing her sister. "Do you want Mr. Wade to follow you?"

"If he follows, it's because I'm simply a different sort of challenge for him. I don't find him terribly amusing, and I'm certain that he's flirted with ladies who are much more accomplished at it than I. He will tire of me and the game quickly."

"Then you don't know men," Rebecca warned her. She looked at her sister and her cousin in turn. "Should I wish us all good luck, even though we won't need it?"

They held each other's hands for a moment, smiling.

Early the next afternoon, Julian leaned against the wall in Lady Thurlow's drawing room, waiting for Rebecca to arrive. He'd already been to Madingley House, and managed to discover from a stableboy that the ducal carriage would be going to the home of the elderly earl of Banstead. It was easy enough to change his mind and attend, and Lady Thurlow, the earl's daughter-in-law, had seemed surprised and pleased to see him.

He really had no idea that the ladies of Society had

forgotten the scandals of the past. His mother had tried to tell him of course, but since he intended to find a suitable wife on his own accord, he'd avoided the matchmaking mamas as much as possible.

He idly wondered which of the women in attendance he'd been considering for marriage. Not that he'd recognize any of them. Their looks and comportment were not nearly so important as their family backgrounds and their temperaments. He'd already met many of their fathers, of course, and smoothly persuaded the men to discuss their daughters in a frank manner. Occasionally he rearranged his list of eligible prospects as he gathered more information. He didn't understand the dilemma of other men where choosing a wife was concerned. The selection was practically mathematical.

It didn't take him long to realize why Lady Thurlow was so surprised at his attendance that afternoon. This was not a regular luncheon, but a reception to discuss the arts. There were women taking turns playing the piano and singing, groups of people discussing the paintings on the walls, even an easel set up in one corner with clusters of budding artists.

He felt very out of place, for this regularly held event was obviously well used by young men blatantly looking for a wife, something he was always very careful not to advertise. And he was by far the most titled man here. When he saw his brothers arrive, they scowled at him as if he might interfere with whatever flirtation they had planned for the afternoon. He felt . . . old. But then he'd felt like their parent since he was eighteen.

He was hardly acting as an established businessman and earl. He knew his businesses and properties could run without him, but he'd neglected meetings and paperwork these last few days. He told himself it wasn't just about the foolish wager but about the stolen diamond, and family honor.

But it was about Rebecca Leland, too, he realized, straightening away from the wall when he saw her enter at last. She stood in the hall, speaking animatedly to Lady Thurlow while her sister Susanna was called away to the group by the easel.

Julian simply waited, his gaze on Rebecca. More than one person approached him, then thought better of it. He almost followed Susanna for an interrogation, then realized he'd be irritating her sister. Why did he enjoy the prospect of that so much? Was it the fire in Rebecca's eyes, the verbal challenges between them? He told himself he needed to win her trust, not irritate her. The wager meant nothing compared to the ultimate prize of discovering what had happened to the Scandalous Lady after all these years.

And then Rebecca saw him, and he felt the power of the moment hold him still. She gave him a wicked smile, and he nodded in return. Her dark hair gleamed in the afternoon light, and she wore a dress as yellow as a sunbeam.

So when had he bothered to notice a dress unless it was to divest a woman of it?

But not usually an unmarried miss of the *ton*. But that's what he wanted to do to her, lay her delicate body across his big bed and then—

And then she was coming toward him, direct as always, and he was relieved to have his fantasies interrupted. He had to keep his mind focused, more so with her than any other woman of his acquaintance.

Her scent of jasmine enveloped him as she came to a stop. He blinked at her.

She smiled. "Lord Parkhurst, how unusual to meet you at a reception for the arts."

He leaned a shoulder against the wall. "I like the arts."

She smirked, but only said, "It is my sister's passion. She is a brilliant artist."

"Does she have paintings for sale? I'm sure she'd speak to me in depth if I purchased some."

Rebecca tsked as she shook her head. "Bribery will not work, my lord. She makes gifts of her art, and she assists our father."

"Your father is a professor . . ." he began, faintly confused.

She looked away, and he realized that she regretted being so free with information.

Then she took a deep breath. "He lectures and researches on the topic of anatomy."

"Does she take notes for him? Perhaps transcribe his work?"

Rebecca tilted her chin so their eyes could meet. "She sketches."

"What does she—ah," he said with sudden understanding and growing interest. "She sketches *his work*. His dissections?"

She nodded. "It is not common knowledge, my lord. I only tell you so that you will not pursue such a subject with her. She is sensitive to the fact that our mother is mortified by what she's done, seen the human form so completely—"

"Nude?" he interrupted, glancing leisurely down her body. He enjoyed her blushes, and she didn't disappoint. He didn't linger on his thoughts of the painting of course, for his trousers would soon be too tight. Not that he didn't battle that regardless whenever she was around, as if he were a schoolboy again.

"Not quite the same thing as my painting at the club," she said dryly. "I stayed away from the laboratory. It was rather . . . messy."

"I can imagine." Feeling a prickling of awareness, Julian glanced up to see his brothers frowning at him. He hadn't told them he was attending, and he certainly didn't want them to know anything about his current plans. Without asking, he took Rebecca's arm. "Since you're not the artist of the family, care to walk the gardens with me?"

She seemed startled but smiled readily enough. He liked that she wasn't afraid of him, that she welcomed the challenge of the wager. It would make his search for information so much easier.

They remained silent as they walked through the house, across the terrace and onto a garden path. A cool, spring breeze ruffled their clothing, but Rebecca didn't seem to mind it as she lifted her face to the sun.

"A fine day, after all the rain," she said, walking at his side, her hand still lightly on his arm.

"We're going to discuss the weather?" he asked dubiously.

She continued as if he hadn't spoken. "A good day for traveling." She gave him a provocative glance.

He frowned. "Traveling? Are you journeying somewhere?"

"I might be."

"At the height of the Season?"

She shrugged. "Family duty calls. A silly wager can't be more important than that."

"A silly wager? Are you fleeing notoriety? Worried that awareness of the painting will spread?"

She clenched her jaw, but the smile never left her face.

He felt frustrated. Now that the truth of the diamond was so close, how could he permit it—or her—to elude him? He had to make her reveal the truth. But how to coerce a lady into doing anything?

But she wasn't behaving like a lady, and that gave him more freedom.

"I won't allow you to flee from me," he said in a low voice.

He pulled her against him. She gasped, but didn't cry out, didn't push him away, even though her hands were on his chest. Very slowly she lifted her face until their eyes met. For a suspended moment, he let himself simply feel the delicateness of her bones, the way her thighs touched his. Because of his height, his hips were pressed into the softness of her stomach. He had his hands on her back, but he didn't need to hold her to him, for she remained still.

He forgot about his questions, his goals. There was only her nearness, the jasmine that enticed his senses, the warmth of her in his arms. He forgot where they were, who might see them—and what the consequences might be. He found himself bending over her, longing to taste the sweetness of her lips. And surely she wanted the same, for she raised herself up on tiptoe to reach him, began to slide her hands along his ribs to his back—

"Look what Julian is doing!" cried an appalled male voice.

With a gasp, Rebecca practically leapt away from him, and he let her go, feeling sluggish and dazed. Wide-eyed, she covered her mouth, and he saw her fear.

He put out a hand but didn't touch her. "It's only my brother Gavin."

She let out a breath, closed her eyes. Then they both turned to find the twins bearing down on them, rounding the fountain.

To others, the twins were identical, but Julian knew their every difference in personality and expression, and even the way they wore their dark hair. Gavin was in the lead, but Joseph was right behind. Both of them ogled Rebecca with interest, even as they came to a stop, hands on their hips in the same pose.

"I am rather surprised at such behavior," Joseph said.

Gavin snorted. "Julian, you're hardly the model of propriety you've always held yourself to be."

Julian found himself growing angrier by the moment at their rude behavior. He let his frown speak for him. *"Gentlemen,"* he said, stressing the word. "Allow me to introduce a *lady.*"

They both stiffened and blinked, and any sheepish expression on their part was mostly hidden.

"Miss Leland, these are my brothers, Gavin and Joseph Delane."

He wondered if she would be embarrassed, but her worried expression had given way to one of amusement. She gave each of the boys her hand and an elegant curtsy, even though her cheeks were still a flushed from the intimacy of their near kiss.

"Mr. Delane." She nodded to one, then the other. "Mr. Delane."

Her easy elegance seemed to make them tongue-tied, and they looked between Julian and Rebecca with new hesitation.

"Are you both an admirer of the arts?" Rebecca asked, giving Julian a sidelong glance. "Is that why you're attending Lady Thurlow's reception?"

He was impressed by her daring, as if she challenged him to bring up a certain painting.

"Art is . . . fine," Gavin said. "But the ladies make it better."

Joseph covered a snort of laughter. Julian could have groaned at their immaturity.

Rebecca smiled. "Your brother tells me the same thing." Tossing her head, she walked away from them all, calling behind her, "Good day, Lord Parkhurst."

Damn, but he'd lost the chance to discover where she was journeying—and when. He would have followed her, but Gavin caught his arm.

"Could this really be our brother?" Gavin said to Joseph, his face full of mock surprise.

"What a terrible example he sets." Joseph shook his head.

Julian wondered if his focus on Rebecca was being noticed by more than just his brothers. He didn't want gossip to harm her—he only wanted the diamond, and to enjoy teasing her.

He would have to follow her closely and discover her plans.

"Oh, he has it bad," Gavin said behind him. "The mighty are about to fall."

The boys laughed, but he ignored them.

Chapter 5

Rebecca didn't think Lord Parkhurst saw her as she slipped out the front door of Banstead House. She left Susanna behind, knowing how much her sister enjoyed this particular reception when they were in town.

Rebecca knew herself too well. She would have confessed to her sister that the earl had tried to kiss her, and that she would have allowed it but for the interruption of his puppyish brothers.

She waited on the front step for her carriage to be brought around, her mind dizzy, her body flushed and somehow unsettled.

She'd *wanted* his kiss, and not simply because it would have distracted him from his questions. How could she think that succumbing to temptation would in any way help her win the wager?

In that moment, she simply hadn't *cared* about the wager. She'd wanted to experience a man's kiss. She'd spent her life on the outside, hidden away from the possibility of drafts and exposure to illness—and from the risk of giving to others what she suffered with.

No man had ever held her; they'd always treated her like blown glass that might break if handled too roughly. That was the impression her family gave everyone.

But all Julian Delane knew of her was a nude portrait and her spirited response to his wager.

And he liked it.

Feeling giddy, she hugged herself as the carriage pulled up. The footman folded down the step, opened the door, then held out a hand to help her inside. She looked over her shoulder to smile her thanks, and didn't realize how gloomy the interior was until she sat down and the door closed behind her.

Why were the blinds lowered and the glass raised on such a beautiful day? She could barely see anything. When she reached for the window, a hand suddenly gripped her wrist. Before she could scream, another hand covered her mouth, pressing her back into the bench as a man rose up over her.

The first thing she noticed was the smell of used garments and unwashed skin—and then terror swept through her, shaking her limbs, turning her stomach until she wanted to gag.

"Quiet!" the man said, his voice impassive and cool though she struggled. "Ye'll not be hurt if ye do what I say."

She forced herself to stop fighting, though she could not control her quivering.

"I'll release yer mouth if ye promise not to scream. One scream and I'll silence ye fer good."

She nodded, even as fearful words fluttered inside her head, urging to scream for help, to flee. But he had her pinned to the bench. All she could hope to do was to stall him. Madingley House was not so far across Mayfair, and the coachman had been one of their trusted servants, not a man in league with this thief.

His gloved hand left her mouth, and she gasped.

"Easy," he said, as if she were a horse he was trying to break. He sat beside her on the bench, holding both her wrists prisoner in his hands.

He wore a soft-brimmed hat pulled low over his whiskered face, but did not shield his identity from her any other way. That sparked her fears even higher, because it seemed as if he didn't care that she could describe him to the police.

As if he didn't plan to release her at all.

She licked her dry lips and forced herself to speak. "What do you want? I am wearing little in jewelry, and only have a few coins in my—"

"Aye, it's jewelry I want, milady, but I don't see it 'round yer neck. The master wants the one ye wore to a fancy ball several nights ago—the one in the paintin'."

For a moment, she tried to organize her scattered thoughts. Who else could connect her to the painting but Parkhurst and his two friends? Was this some fool-ish attempt on his part to scare her into revealing the truth?

"The painting?" she whispered. "The only painting of me is in Cambridgeshire, in my parents'—"

"Don't play the fool."

He pulled her wrists until she half lay in his lap. A putrid smell rose around her.

"Ye know what paintin' I mean. I ain't seen it, but the master tells me ye bared everythin' God gave ye."

She shuddered and a moan escaped her. Then he took both her wrists in one hand, freeing his own to fumble beneath her cloak. He pinched her breast hard, and she bit her lip to keep from crying out.

This—this thief could not possibly be connected to the earl. She closed her eyes, fighting light-headedness and nausea as doubts assailed her. But what did she know of the earl after all? Evil could lurk within the *ton* as well as in any East End slum.

And the diamond pendant she wore to the ball? Lord Parkhurst hadn't even mentioned it to her. It was made of paste, and she'd only worn it for a lark.

But this man worked for someone who'd seen it, who wanted it. What would he do to get it?

"I—I didn't understand what you meant," she said, trying to placate him. "Please don't hurt me again, and I'll do what you wish."

She thought he would continue to paw her, might

even do worse, but something seemed to stay him. He released one of her wrists and she pushed off his lap, sitting back on the bench where she trembled uncontrollably.

"When we get to yer house, ye'll bring the diamond out to me. No one has to be hurt, includin' yerself." He leaned over her, eyes gleaming with cruelty, his breath foul. "But if ye don't, I'll follow ye inside. Ye may sic a footman on me, but not before I tell everyone about what ye did in that paintin', what kind of doxy ye are. Or maybe I'll hurt yer old mum. Now, is a pricey bauble worth all of that?"

She shook her head, staring at him. "Sic a footman"? Did he not understand how many people worked in a duke's home?

But of course he did. He had no intention of following her inside. He thought she was stupid—or fearful—enough to do anything he said. Yet she couldn't very well let this thief continue to follow her, or terrorize her family. And she couldn't go to the Metropolitan Police without revealing everything—including what had been revealed in that painting!

The carriage jerked to a halt. The thief backed farther into the shadows. "Tell the coachman ye're comin' right back. Get the diamond and bring it to me—or else."

She nodded frantically, rubbing her wrists, easily able to look terrified and cowed. She gathered her shawl about her as the footman opened the door, then gave

him her hand, trying hard not to tremble. She kept waiting for the thief to do something behind her, but he
remained silent.

After descending, she smiled stiffly at the coachman,
who stood near the matched pair of horses. "Hewet,
will you please wait here for me? I have another errand
to run."

"Of course, Miss Leland."

As she hurried up the stairs, she glanced up at the
warrior angels lining the roof, and sent a fervent prayer
heavenward that someone would be watching over her.
Once inside, she walked swiftly up the staircase, her
footsteps echoing in the marble hall. Nodding to the
occasional servant, she was glad when she reached her
bedroom. Just as Susanna promised, there were two
train tickets on her dressing table.

She pawed through her jewelry box, breathless and
shaking, until she found the diamond pendant. It glittered through the light from the window, shining a red-
speckled pattern across the carpet. *Real,* she thought in
amazement. And surely worth a fortune, for she'd not
seen many red diamonds, especially not one so large.
Quickly, she put it around her neck and tucked it within
her bodice. Then she grabbed her train ticket, skimmed
the printed schedule, and found just what she was looking for.

The door to her dressing room opened, and Beatrice,
her maid, entered. The round-faced woman came up

short, and her gaze went right to the tickets in Rebecca's hand.

"Miss Rebecca? Miss Susanna told me to send ahead your trunk for the goods train, and that has been done. But you aren't scheduled to leave for several more—"

"I know, Beatrice," Rebecca interrupted, forcing another smile, "but there has been a change of plans. My dear friend Rose decided to go with me, so I'm giving you a holiday."

Beatrice blinked, even as a slow smile touched her mouth. "But, miss, won't you need me?"

"Surely my great-aunt has plenty of servants. You haven't been to York to see your family in ages, have you?" Thinking quickly, she held out a train ticket. "Take this and have it transferred to something you can use. I won't need you for several weeks."

She seemed hesitant, thrilled, and Rebecca was so impatient she wanted to shove it into her hand and run.

"But doesn't your friend need this?"

"We'll buy another one. You just get yourself to the railway station so you can get right home."

"I confess, it is my mother's birthday."

"Why didn't you tell me that?" Rebecca asked, in truth this time. "I would have given you a holiday."

"But the Season—"

Rebecca snorted. "The Season will go on without us.

Now go!" With both hands she shooed her maid back the way she'd come.

Beatrice sent one more smile over her shoulder. "Thank you, miss! Enjoy your holiday!"

With a groan, Rebecca stuffed the ticket and schedule into her reticule, picked up her cloak, and left her bedchamber. But instead of heading for the front of the town house, she went down the rear stairway to the corridor that led out onto the terrace. She hurried down through the garden to the stables. A groom was happy to prepare a cabriolet that she could drive herself. She asked him to accompany her to the train station so that he could return the carriage.

"Ye'll not wait for yer maid, Miss Rebecca?"

She shook her head, using the power of her smile. "I've given her a holiday. It's Great-aunt Rianette and I alone in the Lake District."

Before she knew it, she was out in the alley, the groom holding on at her side as she turned up one street, and then the next until she was driving parallel to the town house.

She'd kept the top down on the carriage, and made certain she called loudly to her coachman, "Ho, there, Hewet, I decided to drive myself. I'm so late!"

Even as the coachman saluted and climbed up into the box, she saw the shutters in the carriage move and knew the thief had seen her. She urged her horse faster, not bothering to see how he got out of the carriage, or if someone was waiting nearby for him. There was no time to waste as she led him away from Madingley House and her family.

It hadn't been difficult to notice when Rebecca left Lady Thurlow's reception. Julian followed on his horse as she returned in the enclosed carriage. She was not going to leave town without him knowing about it. At the duke's town house, he took the opportunity for a little exploring, leaving his horse on the street to follow the garden wall back toward the alley. Over the top he could count the windows on the second floor to estimate the number of bedrooms.

He wasn't certain what he planned to do with such information—steal into her bedroom beneath the nose of the dowager duchess? Or should he try to find a way into the garden? Somehow he needed to keep track of her, to discover if she truly meant to leave London. He came upon a wrought-iron door, but it was well locked.

And that's when he saw Rebecca hurrying through the garden, wearing her cloak, heading for the stables. He didn't bother calling out, only began to run toward the back alley. He crept the width of the garden wall toward the great double doors that led to the stables. It seemed to take forever. Surely Madingley House was the largest palace in London. Before he even reached the doors, a horse emerged with a cabriolet behind it. And there was Rebecca driving, her expression intent, even though a wide-eyed groom sat at her side. She was past Julian without even seeing him, and he took off at a run for the front of the house and his horse.

By the time he caught up to her carriage in the London traffic, he was feeling like a fool. Did he plan to follow her night and day?

But he just had a bad feeling about all of this. She'd left a carriage sitting out front, only to take another one she could drive herself. Why? He didn't believe for a moment that she was teasing him about traveling. She had something planned.

And his instincts were confirmed when she pulled up to the Euston Railway Station, with its massive columns holding up an arch like a Greek temple. She hopped down without waiting for her groom, and more than one man had a fleeting, impressive view of her trim ankles.

At the entrance to the train station, she looked back one more time at the street—and saw him.

Julian saluted and smiled, even as he dismounted near her carriage. But to his surprise, her face drained of blood. She picked up her skirts and practically ran inside.

Frowning, his sense of urgency increasing, Julian caught the Madingley groom before he could step up into the cabriolet.

"You there," Julian said. For once he was glad he could say, "I am Parkhurst. I need you to return my horse to my town house on Berkeley Square." He handed over several coins.

The boy's jaw dropped. "A-aye, milord."

To Julian's surprise, he almost didn't catch up with Rebecca. She had a train ticket, and he didn't, and she was able to show hers at the gate and hurry toward the waiting train. At least he knew they were headed north, for this station only served the London and Birmingham Railway.

Was he really going to do this? he thought, even as he purchased his own first-class ticket at the counter. Get on a train without luggage and see what happened, in pursuit of Rebecca Leland?

Her face flashed in his mind, all pink and languid and expectant just before he'd been about to kiss her. And then he saw a more recent memory, where she'd looked almost terrified to see him. What had happened in the space of an hour?

Chapter 6

Rebecca found it terribly easy to switch her train ticket from the 5:10 to the 3:15, even though she dropped her ticket in the booking office from sheer nerves. Two men fell to their knees to retrieve it, and she concentrated on them gratefully, afraid to look behind her.

The Earl of Parkhurst had been following her.

She had wanted that to happen, hadn't she? She'd practically *told* him she was going on a journey. She'd wanted a grand adventure—

And then she'd been held captive in her carriage, threatened, forced to run—surely not at his behest. She couldn't believe that of a peer. Or his friends, men she and her family had socialized with their whole lives.

But he'd seen the painting and the diamond. Who else could connect that to her?

She reminded herself she'd worn the necklace to a ball before knowing that the painting wasn't in a French collection. Probably any number of men, members at the same club, might have connected her to the jewel, once they'd heard that a Society woman had posed.

But it was Lord Parkhurst following her, no one else. Was the thief following separately, or were they together?

She prayed that his lordship didn't have a ticket, that he wouldn't make the train. She needed to figure out what she was going to do next.

The London and Birmingham train was already there, steaming in the sunlight. Men and women bustled to their carriages, carrying portmanteaus or having their luggage loaded on carts pushed by porters. Not her, she thought, resisting the urge to give in to a grim laugh.

But as she was assisted into her compartment in the first-class carriages, she looked behind her and saw the thief. She almost stumbled going up the stair. In daylight, he'd looked more respectable than she'd imagined, in his coat and trousers and white shirt, like a working-class man taking the train to another working-class town, perhaps Birmingham or even farther to Manchester. But from her window she could see him watching her, even as he stood back near the third-class carriage. There were no seats in that carriage; they'd only recently put roofs on the cars to protect the passengers from the elements. He didn't enter, as if he were waiting to see if she'd run for it now that she'd seen him.

He was shoulder to shoulder with another man, she

realized with dismay. They even spoke together; they wanted her to see she was outnumbered. Had the second thief been waiting near Madingley House and together they'd followed her?

Did that mean that the earl wasn't involved with the attempted robbery and kidnapping? She didn't know what to think. There were always a rare few of the nobility who believed that their title allowed them to do anything in their own interest. Just then, she saw Lord Parkhurst leave the railway booking office, ticket in hand. She wasn't certain he could see into her compartment, but he walked right toward her. Only six people fit in each carriage, and there was already a family seated in hers: mother, father and two children. Their clothes displayed a rather open wealth, and she imagined they were of the newly rich industrial class since they didn't seem familiar.

There was one extra place on the bench, directly across from her. She gritted her teeth as Lord Parkhurst opened the door and leaned in.

"Is there an open seat?" he asked politely.

The man already inside went a little wide-eyed on seeing the earl. He must have recognized him, for he nodded and said, "Of course, my lord."

Rebecca wanted to ignore them all. She wanted to chew her fingernails; instead she plastered her face to the window to see what her two shadows were doing. Surely they were waiting until the last possible moment to board their carriage, just to make certain she did.

She had led them away from her family—what was she supposed to do now? She could hardly go all the way to Aunt Rianette's home and put even more family in danger. She had hoped something brilliant would occur to her. It didn't. She put a hand to her upper chest, where beneath her cloak and gown she could feel the outline of the jewel, warm against her flesh.

She could hear Lord Parkhurst settling in, even as the train whistle sounded. Porters hurriedly loaded the last of the luggage above the train carriages, those that hadn't been sent with the earlier goods train, as hers had been.

She had no other clothing but what she was wearing. She pressed her lips together, still feeling a little hysterical amusement.

And then something brushed her foot and, startled, she was forced to stop looking out the window. Lord Parkhurst's great legs were sprawled before her, his knees almost reaching hers, his feet beneath her skirts. He was watching her, a faint smile on his broad mouth. She hastily dropped her hand from the hidden diamond.

At last, with a jerk and a shudder, the train began to move, heading north out of London. She turned to look out the window again. She didn't want to talk to the earl, didn't know what she could possibly say to him without revealing their strange connection to the small family traveling with them.

At least he seemed to realize the same, for he didn't speak to her either. Yet she could not forget him, for the rumbling and vibrating of the train sometimes let their legs briefly touch—or was he instigating it? She wouldn't put it past him as he tried to unnerve her.

At last the father of the little family, Mr. Seymour, struck up a conversation with the earl about the expansion of the railways, and Rebecca felt a bit of her tension ease. She huddled within her cloak, wishing she had a rug across her lap as each member of the little family did. It was always so drafty on a train.

Within the next hour, after several brief stops at railway stations in Middlesex and Hertfordshire, the little children, a boy and a girl, became bored with the countryside and their confinement and began to pick fights with each other. At one stop, the Seymour family's maid came up from second class to bring them sandwiches and beverages from the dining car. That helped occupy the children. After a while, Rebecca couldn't conceal that a maid wasn't traveling with her, for no one brought her food. Mrs. Seymour offered to share, but Rebecca declined politely.

Always Lord Parkhurst was watching her, smiling as if she amused him.

As if he had her right where he wanted her.

She shivered. Hadn't she wanted a grand adventure? How much more adventurous could a sheltered lady be? She was being chased by three men; she was wearing a valuable jewel around her neck; she had no idea where she was going, or what she would do to elude the thieves.

And she was facing a large, powerful man who looked at her as if he could eat her up.

She was almost cowering against the window. That had to stop. Rolling her shoulders for a moment, she repositioned her legs, wishing she could stretch them out. But that would be right between Lord Parkhurst's legs. Lifting her chin, she met his gaze, then straightened her stiff limbs anyway. He arched a brow, a smile playing on his mouth, but he made no physical response as she invaded his territory.

The little boy, perhaps five, chose that moment to have a tantrum that his red-faced mother could not hush. He seemed to forget where he was as he ducked away from his mother, then tripped over Lord Parkhurst's legs. The boy fell right between Rebecca and the earl, and as they both leaned forward to help him, their heads banged together. She straightened, hand to her head to readjust her hat even as the earl came up with the boy in his big hands. Lord Parkhurst surely didn't notice their collision, while she felt as if she'd hit a great big rock.

"Oh my!" said Mrs. Seymour, wringing her hands together. "My lord, I am so sorry!"

To Rebecca's surprise, Lord Parkhurst put the boy on his knee and gestured out his window.

"It doesn't look much different on this side of the train, does it?" he said soothingly. "We're passing through the Chilterns now. Do you know what they are?"

Rebecca gaped—along with Mr. and Mrs. Seymour—as his lordship held a conversation about the chalk hills with a five-year-old. The man had no children of his own. He'd been seeing to the business of his title for almost ten years. Had he made time for his brothers and sisters? She wouldn't have thought so, with the tension she sensed between him and his twin brothers.

Could a man who so easily conversed with a child be involved with the thief who'd kidnapped her today? What was she supposed to do with him—and the other two men whom she'd seen waiting for her to disembark at each station?

Julian watched as Rebecca's stiff, tense body finally yielded to sleep. They'd been traveling almost three hours, and they hadn't had a conversation yet. She hadn't left the train, not even for a moment's privacy in a railway station. She had to be hungry—he certainly was. What was the point of her behavior, if she were simply fleeing London and the wager?

He still couldn't erase the image from his mind of how frightened she'd looked when she'd first seen him

at the station. Something had changed—and he hated
being ignorant of it. He was a man who left nothing to
chance, even if it was the smallest business decision. He
over-researched everything. And now he was turning
that focus on Rebecca Leland. He knew she was cold,
the drafts going up her skirt, but too proud to ask for
help—or to purchase a lap rug at a station.

More than once, he'd seen her hand go unconsciously
to her bodice, fingering something beneath her cloak.
She hadn't worn the diamond to Lady Thurlow's reception; why should he believe she'd donned it for the
journey?

Because he always trusted his instincts.

At last they reached a railway station in Warwick-
shire, and the entire Seymour family temporarily departed, leaving their cloaks and gloves behind. Rebecca
looked out the window, her expression pensive.

He folded his arms over his chest. "So where are you
going without a maid?"

Her gaze shot to him, cool—but a touch hesitant.
Was he about to hear something resembling the truth?

"You followed me," she said in a low voice.

"I do not take wagers lightly. And you deliberately
led me on with your talk of a journey. You *wanted* me
to follow you."

She took a breath, then leaned toward him, eyes suddenly earnest. "You're not the only one following me."

He went still, staring at her, taking her measure. Was

this a game, part of some plan to keep all her secrets hidden?

But then she glanced out the window, and her face paled. Could she be telling the truth? He thought again of how she'd gone in the front entrance of Madingley House, leaving a carriage waiting, then emerged from the rear, driving as fast as she could in traffic.

"Are you with them?" she asked, gesturing with her head out the window.

He looked past her. The platform was crowded but, after a moment, he realized most people were milling about, stretching their legs, or walking briskly to and from the station.

But two roughly dressed men stood alone, unmoving near the first-class carriages. And they were looking right into Julian and Rebecca's compartment.

He arched a brow. "How long have they been following you?" Someone else must have made the connection between the painting, the diamond, and Rebecca. Did she even realize what was going on?

Or perhaps the heirs to the maharajah, who'd given the Scandalous Lady to his father, had never let their interest in the diamond die.

She studied him. "You do not even ask if I'm making things up, or letting my feminine nerves get the best of me. I cannot tell if it's because you're treating me as a responsible adult—or because you already *know* they're following me."

"You're accusing me of being in league with them," he said calmly, wanting to take offense, but not wanting to frighten her into silence. "Why ever would you believe such a thing?"

She linked her hands in her lap, and he had to be impressed by the cool way she faced this situation.

"Aren't *all* of you following me?" she asked with sarcasm.

He gave her a faint smile. "You have a point. But you know why I'm following you. Do you have any knowledge of those two men?"

She hesitated, worrying her lower lip between her teeth. Then she seemed to make a decision, for she let out her breath and said, "One of them was hiding inside my carriage when I left the reception."

He straightened. "Are you well?" he asked in a harsh voice.

She blinked at him. "Don't I look well?"

"You're proud enough to hide what you wish to. Answer my question."

"I'm well," she said, still looking at him as if surprised.

"Tell me everything he did from the moment you entered the carriage."

So she recited her afternoon adventure, step by step, and Julian's anger increased with each revelation. She acted as if the diamond she'd worn was hardly worth this kind of determination.

"You didn't see the second man earlier?" he asked.

She shook her head. "Not until just before we boarded. If you didn't bring the thief with you—"

He actually emitted a growl, surprising himself and startling her.

Quickly, she continued, "Then he had to have traveled to the station with that second man."

"And you simply boarded the train, rather than go to the authorities," he said with disbelief.

"And what would you have me say?" she asked coolly. " 'Yes, Officer, I was wearing the aforementioned diamond when I posed nude. Shall I show the painting to you, so you can parade it before all of London?' "

Of course she wouldn't have thought of her own safety—only the scandal of it all, and what it would do to her family.

She'd been protecting her family by leading the thieves away from Madingley House. He didn't want to admire her right now, not when he was still furious that she'd put herself in worse danger.

"Did you have any plan at all?" he demanded, spreading his hands wide.

She lifted her chin. "I would have thought of one. But you kept distracting me."

He let that curious idea go without comment. He rubbed a hand down his face.

"Your friends are returning," she suddenly said, her body stiff.

He saw the Seymours escorting their children toward the train.

"We won't be able to talk," he said swiftly. "I'll remove you from this situation. Be ready—and for God's sake, do whatever I say, immediately, with no questions asked."

He could see her bristling, like a cat with its fur standing on end. But she pinched her mouth into a straight line and said nothing as the compartment door opened and the family piled back in.

Lord Parkhurst had actually fallen asleep. Rebecca stared at him, dismayed and angry, as the train chugged closer and closer to Birmingham, where she'd be forced to disembark to change railways.

That is if she continued to head north, as her ticket permitted her to. She might have once planned to lead the earl to Great-aunt Rianette, but she didn't want two thieves tagging along.

Part of her longed to stand up, to ease her bodily discomforts, to quiet her gurgling stomach. Lord Parkhurst had to be just as uncomfortable—but he was sleeping, his deep-set eyes closed, the tension gone from his frame.

If she could have woken him with her angry stare, he'd have a smoking hole between his eyes.

What did he have in mind? She wanted to be a part

of his decision-making—not dragged about like a helpless girl.

She wasn't helpless; she'd outwitted a thief who'd
threatened to harm her family.

"Do you know his lordship, miss?"

Startled, Rebecca glanced to her side, at the mother
who held her sleeping daughter in her lap. They'd sat
practically shoulder to shoulder for several hours, and
Mrs. Seymour had at first seemed to realize that Rebecca wasn't in a talkative mood.

Rebecca was about to claim a mere acquaintanceship
with the earl and turn back to her window, when she
suddenly realized that she had in her hands the ability
to control what people thought of her—should someone
ever question her presence on the train.

And she was still simmering with irritation that Lord
Parkhurst held all the power, while she was helpless to
do anything other than allow him to save her. It grated
on her.

Rebecca smiled at Mrs. Seymour. "We are ac-
quainted, ma'am. But . . . it is difficult for Lord Parkhurst
and me to talk. He's still angry because I rejected his
suit."

The woman gasped. "Why would you reject an
earl?"

Rebecca noticed that Lord Parkhurst did not seem
quite so relaxed. Had he been sleeping at all, or merely

dozing? Why would he do so, unless to make her angry? Well, then, he'd succeeded.

Rebecca dropped her voice, even though she knew he would certainly hear her whisper. "He's not a very romantic sort, ma'am. A woman needs flowers and courtship. He seemed to think that his wealth alone would have me begging for marriage."

Mrs. Seymour spoke doubtfully. "Then you are a better woman than most. You do not seem to be traveling together," she added.

"We're not. But I think he realized the error of his ways, and now he's trying to pursue me."

"You'd think he'd try a bit harder. He hasn't even spoken to you."

Rebecca sighed. "Do you see what I mean? He's rather dense."

The train hit an uneven part of the track, jolting them all, and Lord Parkhurst obviously used that opportunity to pretend to awaken.

He smiled at them. "Did I sleep? Hope I didn't embarrass myself."

"You drooled dreadfully," Rebecca said in a sweet voice. "I could not possibly marry a man who drooled."

Mr. and Mrs. Seymour stared between them, eyes wide. Rebecca imagined they didn't think anyone would ever be so forward with an earl.

And then Lord Parkhurst leaned near and gripped

her hands urgently. "My dearest, how can you tease me so, knowing how I feel about you?"

So he didn't mind her playacting, and committed himself to it. His hands were so large, so strong. He could do anything he wanted to her, now that they were away from London. It was strange how that hadn't occurred to her when she was making plans to lure him away and win the wager.

But now she needed him to escape two others who might be worse—*might,* she reminded herself.

"Come, Lord Parkhurst, you're embarrassing yourself," she said coolly.

The little girl had woken up and now contently sucked her thumb, staring at them from her mother's lap.

"I cannot think of embarrassment, my dear, not when our future is at stake." He glanced apologetically at the Seymours. "But I imagine we shouldn't talk about this now."

"Why? They might have very good opinions," she said, batting her lashes at him. "After all, they're married."

This was certainly a better distraction than wondering how she was going to escape two determined thieves. In fact, she felt positively amused.

But Lord Parkhurst gave her hands another squeeze and sat back. "No, my dear, I'll have a chance to plead my case when we arrive."

"*That* is romantic," Mrs. Seymour said shyly.

Lord Parkhurst bestowed the full force of his grin on the poor woman, who blushed from the roots of her hair to the base of her neck.

Rebecca sighed, and for the next half hour, was forced to put up with the earl "courting" her by nudging her feet. Surely they were presenting the Seymours with a fine show.

The train slowed at Coventry, only a few stops from Birmingham. The Seymours said their good-byes, for this was their destination.

Then Rebecca and the earl were left alone. She waited for him to rebuke her—or perhaps laugh at her antics—but he was concentrating on the view of the platform outside the window.

She glanced that way, saw the two thieves, and gave a soft groan.

"Prepare yourself," he said quietly.

She perked up. "What do you mean to do? That was the whistle, we're departing."

He nodded, then lowered his window and leaned his head out. Smoke seeped in, and she resisted the urge to cough, blinking her stinging eyes.

"Will you close that before we can't breathe?"

But it was still another minute before he closed the window and said, "Our interested friends are back in their carriage. They can't see us. Let's go."

She gasped, for the train jerked and slowly began

to move. But she gamely reached for the door handle toward the platform.

"Not that one. We don't want the world knowing we've left."

He opened the opposite door, which led to the right side of the track—in the dangerous area between the up and down railway lines.

"But—there's no platform!" she cried. "We're starting to move too fast."

He had the door open and his foot on the single stair below. He reached for her. "We need to jump—now!"

Chapter 7

Rebecca felt like she was flying. It wasn't that long a fall, but the fact that the train was moving made everything worse. She stumbled and landed hard onto her stomach, rolling several times. Her cloak became entangled around her, and with a gasp she yanked it away from her face. Lord Parkhurst dragged her to her feet and to the far side of a shed between the rail lines.

Breathing heavily, her heart pounding, she waited with her eyes closed as the train picked up speed. Her whole body seemed to vibrate, and a fierce wind ruffled her skirts. She was still clutching the earl's hand, and she didn't let go.

At last the noise and rumbling lessened, and she slowly opened her eyes. Lord Parkhurst was beside her, his back to the shed. With a gasp she looked across the other track to the northwest, from where another train could have arrived.

He gave a soft laugh. "It's a good thing I'd already

checked if another train was in the distance. We might have been swept under the wheels."

She yanked her hand away.

His amusement faded, and he looked down her body. "Are you injured? You have a scrape on your face."

He gently touched her cheek. She ducked away from his hand. Her cloak was still thrown back over one shoulder, and to her dismay, the delicate yellow silk of her gown was torn in several places, and filthy in many others. She could see her hair tumbling down around her shoulders. Her hat was crushed on the ground. Frustrated, she yanked closed her cloak, noticing that the earl looked unscathed.

"I am fine." Then she coughed. The air was foul with the smell of the train, and she started to move away from the shed.

"Wait."

His voice was a command to be obeyed, and she imagined he was used to giving orders. Begrudgingly, she waited while he looked around the corner of the shed, toward the platform.

"Do you see the thieves?" she asked.

"No. I'm certain they never left the train."

"Well, they certainly thought we stayed on it," she said dryly. "We took quite the risk of being pulled beneath the wheels."

"It was moving slow enough. We were safe."

They looked at each other, and for a moment, she

wondered if she was really safe at all. But it was too late to have doubts. She ran her hands through her hair, slipping the remainder of the pins into her reticule. She found weeds caught in her curls, and even a bit of gravel. But she finger-combed it as best she could.

"If we're lucky," he said, "the thieves will believe we jumped from the train on our arrival at the next station. It may take them days of searching before they realize their error."

She gave a reluctant smile. "An ingenious plan."

He nodded, and said in a serious voice, "I know."

She frowned at his arrogance.

"Hey, mate!"

They both started. A porter on the deserted platform for the down line was gaping at them.

"Ye can't cross between the lines there!" the man cried. "Ye could have been killed."

Before Lord Parkhurst could speak, she called, "Oh, sir, I've never ridden a train before. This man only tried to stop me, and surely he saved me from being run over by the train!"

The porter grumbled and motioned for them. After they crossed the tracks, the porter reached down to help her, for she could not jump onto the platform in her unwieldy skirts. Lord Parkhurst moved behind her and put his hands directly on her backside to boost her up with the porter's help. Her mouth tightened at such familiarity, and she could not escape the intimacy quick enough.

How much had he been able to see beneath her skirts?

She tossed a glare at him over her shoulder when she was safe on the platform. With ease, he boosted himself up, going from a squat to standing with graceful energy, the sleeves of his coat tightening over thick muscles. Ruefully, she imagined anything physical was never a challenge for him.

And then she blushed as he looked at her, as if he could read her mind. She quickly turned away.

The porter gave them another incredulous look and stomped away, leaving them alone on the platform. Her reticule dangled from her wrist, but that was all the luggage they had between them.

She gave him a bright smile. "Shall you buy your return ticket?"

He frowned. "Two men were following you, Rebecca. You expect me to leave you here?"

"I will be fine. I'll get back on the next train and go to my aunt's."

"It will have been easy for them to discover where you were journeying. Servants talk."

"Not our servants!"

"*Your* servants told me you were at Banstead House this afternoon."

"You *are* an earl. Of course they'd feel they must obey you—and you used that against them. Regardless, I certainly cannot be seen traveling with a man."

To her shock, he lifted his hand and set his fingers

on her bodice, right where the jewel hung just at the top of her breasts. She gasped, and her breathing picked up again, which only made her breasts touch his sleeve with rapid little flutters. A strange and almost achy sensation flushed through her.

"And what were you going to do with the diamond?" he asked in a low voice.

She batted his hand away and renewed her smile. "That's my problem, my lord."

He looked behind himself, but the platform was yet deserted. He spoke softly. "From now on, you cannot call me that. I am Julian, Rebecca."

His tone was too intimate—as had been his touch. He'd rescued her from one situation, and thrown her into the fire of another.

"The sun is setting, and we cannot remain in the open," he continued. "Your thieves might already have deduced what we did and know where to come."

Could she trust him? She still knew nothing about him except gossip—and that had only been about some scandal of which she didn't know the details. He was reclusive in Society—what was he concealing? Did he just "happen" to be following her when the thieves were?

All she could do was bide her time. "So we find an inn? Surely there is one near the railway station."

"We can't use that. We need to conceal ourselves, not appear as an earl and a gentlewoman."

She gave him an ironic glance. "In my present disheveled state, that will be easier for me."

He rubbed his chin. "True, you look like a doxy who found a fine gown in the rubbish."

She resisted the urge to slap him. "Did no one ever tell you that insulting a lady is bad form?"

"No insult meant—I simply told the truth." He looked down at himself. "For myself, it will be difficult to blend in wearing such garments."

"A shame we didn't bring luggage," she said dryly, hands on her hips. "Very well, let us find an inn before our friends return. Have you ever been here before?"

He shook his head. "If only it were that easy. Since we still have an hour or so of daylight, we'll start walking, looking for the oldest section of the city. We'll ask for directions there, rather than here, where railway employees might remember us."

She grinned. "Well thought out, Lord— Julian."

They walked through the crooked, narrow streets of an unfamiliar town, with its medieval timber-framed houses that almost overlapped each other. Julian followed those streets as much as possible, as the light disappeared down dark alleys. The ground sloped gently upward, toward an old church that sat at the summit of Coventry.

They received many suspicious stares, even though

he'd removed his cravat and waistcoat and smeared dirt on his well-polished boots. He'd even torn the shoulder of his coat and the hem of Rebecca's cloak.

But it was difficult to hide her natural, ladylike grace, the proud way she carried herself. And although he kept warning her of the seriousness of their situation, she actually seemed to be enjoying herself. Other women would protest as they entered narrower, more decrepit lanes, but she only looked about with interest, studying everything she could.

Or memorizing the path they'd taken. Intelligent of her. But although he kept reminding her to lower her gaze in a docile fashion, she couldn't seem to remember.

At last he thought they were far enough from the train station that he felt safe entering a tavern to ask for the nearest inn. His size tended to inspire quick answers, so he didn't have to leave Rebecca standing outside the door for any length of time. And although his garments called attention to himself, his rural accent was flawless.

When he emerged back onto the twilit street, Rebecca looked up at him with grudging interest. "That was well done," she said softly. "And I thought I was the only one who could mimic the servants."

"The talent will come in handy," he said. "This way."

They walked side by side and he considered her. "Why did you learn to mimic the servants?"

She shrugged. "If you know anything about me, you know that I was ill often as a child. That left me with much free time. I learned to read aloud and alter my voice to fit the parts. It was a game my brother and I played. We became very good at it. And you?"

She seemed so vibrant that it was difficult to imagine her pale and ill. He looked ahead of him, at a lounging man who came to his feet when he saw them. Julian frowned, and the man promptly sat back down on his crate and hunched his shoulders.

"Accents came quite naturally to me," Julian said, "probably because I was with the servants more than anyone else."

He sensed her curiosity, but didn't see the need to satisfy it.

"You have a large family," she said, "or so my mother tells me. One would think *they* would take up most of your time."

"The inn should be nearby."

She was still studying him too intently, but she didn't continue her questions.

On the next block, they found the inn, The White Hare, whose faded sign hung crookedly. There was an arch leading into a stabling yard where several broken-down carriages sat among the weeds. The stables stood open and empty, without horses to rent.

"You have investments in railways?" she asked quietly.

He frowned down at her. "You heard me discuss it with Mr. Seymour. Why?"

"*This* is what happened to small towns because of the railways."

He nodded. Coaches no longer moved up and down England, leaving posting inns to fade into oblivion.

"But how many days would it have taken us to get here by coach?" he countered.

"I didn't say there weren't benefits. I enjoy the train. Someday I'd like to travel it as far north as I can and see even more of England."

Now she seemed to be babbling, and he couldn't blame her. They stepped into the hall of the inn, with its unswept floor and empty sideboards. A lone young man occupied the counter, propped on a stool and looking bored. The youth barely glanced at them when Julian signed the register.

Rebecca peered over his shoulder, and he knew she saw the signature, "Mr. and Mrs. Bacon." She only arched a brow and turned away.

He needed to be alone with her and keep both her and the diamond safe. But it didn't seem to bother her to be labeled his wife.

And his groin tightened at the thought.

A shuffling chambermaid showed them to their room and started a fire in the coal grate. She turned down the bed, not meeting their eyes.

"We'll be needin' a meal," Julian said, handing over a coin for her trouble.

The girl looked at it in surprise. "Aye, sir. Me mum made a fine mutton and pudding." Then she truly looked at him, and bobbed a curtsy.

When she had gone, Rebecca said, "I imagine you tipped her far too well, which made her notice your garments—and remember us."

He glanced at her and gave a faint smile. "I will not make that mistake again."

"We won't be dressed like this for long. For more coin, she will be able to find clothing for us, so your generosity won't go to waste."

He stood in the center of the room, watching as Rebecca prowled about. She ducked her head behind a changing screen, partially torn. The chamber pot must have been hidden behind, for her cheeks were a delicate pink when she straightened. There was one bed, and he wasn't even sure his shoulders would fit across it, let alone the two of them.

Had she realized yet?

She stumbled to a halt at the foot of the bed. "Lord— Julian," she began. After a pause, she turned away from the bed. "I need a moment's privacy. Would you wait in the hall?"

He used the privy in the stable yard, and by the time he returned, she was seated before the grate, finally looking uncertain. She'd lit several coarse candles, but there wasn't a lamp. Her hair, though disheveled, gleamed in the warm yellow light, and her eyes, great pools of mystery, regarded him steadily. She'd removed her cloak, and with the shadows, he could see the faint lump of the diamond, the Scandalous Lady, she kept hidden. How much should he reveal to her? And what should be their next move?

But before he had to think about it, the maid returned with a tray, and the two of them sat down on stools at the wobbly, rough table and began to eat.

They were both clearly famished, for even the pudding was appetizing, though it tasted of onions. The coarse bread steamed, and the butter was fresh.

"Oh, heavens, this tastes like the best feast," she said, speaking with her mouth full. "I didn't even have time to eat the luncheon at the reception."

"You mean before you ran away from me?"

"I don't run away."

But she had, he thought, not arguing the point, for she knew it well. But now the specter of the near kiss rose between them—at least in his mind. She seemed determined to devour every last crumb, then washed it all down with ale.

"Do you usually drink such a strong beverage?" he asked as she wiped the foam from her lip.

"I have sampled it, but it is not my first choice. Tonight it tastes like the nectar of the gods."

He didn't want to laugh, for this was no journey of amusement. Yet, she kept surprising him, even her performance on the train, where she'd pretended he was her ardent suitor.

She leaned back against the wall, her arm across her stomach. "I am sated at last," she murmured, eyes closed with weariness.

He arched a brow, thinking of far more wicked ways she could be "sated."

Being alone with her was giving him interesting ideas, he told himself. Perhaps it was because for the first time in almost ten years, he didn't know what would happen next, had no plan for the coming moments, hours—night. There were so many ways they could amuse themselves.

She suddenly shivered and hugged herself. "Julian—" She broke off, as if surprised to hear his Christian name from her lips.

He'd never heard another woman call him such, except for family. It sounded intimate here in this room where they pretended to be husband and wife.

She gave a rueful smile and started again, "Julian, when you take the tray down, will you fetch me another blanket? The coal grate is only meagerly filled."

He noticed the extra blanket on the end of the bed. And she did not? And why not leave the tray for the maid in the morning?

Something made him agree and lift up the tray. She

gave him a grateful smile, dazzling him. He held the tray one-handed while he stepped into the hall, closing the door behind him. And then he stopped, his ear to the door.

She seemed to be moving around, for her footsteps tapped regularly. Then he heard something squeak, and wood being dragged across the floor.

He set the tray on the hall floor, then opened their door, only to find her standing on a stool, head and shoulders out the window.

Chapter 8

When she felt big hands around her waist, Rebecca gasped and tried to kick, but Julian eluded her blows, hauling her back inside. To her mortification, she slid down his body, her backside to his front. She fought his restraining hands and he let her go. Over her head, he slammed the shutters closed, even as she stumbled away from him and caught herself on the bedpost.

"What was the meaning of that?" he demanded.

She faced him, hands on her hips. "Why ever would I trust you? I told you I was leaving London, and suddenly men are following me—including you!"

"According to you, the thief was in your carriage at Lady Thurlow's. I didn't even know you were leaving before that."

"But you have an unscrupulous wager about me. And you saw the diamond in the painting."

"And around your neck at a ball, *before* I saw the painting," he added grimly.

She narrowed her eyes. "The thief said that his master saw the jewel in both places, too."

"Many men could have seen the same thing. You cannot be accusing me of hiring a man to terrorize you."

He seemed outraged as he drew himself up, but that only reminded Rebecca how very large he was, how he seemed to dwarf the tiny room—the tiny bed. With his clothing dirty, his hair windblown, whiskers darkening his face, he seemed far too dangerous, not like a civilized earl.

"Why shouldn't I accuse you?" she demanded. "I left the thief in my carriage, and he turns up at the railway station at the same time as you!"

"We were both following you—separately."

"And why should I believe you?" she demanded, feeling frustrated. "How am I supposed to know the truth?"

He took a deep breath, as if he were trying to control his temper. She had seen no evidence of an unruly one—but she didn't know him at all.

"I'll tell you what you need to know."

That could mean many things, but she refrained from pointing that out. "Please do."

She thought he would pace the room to work off his anger, but he remained utterly still as he spoke.

"The name of the diamond is the Scandalous Lady."

Whatever she'd thought he would say to excuse himself, it wasn't that. "You know the name?"

"It was my father's. It had been missing for almost ten years—and then I saw you wearing it at the ball."

She sank down slowly on the bed. "Your father's?" She couldn't even make a connection between the painting, Roger Eastfield the artist, and the last earl of Parkhurst.

Julian nodded. "It was a gift to my father from an Indian maharajah who was visiting London. My father served as his official escort on behalf of the king."

"When I wore it, I thought it was paste," she said lamely.

"My father was honored to accept it, but when the maharajah died, his heirs tried to say that my father had coerced an old man out of a precious heirloom."

She held her breath in surprise. Julian looked toward the hearth, his heavy brows lowered, his gray eyes focused far away. She sensed . . . something within him, an old pain he kept buried. It was close to the surface now; he yet struggled with it. He was a proud man, and she imagined his father had been the same.

"That must have been terrible for the earl," she said softly. "What happened?"

"My father disagreed, and he kept the jewel. Society being as it was, the gossip was brief and then gone, especially since it dealt with Indians," he added sardonically. "But my father was humiliated."

"Of course he was," she murmured.

"Just before my eighteenth birthday, the Scandalous Lady was stolen. And then my father died."

She didn't try to hide her sympathy now, but he wasn't looking at her. She knew she was lucky that her parents were still alive, and thankfully, more in love with each other now than for most of their marriage.

"I inherited money from my mother's side of the family," Julian continued, "enough to save our property and to begin again."

She wanted to ask what had happened to their wealth, but sensed it wasn't a good time. He was speaking so impassively, as if reciting history written in a book, instead of the personal, painful things that had happened to him and his family.

His eyes narrowed as he considered the past. "But the rumors of the Scandalous lady wouldn't die. People said it had not been stolen, that either I or my father had sold it, and used the proceeds to resurrect our fortunes."

"I imagine that as a young man, you didn't appreciate people ignoring the hard work you were doing."

He frowned at her, but only in consideration. "I didn't care what they thought of my work. I simply wanted them to believe the truth."

"You know by now that people believe what they want, Julian. We can't change that. We can only accept it and move forward." She'd learned that lesson over and over since childhood.

He crossed his arms over his chest. "This all took place almost ten years ago."

"I was still in the schoolroom," she said mildly.

He rolled his eyes, and she saw that he'd regained control of the emotions battling inside him—emotions that he'd spent his adulthood keeping locked away, she guessed. She heard he was in control of an empire he'd resurrected, and she saw how firmly he managed the people all around him. He was certainly taking control of her, too. But his feelings? Mastering them was a different matter, and she felt it must frustrate him. It seemed so . . . foreign to her. She was a member of a family that loved openly, fought openly, expressed every emotion.

"So if you're not accusing me of theft . . ." Her voice trailed off expectantly.

"I need to find out how the Scandalous Lady came to you."

Julian watched Rebecca's hazel, changeable eyes, looking for a clue to her thoughts. He didn't know her well enough to read the truth, but he was a good judge of the measure of a person. Yet . . . the depth of her eluded him. It was too soon in their acquaintance, but it frustrated him nonetheless.

She sighed and leaned back on her hands as she sat on the bed. Though her gown was torn and dirty, in the soft candlelight he didn't notice such things, only the curves of her breasts, the smooth line of her cheek.

He couldn't afford to lose track of the importance of this conversation. "Well?" he asked, keeping his voice even. "How did you come by the diamond?"

"Roger Eastfield had it. He suggested I wear it when I posed for the painting." She shrugged, her smile wry. "He was the artist, so I obeyed. When I asked to borrow it, he agreed, telling me it was only paste. It was such a good piece of craftsmanship that I thought it would work well with one of my gowns—as you saw."

"It drew a man's eyes where you wanted them to go."

She inhaled swiftly, eyes widening.

He smiled. "I meant no disrespect. Women dress to be seen, and to emphasize their best assets."

"I would like to think my best asset is my mind," she said.

"Conversation would show that, of course." He hesitated, momentarily remembering the wager. "Then again, you'd already had a painting show *several* of your best assets."

"Believe what you will," she said firmly, frowning. "So do you want to talk about the painting again, or the diamond?"

He sank down slowly onto a stool at the table. He had so many questions about why she'd chosen to pose nude—but now wasn't the time. "The artist never spoke of the diamond, or how he came by it?"

She shook her head. "I'm sorry. And I didn't think to ask. It was in a box with other jewelry."

"Perhaps he was a thief," Julian mused.

"He was a creative person, passionate about his work. Why would he do such a thing?"

"To support his art. I understand that demand is now growing for his paintings, but ten years ago, perhaps that wasn't true."

"He never sold it, which negates your theory. Would he have had access to the jewel by painting a portrait for someone in your family?"

"Not that I know of," he conceded. "But he could have heard the tale of the Scandalous Lady, the argument over its rightful owner, and decided to use it to his advantage."

"Anyone could have done that, Julian," she said softly. "And wouldn't the thief most likely be someone your family entertained?"

"I always thought so. Then I saw the diamond displayed on your neck."

She cocked her head. "Did you think someone in my family had stolen it?"

"I considered it. And then I did my research. There would be no reason, for your family certainly has wealth aplenty."

"Most of that is the duke's. My father is a mere professor," she reminded him.

"I know, but your mother is the daughter of a duke, and you grew up in a palace. Yet nowhere did I come upon anyone in your family ever accused of evil intentions. Stupidity perhaps, or thoughtlessness."

He thought her shocked gasp rather forced, because she bestowed a slow, teasing smile on him that made his heart pick up speed. By the devil, if she ever knew what she did to him, she would wield power over him.

"Julian, you know that we are each telling stories that cannot be corroborated."

He stiffened.

"I don't believe you're lying," she quickly said, "but I just cannot hand over the Scandalous Lady and be done with it."

"If you do, your worries—and the danger to you—will be finished. I will proclaim the jewel found, so that everyone will know you don't have it."

"You're going to do that immediately?" she asked with doubt. "But you won't ever know the identity of the thief that way, will you."

He said nothing.

"Ah, but you don't plan to announce the jewel's recovery right now. A man like you cannot be content with anything less than the truth, especially if the scandal harmed your father."

For a moment, he relived the depth of the harm, but he wasn't about to put those memories into words.

He simply locked them away, as he was very good at doing.

"So you want to know how the jewel got from your father to me," she continued. "But I borrowed the item in question, and I must give it back to Roger, as I promised."

"He's not the owner."

"He doesn't know that. Perhaps we can talk to him and find out how he came by the diamond." She smiled. "But of course you already planned to do that without me."

He crossed his arms over his chest, feeling a trap settle around him.

"Together, we can solve both our dilemmas," she said. "You agree to take me with you, and I'll tell you where Roger has gone."

He came swiftly to his feet and approached the bed. "You know?"

To her credit she didn't cower or shy away from him. Instead, she rose slowly to her feet. They stood far too close together, staring at each other. "He told me." She gave him a deep, knowing smile. "Do we have an agreement? I need your word, my lord."

"*Now* you trust my word?" he shot back. "Just moments ago you thought I was in league with two common thieves."

"I feel you've been truthful—with the things you've revealed."

He felt a reluctant sense of admiration. She saw far deeper into him than he wanted. She had surely led a privileged life compared to him, but there was a wisdom in her eyes that seemed well earned. His curiosity about her wouldn't die any time soon.

"So what shall it be, my lord?" she asked, touching his chest with a single finger, her manner saucy. "Will you accompany me to question the man from whom I borrowed the jewel?"

He caught her hand. "This is dangerous, Rebecca. Not a social outing for a young miss."

"I know, but it's also more exciting than anything I've ever done. I want to experience it all, Julian." Her eyes gleamed in the candlelight.

He wanted to refuse, to shake the answers out of her and send her back to the safety of London.

But was he supposed to rip the diamond from around her neck? And how could he trust that she wouldn't simply follow him? What made a gently bred woman want to brave danger, all for a jewel she wasn't even connected to?

And what made this same girl pose nude, revealing everything a young lady had been taught to save for marriage?

And would she want to try other things, now that she'd been ruined?

At last, he heaved a deep sigh. "Very well. You may accompany me, but you must agree to certain conditions."

She groaned and whirled away from him, going to the table to pour herself another tankard of ale from the pitcher. "From the beginning I've sensed you're a man who thinks he's in charge of everything—and everyone."

"And in this, I am. You could bring about our deaths with one wrong move."

"So could you," she muttered, not meeting his eyes. "Go ahead, spell everything out for me, even though I know what you're going to say."

"You do."

"Of course I do! You want to make every decision. We have to follow *your* plans."

"I would certainly consider any suggestions on your part."

"How gracious of you, my lord!"

But she spoke too loudly in an old inn with thin walls. He put a hand over her mouth, and she went still. He cocked his head, listening. On their arrival, the inn was vacant but for them, according to the register. But anyone could have arrived in the last hour or two.

Quietly, he said, "It will be very important to keep to whatever story we're going by."

She nodded. When he removed his hand, she looked guilty, murmuring, "Sorry."

And then she licked her lips, undoing all his own concentration. Night after night, he would be alone with her, this woman he'd seen nude in a painting. All he wanted to do was examine the real thing with his eyes and hands and mouth, all laid out before him like a feast.

"Do you think someone heard me?" she asked breathlessly. "After all, if they believe you're my husband, they might certainly believe I could call you 'my lord' with complete sarcasm."

"Very amusing. But this is serious, Rebecca."

"I know it is, and I will treat it that way. As long as you listen to my suggestions, and we make decisions by compromising—"

"That wasn't going to be one of the conditions."

She smiled and batted her lashes playfully. "Please?"

"I agree to listen to you, and I agree to compromise, if I feel it won't endanger us."

"Or the mission, sir?" she asked, saluting.

He ignored her. "So now fulfill your end of the bargain. Tell me where Roger Eastfield has gone to visit his sick mother."

"Oh, you remembered the part about his mother, did you?"

"I have a good memory, especially when the club proprietor was explaining the history of a new, scandalous painting."

It was her turn to roll her eyes. "Very well. He's gone to Manchester."

"And if we could have stayed on the train, we would

have eventually been there," he said, briefly closing his eyes. "Is that where you meant to go?"

"Not at first. I was simply running away using the only train ticket I had."

"Going to . . ."

"Visit my Great-aunt Rianette in the Lake District." She grimaced. "It was Susanna's idea to separate so that it wouldn't be so easy for you and your friends to consolidate your resources against us."

"My friends and I are in a wager against each other," he reminded her.

"I saw the way you were with each other last night."

"I think you didn't want me to talk to your sister and cousin," he said slowly. "I wonder why."

She suddenly gave a great yawn. "Do you know what time it is?"

He took his watch out of his coat pocket, where he'd hidden it when he'd taken off his waistcoat. "Almost eleven o'clock."

"I'm suddenly very tired. I'll surely sleep like the dead."

Was she telling *him* that—or herself?

Chapter 9

For Rebecca, the lone bed had begun to encroach more and more on her mind as their conversation waned. Julian was too honorable to try to seduce a virgin—and that was almost disappointing.

What was wrong with her? she thought, taking another sip of ale. She was strangely parched.

Julian plucked the tankard from her hand. "I think you've had enough."

"Trying to control me already?" she demanded.

"Trying to make certain you don't embarrass yourself."

"I would never—" She broke off, remembering her disappointment that he wouldn't try to seduce her. Grudgingly, she admitted, "You're right. The brew is rather potent."

He leaned over her. "Did I hear correctly? You admitted I'm right?"

"About this," she muttered. She looked at the bed, hands on her hips, then faced Julian again. "So what are we going to do about the sleeping arrangements? And if you say again that we're pretending to be married—"

His smile was slow and dangerous.

One of the candles sputtered and went out, leaving the room just a bit darker. His shadow seemed enormous on the wall. But she wasn't afraid of him. Afraid of herself, perhaps, for what went on between a man and a woman had always intrigued her.

But she'd never truly felt the lure of it, the feelings that made couples risk everything to be together. Yet when Julian had almost kissed her in Lady Thurlow's garden, she'd felt a power greater than herself, one that made her long for his touch. If that was a sampling of desire, then she should be more wary.

"There is nowhere else to sleep," Julian said. "I suggest we practice the ancient art of bundling."

"Bundling? We're hardly courting."

"But the point of bundling was to lie in bed and simply talk, getting to know one another. We'd each have our own blanket."

"And we're clothed," she pointed out.

A faint smile touched his lips. "We're clothed." His mood sobered. "We'll have to be together night and day, Rebecca, and this won't be the last time we sleep in the same bed. That jewel around your neck puts you in too much danger. Perhaps I'd better—"

"No." She smiled sweetly.

"Very well," he said with resignation. "I'll step out

again to leave you some privacy. I assume you will remain in the room this time."

"You have my word."

He nodded and departed.

She let out her breath in a whoosh, feeling a bit light-headed from the ale. She spent the next several minutes struggling to unhook her gown so that she could be more comfortable, but she couldn't reach most of the fastenings. She wished she had her toothbrush, she lamented, but resigned herself to only washing her face and hands. Then she remade the bed, laying out a blanket for each side, and crawled beneath hers.

At first she pulled it up to her chin, then thought that made her appear frightened. She tried her waist, but that was too drafty—and might make him think undesirable things. At last she arranged it just above her chest, but with her arms lying on top of the blanket. Her corset cut into her flesh uncomfortably, but she pushed it from her mind.

Should she pretend to be asleep? But that seemed cowardly, and surely she couldn't carry off the deception.

After a soft knock, the door opened. Julian returned, his coat hung over his arm. He'd rolled his shirtsleeves up his forearms and opened his collar wider. His face was still damp.

"You could have washed here," she said softly.

"I didn't mind."

She watched with interest as he removed his boots—
she knew some gentlemen needed their valet's help for
such a task. Should she volunteer? But he managed it
himself. As he sat on a stool, facing away from her,
his back looked so broad. He obviously didn't need
padding in his coat to define the width of his shoulders. His height was inherited, but how had he gotten
so very muscular, managing an estate and business investments? She wondered if he fenced or boxed or even
wrestled—

And then he was blowing out the candles.

After telling herself not to tense, she promptly did so
anyway. She thought about how she would tell the story
of this journey to Susanna and Elizabeth later, relating
it as an exciting adventure.

But in the pit of her stomach, it didn't seem adventurous so much as daring, filled with the excitement of the
unknown. She lay on her back, fighting to control her
breathing, then exhaled on a gasp as he seated himself
and the bed sank beneath his weight. She barely kept
from rolling into him. Then he stretched out, and their
shoulders brushed, making her jump.

"This bed is not very wide," he murmured in the
dark.

"No, it's not." She could have groaned at the breathless sound of her voice. What must he be thinking? To
him, she was a woman of such loose virtue that she'd

pose nude. Then she'd insisted on traveling with him, and hadn't even blinked when he'd claimed them married. Did he assume . . . ?

After several minutes of tense silence, he cleared his throat. "So how did you hear about bundling?"

She was grateful for the distraction of conversation, even if it was about sharing a bed. "I read about it, of course. My mother may want me to marry well and soon, but she would never mention this as a method of courtship."

"It does seem . . . different here in the dark. I believe that was the point, allowing couples to relax after a strenuous day of work and just learn to know each other."

"You don't want to learn to know me," she said, staring up at the dark ceiling.

"And now you think to read minds?"

She heard the amusement in his voice. "Julian, I know you don't want me here, that I'm forcing myself on you. You don't have to try so hard to dissipate the tension between us. We can just sleep."

"So you feel tension?"

She crossed her arms over her chest, even though moving her shoulder meant she rubbed against his arm. "Of course there's tension. We're sleeping in the same bed! But you don't have to worry about me. I will hardly demand that you marry me for such behavior. I am frankly in no hurry to marry at all."

"I have never heard such a thing from a marriageable young lady."

"Oh, do not doubt me. I may have gone along with my mother's wishes when I first left the schoolroom, but that was only because I'd never been to many parties as a girl, even ones for other children. Dressing up and flirting and dancing were all a new experience to me."

"And the experience grew old," he said dryly.

She gave a soft laugh. "You sound sympathetic. Perhaps we feel the same about some things. I've told you about Susanna's sketching. Mama has given up on her becoming engaged, and for a while I thought Susanna was relieved. But now I'm not so certain."

"Because of Leo Wade?"

"Heavens, no. Her change in attitude started with our brother's miraculous return. She seems willing to give men a chance again, since Matthew and Emily are so happy. But when it seemed like she was determined to be a spinster, Mama focused all her zealous attention on me. So far, it has been too difficult to tell her I've changed my mind."

"So you want to put off marriage, when every other lady your age is jumping into it giddily."

"Well, I don't need money or security. I know my cousin and his wife will never deny me a place to live. It's just that . . . there is so much to see in this world. All I could ever do was read about it. But now I want to experience it."

"By luring thieves out of London while wearing the most valuable diamond in the kingdom."

She laughed. "That's one way. Now if I were allowed to choose my own husband, he would have to be a world traveler, knowledgeable about history and archaeology and dozens of countries."

"A paragon of an adventurer," he said dryly.

"Of course! What about you? You're not married, and certainly you need to have an heir someday."

"Such an important selection should never be left to chance."

Rebecca felt strange bringing up . . . procreation, considering they were lying in a bed. But he'd continued the conversation as if he didn't notice. That was strangely deflating.

"It sounds as if you have a detailed plan."

"I always plan for every possible outcome."

"You can't simply *live*?"

"I am living," he said dryly. "Through my efforts to discover the perfect qualities for a wife, I'll marry an *obedient, respectful* woman."

She knew he emphasized those characteristics to rebuke her, but she ignored the taunting. "If you're actually interested in finding a wife, why have I not seen you at more events?"

"I have not reached that phase of courtship yet."

" 'That phase'?" she echoed in confusion. "How can

you claim to be looking for a wife while not actually *looking*?"

"But I am looking, through research."

"Research?" She didn't understand him at all.

"I would not buy a horse without knowing its blood-lines and temperament."

"Did you just compare a woman to a horse?" she demanded.

"The process of selecting one, perhaps. Family background is of crucial importance, much more so than the chance of love."

"The *chance* of love?" she echoed. "Were not your parents in love?"

"I believe so, and it did not help them have a success-ful marriage. But we don't need to discuss something so private."

He sounded so certain of himself, so ridiculous, that she couldn't even be angry, only bemused. She lay still for several minutes, as the sound of his breath-ing invaded her consciousness. She could still feel his shoulder against hers. Just touching him in that one spot made her feel far too warm, almost . . . restless. Yet, she didn't move, didn't break the contact. The tension be-tween them began to rise again, a dangerous awareness that made her think forbidden thoughts. It seemed best to address the situation.

"Julian."

"Yes?"

The amusement in his voice annoyed her.

"We are lying here in bed, both worried as if we're . . . expecting something."

"We're worried?" he asked.

She ignored him. "It's only natural, being that we're two healthy people sleeping in the same bed. It might . . . dissipate the tension if you get it over with and just kiss me."

He made some kind of strangled noise—and then she realized that he was trying to hide his laughter. She hit him in the arm.

"Rebecca," he spoke in a soothing voice, even as he gripped her hand.

Had he sensed she would have gladly hit him again for teasing her?

"If I were to kiss you, things would not be the same between us. It might only make everything worse."

She went still, feeling his warm hand in hers in the dark. "Why would it make everything worse?" she whispered. "Is the thought of kissing me so repulsive? You didn't seem to think so this afternoon."

She remembered him looming over her in Lady Thurlow's garden, the way her breathing had become uneven, the way her world had narrowed until she only saw his dark, attractive face, coming ever closer. She'd been full of anticipation and eagerness, even as she'd pushed away the part of her mind that shouted a warning.

Before he could speak, she said bitterly, "Ah, but I was mistaken. You only tried to kiss me to further your victory in your wager. Or to find out more about the Scandalous Lady." She tried to pull her hand away but he wouldn't release her.

"It started out that way," he said, his voice low and husky in the dark. "I meant to distract you, and instead, I was the one distracted."

Her spirits brightened a bit.

"And if I kiss you"—his breath was warm on her cheek, as if he'd moved closer—"what if *you* don't wish to stop?"

"You think I'm so weak? Or are you deflecting your own worries on to me?"

He chuckled even as he rolled onto his side, away from her. It certainly gave her more room in the bed. She told herself she appreciated the gesture, that she wasn't offended—or hurt. Perhaps he really didn't want to kiss her and couldn't find a way to say so? Listening to his deep, even breathing, she fell asleep at last.

Julian awoke at the first light of dawn, with Rebecca curled around him, her thighs behind his, her arms about his waist, her cheek pressed to his back. He felt every curve of her body, especially the softness of her breasts. Occasionally she had moved in her sleep, rubbing against him, teasing him. But she wouldn't tease him into a loss of control. No woman ever had. He gave pleasure, received it, but knew when to stop.

He'd bedded many women in his life, but none had ever made him feel such overwhelming desire, as if he hadn't been truly alive before he met Rebecca. He kept remembering that painting, and thinking about the kind of woman who would pose nude.

She might not even be a virgin. Yet even if she was, she had put herself beyond the bounds of decent women with the painting, and by fleeing London. Yet, when she'd asked him to kiss her, there'd been a wistfulness in her demeanor. Was she innocent, perhaps even innocent of a man's kiss?

And something dark inside him was lured by that. He'd never bedded a virgin before. What would it be like to be the first to taste her, to show her—

He closed his eyes and gritted his teeth. Enough of that. He would never deflower a virgin unless he meant to marry her. Such a loss of control would change all of his carefully laid plans for his family's return to true respectability.

And then he noticed that she was awake. Her breathing changed, although she didn't speak or roll away. Her hand still dangled loosely in front of his stomach.

"Are you wondering how you can escape this?" he asked softly.

With a groan, she rolled away from him. "I am so sorry!" she whispered.

He sat up and turned to look back at her. She was covering her face with both hands, her tangled hair spilling out all over her pillow, her yellow gown filthy and torn. Yet to him, she looked so inviting, so desirable.

And miserable.

He leaned over, bracing himself on one elbow, and tried to pry her fingers away from her face. "You have nothing to apologize for. We were both asleep. We could not predict what would happen in the night."

At last she slid her hands away and stared up at him. "Really? You don't think I was deliberately . . ."

"Of course not." But as he looked down into her hazel eyes, framed with dark lashes, he began to lose track of the conversation. She was almost beneath him, her mouth so close. She'd wanted him to kiss her.

But now was not the time, he thought with resignation, remembering the diamond. He rose to his feet, ran his hands through his rumpled hair, then turned to face her.

As she sat up, he thought she winced. She might simply have slept in a funny position—although she'd seemed awfully comfortable pressed up against him, he reminded himself with satisfaction.

"The first thing we need is clothing," Rebecca said, trying to smile as if nothing was wrong.

He appreciated that. "We'll have to buy them."

"The maid will help, after your generous tip. I'll speak with her."

"I'll send her up with a tray when I go below. Until I return, don't leave the room. Have her bring the garments to us. And then we're going to have a discussion about our money, and how to make it last."

"Budgeting," she said with a smile. "You must be very good at that."

"I am."

"And humble, as usual."

He laughed as he donned his damaged coat and left the room. He wasn't used to being teased by women; they'd always been so respectful and in awe of his title that it was almost boring.

But not Rebecca. She openly asked for kisses and willingly slept in his bed. He was looking forward to the coming night.

Chapter 10

After Julian had gone, Rebecca groaned and put her head on her bent knees. She'd tried to behave normally, but she could still feel his big, warm body against hers. Heavens, his backside had been against—

Collapsing back on the bed, she covered her face again. Why hadn't he simply kissed her and put her out of her misery? Surely she'd stop feeling this way once she knew how it felt—how he tasted.

She shuddered, feeling too warm, too sensitive down between her thighs, a strange, unsettling feeling. But she welcomed the sensations, for she wanted to experience everything.

He was able to control himself, a feat that seemed far too easy for him to do, she thought begrudgingly. She needed to do the same.

By the time she washed her face, the chambermaid was already knocking on the door. Rebecca didn't open it without hearing the woman's voice—Julian would be proud of her caution—but at last she bade the woman enter. After setting the covered breakfast tray on the table, Rebecca explained her dilemma.

"—and our luggage broke apart in the mud," she finished, spreading her hands wide. "My husband threw everything away, and now we have nothing. Would you be able to find clothing for us to purchase?"

"Of course, ma'am. Tell me what ye need."

By the time Julian returned, she was feeling very proud of herself. They sat down together, sharing a loaf of bread as they ate their fried eggs.

Rebecca took a sip of strong coffee. "Let me tell you about my conversation with the maid. She's off to find us three sets of—"

"Stop right there," he said.

She stared at him.

"Did I mention we have little funds? Only what was in my pockets and your reticule. We have to conserve it as much as possible. We need clothing—but not three additional sets. And how would we carry it all? We certainly won't be in a hired carriage—or a train."

She cocked her head, intrigued. "Do you plan to walk?"

"Of course not. We'll ride in a public wagon, as rural people have done for centuries. I already discovered that one stops here at midmorn. It will take us longer to reach Manchester, but that's for the best. The longer we stay away from the main railways and roads, the better the chance we'll remain hidden from the thieves."

"And their master."

He slowly smiled. "Exactly."

"So if we ride the wagon, and buy fewer garments, will we have enough money?"

"Not likely."

"You could have lied," she said, shoulders slumping.

"To protect your sensibilities? You, the great adventurer, a woman who dares—anything?"

She was about to smile, but his voice seemed to change as he spoke. She studied him, but his eyes were lowered as he ate the last of his eggs.

"So then we'll work for money," she said.

" 'We'? *I* will work for money."

Nodding, she did not protest, knowing it was pointless. Already he frowned at her, but she tried to blink innocently as she finished chewing her bread. She could not imagine sitting in a room alone all day, doing nothing, while he supported them.

But what could she do? She was intrigued by the notion, and intended to give it some thought, especially on the long wagon ride north.

When the maid returned, Rebecca allowed Julian to negotiate the price for her goods, knowing he enjoyed it. He obviously wanted to take care of her, so she would let him—to a point. But there was no need to tell him that now.

They went through the clothing made of plain linen and course wool, choosing what would fit them best.

The maid surely knew someone of a large stature, for several items seemed like they would fit Julian well. And she'd included toothbrushes and a comb! Rebecca could have hugged her.

At last the maid took her earnings, the garments, the tray and left.

"Oh, I forgot," Rebecca said, starting toward the door. "I need her to unhook my gown."

"Won't she wonder how you fastened it this morning?" he asked doubtfully. "After all, she probably doesn't think you slept in it."

She glanced at him. "You would have had to do it."

He nodded. "So I cannot allow her to think otherwise. Come here into the light."

"It's very complicated . . ." she said, presenting him her back self-consciously.

Was that a chuckle? She turned around, but his expression was composed. Still suspicious, she turned away again.

He was as competent with women's clothing as he was with everything else. "You've had practice," she accused, feeling curious. It was better to feel so than to imagine what he was thinking as he performed such an intimate task.

He remained silent.

"I know men enjoy relations with certain women before they marry. I do have a brother and male cousins, you know."

"And they discuss such things in front of you?"

"Of course not, but one . . . overhears things. Do you have a mistress?"

"No."

She felt strangely relieved. She felt the last hook give way, and she quickly caught her gown at the shoulders. "That is helpful, thank you. I'm certain I can do the rest."

But he was already tugging on the laces and tapes of her corset. When he separated it, she took a deep, welcome breath. She'd never slept the night wearing a corset, and now she knew why. It was terribly uncomfortable.

"What is this?" he asked in a soft voice.

She tensed. And then she felt his hands, sliding her chemise off at one shoulder. She was only holding her gown up above her breasts.

"Julian?" she demanded, looking over her shoulder.

He rubbed his finger along her upper back, and she hissed at the slice of pain.

"The corset abraded you. Why did you not say something last night?"

"You mean while I was asking you to kiss me?" she asked dryly.

"Keeping silent was foolish on your part, and now you will suffer when it was unnecessary."

"Julian—"

To her surprise, he followed the line of her corset,

pulling her chemise away from her skin above it.

"It continues beneath your arm," he said. "You'll have to bathe and cleanse this."

She gasped as he pulled her back against him so he could look over her shoulder. His head was so near hers that she felt the brush of his hair.

"And the abrasion continues," he said.

She tried to hold her gown above her breasts, but he tugged at her hand until he could see where the corset met her chemise. The Scandalous Lady glimmered in her cleavage, and she wondered if he was tempted to take it from her. But he didn't even seem to notice it.

"Julian—"

Then words failed her. Just in front of her arm, he slid his finger into the neckline of her chemise, and separated it from her skin. There was a welt on the upper, outside edge of her breast. She reminded herself that she'd revealed more of her breasts in the ball gown he'd recently seen her in, but such practicalities didn't seem to matter to her overheated emotions. She was breathing too hard, feeling him all around her, against her back, over her shoulder, his hands at her breasts, as if he was about to touch the injured skin.

She pulled away, holding her garments in front of her as she smiled over her shoulder. "I'll be fine," she said unsteadily. She could not let him think he affected her, or he might put her on the first train—wagon—back to London.

"You need to bathe."

His voice didn't even sound his own as it rumbled through her.

"We don't have time," she said. "I still have soap and clean linen. I'll use that. Turn your back."

"I beg your pardon?"

She sighed. "You cannot keep running out of the room every time I'm changing. I might need you to fasten the clothing anyway. And when it's your turn to change, do you wish me to stand in the corridor alone?"

"Brilliant reasoning." He turned his back on her.

"You could look out the window if you like. This might take me a few minutes."

"An excellent idea," he said, walking to the window and leaning his arms on the ledge.

Quickly, she peeled off her filthy dress and wiggled out of her loosened corset. She removed her drawers and donned new ones, rough linen compared to the silk of her own. But at least they were clean. The maid had seemed surprised she wanted them, but had obligingly found them for her. Rebecca had thought every woman wore them, and would certainly feel naked without them, especially with no petticoats.

She was desperate for a bath, but would save that maneuvering for another night. Lowering her old chemise and washing the scrapes as best as she could, Rebecca bit her lip to hide a laugh as she imagined asking him to reach the ones on her back. She managed alone, and at last she was dressed in a clean chemise.

"Don't wear the corset," Julian said.

She had just picked it up. Was he so familiar with women's undergarments that he knew how each one sounded as she donned them? "But—"

"You'll only increase the chafing. Put it in the portmanteau if you must, but please don't wear it."

It was the "please" that placated her. "Very well." She donned the brown gown, lacing it up the front, enjoying the feeling of freedom as she took a deep breath. "You can turn around now."

He did, looking her up and down. "You'll wear a bonnet to shield your face and hide your hair?"

She held one up. "Am I presentable? Do I look suitably working class?"

"You'll want to speak as little as possible—as will I," he added before she could take offense. "Even if we mimic the correct accent, our choice of words could easily make people suspicious." He lifted her hand and studied it, rubbing his rough thumb over her delicate palm. "You don't look like you've worked a day in your life."

"You took good care of me," she said, lifting her chin. Then she grinned. "Or so I will tell everyone. Will we have stories about our lives that we have to memorize? Who are we? Where have we come from and where are we going?"

"I've been giving it some thought. Allow me to change first. Put your clever mind to work."

He didn't ask her to look out the window, but she did so anyway, seeing a yard that sloped down to a narrow river. It was difficult to ignore what was going on behind her. She could hear the rustling of his clothing, and it gave her flashes of heated embarrassment—and curiosity—to be witness, even if only by her ears, to such an intimate act.

At last he called for her, and she turned around—and froze in astonishment. Lord Parkhurst had simply vanished, and in his place was a tall, hulking man, rough around the edges, his face unshaven, a cap shadowing his dangerous-looking, East End eyes. It was as if changing clothing revealed something more primitive inside him. He wore thick trousers and heavy boots, a simple waistcoat and jacket, and an open-necked shirt.

"Oh dear," she murmured.

"Is something wrong?" he asked, in Lord Parkhurst's cultured voice.

She laughed softly. "No, of course not, but you have succeeded admirably in changing your appearance. No one would ever know you were a member of the *ton*."

"Good. Now let's put the clothing we're keeping in the portmanteau, and I'll carry it. No, not your cloak," he said. "It is too fine to wear. You have a new shawl."

She frowned. "The cloak kept me warm at night."

"I don't think you were cold last night," he said.

They looked at each other for a moment, remembering the way they'd shared the heat of their bodies.

He was the first to turn away, and she accepted his behavior, understanding his dedication. He had a need to discover the truth about the Scandalous Lady, for its saga had obviously hurt him deeply—and not just his pride.

"If I had to choose which extreme," she said, "I'd rather be cold. My mother always kept a fire lit in my bedroom, even at the height of summer, on doctor's orders. They didn't want me to catch any kind of chill."

"Or they were sweating out any chance of sickness."

"That, too. But it was smothering. When I'm overheated now, I feel a little . . . panicky."

"Bad memories," he said. "Best to let them go."

"I'm trying, by creating new memories." She looked at the pile of clothing left on the bed. "I told the maid she could sell what we left behind. Do you think it's dangerous to leave so many obviously expensive garments and fashionable boots?"

"We have no choice. We simply cannot carry it all."

"Can't our identities be young nobles out for an adventure?" Grinning, she lifted a hand. "I know, I know, too close to the truth."

"Hardly."

"Too close to *my* truth."

He eyed her curiously. "Everything's about an adventure for you, isn't it?"

"No, not everything." She lifted her chin. "But why can I not enjoy myself, even through the danger? Why be nervous and afraid when I'm doing something I've always longed to do?"

"Run from criminals?" he asked with sarcasm threading his voice.

"I'm living, Julian," she said earnestly. "Living and experiencing and seeing some of the world, even if it's only the industrial heart of England. That fascinates me, too. I've never been to Manchester." She sat down at the table and tapped the other stool. "Sit down. Let's plan who we're going to be. We've already said we're married, much as I might have chosen brother and sister. But you didn't give me a choice."

He sat down and folded his arms across his chest, saying sternly, "We aren't going to be brother and sister."

She eyed him, folding her arms as well, tempted to tease him by insisting. But . . . she didn't want to be his sister either. And she was secretly glad he didn't want to play her brother. "Very well, since you seem rather insistent about this, I will acquiesce."

"Good of you." He leaned forward, forearms resting on the table. "We might as well stay Mr. and Mrs. Bacon, since the innkeeper will know us as that, and might speak to the wagoner."

"We're going to be someone else tonight?"

"Tonight is full of all kinds of possibilities."

She blinked at him, her mouth suddenly dry, her heart feeling fluttery. What did he mean?

He gave a little smile. "If we want to change identities, we'll have to do so tonight, then take a different wagon tomorrow. I'll think on this. Hopefully, our pursuers will not think to look for us in such circumstances."

"They really want the Scandalous Lady."

"Their master does, and I will need to know who that is."

"Of course. Since I don't want to believe that Roger Eastfield stole it, can we assume this master of theirs was behind the original theft, and somehow lost it to Roger?"

"It's a logical assumption, but I will reserve my judgment on Eastfield."

She sighed. "So, are we Mr. and Mrs. Bacon, come from Canterbury and on our way to visit my mother in Manchester?"

He blinked at her. "Very well. Since you came up with the suggestions, it might make it easier for you to remember."

"I won't have any trouble remembering, Julian. Maybe *you* will. You're so used to being an earl, after all. It will probably be difficult for you not to take charge of the wagon and guide us to our destination on *your* schedule."

"You underestimate me," he said, standing up.

"We'll see."

He glanced at his pocket watch. "Shall we go down to purchase seats on the wagon?"

"I'd keep that watch hidden," she said, teasing even as she scolded.

He only arched a brow.

Chapter 11

The sun peered behind hazy clouds, warming the spring day, as Julian rocked and jerked and lurched with the motion of the wagon. Six sturdy horses pulled them along, and the wagoner hunched on his seat, guiding them, his head lowered within his scarf like a wary turtle. There were benches built down both sides of the wagon, with straw loosely scattered in the center. Rebecca sat at Julian's side, leaning back against the bowed walls of the wagon, her eyes closed, expression peaceful as she lifted her face to the sky. A breeze played with the brown curls that danced at the nape of her neck beneath her bonnet.

Julian thought that other women might be nervous, chased by dangerous thieves, traveling in disguise, away from everything that was familiar—away from a routine schedule. But Rebecca submerged herself into this aberration with almost practiced ease. He couldn't decide if she was courageous or foolhardy.

"Ye seem to be enjoyin' the day, Mrs. Bacon," he said softly.

She opened one eye to look at him, the brim of her bonnet giving her some shade. "The wind is just lovely, Mr. Bacon. I can smell the comin' of summer, the way everythin' is beginnin' to grow and bloom." She lowered her voice. "I was never even allowed to ride in an open carriage, ye know."

They hit a particularly deep hole, and he caught her before she could be thrown to the straw-covered bottom of the wagon. "Ye obviously weren't missin' much."

She grinned and closed her eyes again.

After sweeping his gaze across the horizon in all directions, Julian went back to surreptitiously studying their fellow passengers. Six people had joined them in Coventry, four farmers and craftsmen, and two women who were either their wives or sisters. So far they were an uncommunicative group, which suited Julian just fine.

After a stop to water the horses, Rebecca asked him if she could walk for a while beside the wagon, and he joined her on the side of the road, where they weren't as likely to encounter horse droppings.

Julian walked with his hands behind his back, their pace decent; but it was hardly necessary to race to keep up with the slow wagon. Rebecca strode along with the natural grace of a woman who did much walking. After a while, she let her black shawl slide off her shoulders and dangle from her elbows.

"Why weren't you allowed to ride in an open carriage?" he finally asked.

"I'm certain I mentioned it before," she said, giving him a careless glance. "Illness."

"Just illness? I don't understand."

"I was ill often, to the point of death. I look healthy now, but it wasn't always so. I was lucky to even be permitted to leave the house, so often did I catch whatever sickness was going round. Bronchitis was a specialty of mine," she said dryly. "To combat it, my parents did everything the doctors told them. No riding in an open carriage. I slept with a shawl around my shoulders and neck each night to prevent a draft from taking me under. You have never seen a person so bundled up as me leaving a heated ballroom at night, even when I was an adult and less liable to be ill. I don't even know how to ride."

That took him aback. "Living on an estate in the country, that must have been very difficult."

She shrugged. "I grew used to it. There is a seven-year difference between myself and Susanna, so when she was learning to ride I was still a baby. As I grew older, my brother would occasionally take me up behind him when our parents weren't looking, but that was rare. I was watched far too carefully, if not by my mother, then my nanny, and eventually our governess."

"You seem surprisingly unaffected by the restrictions of your childhood," he said thoughtfully. "Although your longing for adventure is becoming more and more understandable."

She smiled, glancing at him from beneath the brim of her bonnet. "Surely your childhood affected you."

"If so, I don't know how." He looked at the wagon, which had pulled ahead of them. "You must be tired. Perhaps we should—"

"That's a reaction if I ever saw one. You don't want to discuss it."

"My reaction?"

"Your childhood. You mentioned you spent much time with the servants, and I don't think you meant your tutor. So come now, Mr. Bacon, tell your wife your secrets." She linked her arm with his as they walked.

"I have no secrets," he said mildly. He wasn't embarrassed by how he grew up. Yet he hadn't quite explained everything that had happened because of the stolen diamond. There was no reason for him to feel he needed to share something that was so very private.

"So you were just a normal little future earl, who did everything the other future peers did."

"Not quite. I went to school with the village children." Why had *that* slipped out?

Her expression turned curious. "Really? Not Eton or Harrow?"

"I began at Eton. And then my father could no longer afford the tuition."

Her smile faded. "Oh, dear. I am so sorry."

"Your pity is unnecessary."

"I don't pity you! I feel badly for your parents, unable to give you what other sons had. If you began at Eton, did you at least have a year there?"

"I had a term."

"So you went home for the holidays and couldn't return. How terrible for your father to have to inform you." When he hesitated, she latched on to that. "Tell me, Mr. Bacon. No secrets between husband and wife."

"My father didn't inform me. The school did before the holidays began." Why was she able to coerce him into speaking of things he hadn't thought of in years?

When she spoke, he was surprised by her angry tone.

"That's not right," she said. "Your father should have warned you—surely he knew things were not good."

"My father was very good at ignoring things that were right before him."

"And your mother couldn't say anything?"

He frowned, but didn't reply.

"But of course, she might not have known either."

"She'd just had the twins, so there were five of us. She was busy. I should have realized the truth."

"You were probably ten, and had hoped to be like every other boy. Do not put that on yourself."

Rebecca could not believe how evenly Julian spoke of such a sad part of his childhood. It was true that it wasn't as if someone had died, but he must have suffered terribly to not have what the other boys of his station did. And then to go to school in the village— she could only admire such determination to educate himself. And he hadn't even been able to go to university either. And here she was, constantly going on about being unable to do much as a child, and he'd had his own restrictions. She kept imagining a dark-haired little boy, so eager to learn, told not to return to Eton. He never had a chance to develop the friendship with others of his class that were so important in Society. Was that why he seldom bothered to attend the events of the *ton*?

"And this is why you spent much time with the servants," she said, putting things together. "But of course, if there was little money, perhaps there were not so many servants."

"Enough of them agreed to stay," he said calmly.

"Why?"

"Because I asked them to."

She felt the rock hardness of muscle that few noblemen seemed to have. Had he developed this impressive physique spending time with the servants, helping them with their duties? But she could never ask him such a question. He would definitely think she pitied him, when that wasn't the case at all. She admired his determination and work ethic.

"Your people must be very loyal to you," she said slowly.

"They are good people." He picked up their pace again. "Would you care to ride?"

"No. You just don't want to stay here where I can question you as much as I want."

"Then let me question you. You've mentioned this overprotective family—aren't they going to be worried when you don't arrive at your aunt's?"

"I've already thought of that," she said. "When we're in Birmingham tonight, I will write to my aunt, saying that I'm stopping to visit friends along the way—conveniently not telling her where, of course. If I'm a week or two late, she'll think nothing of it."

"Ingenious."

She laughed, knowing he must have thought of a letter, and was allowing her to mention the idea first. "What about you? You didn't even take luggage on this trip. I imagine you aren't known for your spontaneity."

He arched an eyebrow as he looked down at her. "I'm offended."

"How can you be offended by the truth?"

"I often travel to property I own outside London, or to visit my factories in other towns. That's where they'll think I've gone. As you know, my mother is in London. She'll keep the household running smoothly."

"You won't be there to ride roughshod over your brothers."

"They'll be delighted," he said dryly. "My sisters will certainly take turns worrying about them."

"Why do you worry? Whatever monetary problems the earldom had when you were a child, you've obviously banished them with sheer determination."

He said nothing, and she wondered if she'd succeeding in embarrassing him—embarrassing the Earl of Parkhurst!

She grinned up at him. "My point is, that you've probably given your brothers everything you never had. Am I correct?"

He cleared his throat and looked away. "I've done what was required. Perhaps I've done too much."

"Really?" she asked, intrigued.

"You have certainly seen their behavior firsthand."

"Much can be excused by youth and immaturity— but then I imagine you overcame immaturity much sooner than they will. How can they be blamed for that? You have enabled them to have the life you didn't have, growing up."

"Enough, Mrs. Bacon. Such praise is unwarranted."

"One always praises one's husband. Even if he's more interested in a jewel than anything else."

He arched an eyebrow, and she skipped ahead of him to the wagon.

That evening, they arrived in Birmingham, one of the largest towns in Europe, the one place Julian had wished to avoid, but the wagon had its schedule to keep. It was where the train had gone, after all, where the thieves might assume they'd disembarked and would be looking for them. Of course, once again they would hide in a part of town where they weren't expected to be, yet . . . he felt uneasy.

The light was still high enough in the sky for him to see how dark it was down the streets perpendicular to the main road they traveled. The numerous tenements were built too close together, overlooking central courts, blocking out the sun much of each day.

When they were let off at an inn, Julian took Rebecca's arm and told the wagoner they had relatives to visit, so the man didn't have to bother negotiating lodgings for them. And then they left.

Rebecca remained mostly silent as they walked through the streets, now crowded with factory workers returning home for the evening. The smells lingered heavily everywhere, especially coal fires that warmed houses and drove the factories. When they passed a market, he bought each of them a meat pie, and was able to ask directions to another inn.

As Julian entered the receiving hall of the King's Head, Rebecca let go of his arm, and he thought nothing of it—until she strode forward ahead of him and spoke to the innkeeper, a portly man who tiredly informed her that of course there were vacancies.

The innkeeper's midland accent had her blinking a moment, and Julian could see her try to piece the words together.

"Then I will take a room. My name is Mrs. Lambe."

They hadn't discussed new identities, he realized, and was amused that she'd already come up with a new one.

"My servant, Tusser"—she gestured rather imperiously with her head toward Julian, who came up behind her—"will be fine in your servants' quarters."

Julian stiffened. What was the little minx up to? Escape? He could tell nothing by her expression, except that she was trying to portray a woman used to dealing with the world alone.

"Ain't got none," the innkeeper said. "He can bed down in the stables out back."

"Very well."

As she scratched her name in the register—and a hometown, although she hadn't informed him of that either—Julian stood twisting his cap in his hands, knowing he couldn't interrupt. She'd put him in his place as her servant.

As the innkeeper brought a key and started up the stairs, Rebecca said, "Be a good man and carry my portmanteau."

Julian silently handed over the shabby bag to the man, who arched an eyebrow and rolled his eyes at Julian, as if her luggage revealed that she was putting on airs above her station.

Rebecca looked over her shoulder—and gave Julian a wicked smile.

* * *

Rebecca knew her game would be short-lived—at most she'd have a night to herself, and Julian would be indignant with her in the morning—she didn't imagine he ever experienced fury. But it had pleased her to let him know that he couldn't control everything, especially not her. This was her adventure, and she wanted to have fun, even if it meant teasing Julian.

When she was left alone in her bedchamber, she looked about in dismay. No wonder the innkeeper hadn't met her eyes when he'd left the room. There was a layer of dust on the floor and the single chair. He'd said they'd had few guests of late, and would send up a maid to change the bed. Shuddering, Rebecca was afraid to lift the blanket and see what was underneath.

The room was cold, and she saw that little coal had been left in the grate for her comfort. She shook the grate to release the ash, and rubbed her hands together above the meager warmth. When would summer arrive? She looked toward the window, wondering how cold it was in the stables. Surely Julian gave off enough heat that he might not even need a blanket, she thought, trying not to feel guilty. He would have to learn that she was his equal, that they should make decisions together. But of course he'd spent the last ten years making every decision for his entire family himself.

She thought about an eighteen-year-old with such

power. Had he been determined? Relieved? Perhaps even afraid? She couldn't imagine him as such.

When the maid returned to make the bed, Rebecca asked for pen and paper.

"Ma'am, I'll bring it up after yer bath."

Though a bath sounded heavenly, Rebecca said, "But I didn't—"

"Yer manservant said ye'd need it after a day of travelin', ma'am."

Now she truly did feel guilty. "Thank you," she murmured.

When at last the maid had gone, Rebecca removed her bonnet and shawl, then hugged herself. Hot coals gave soft ticking sounds in the grate, and an angry male voice spat incomprehensible words in the room next door. Was she actually feeling lonely? She'd spent her life with her sister and brother, her many cousins. They were all as overprotective as her parents. She'd have thought she'd welcome any chance to be alone.

Then the shutters burst open.

She gasped and jumped back toward the door, heart pounding madly. But it was Julian who put his head and shoulders through the window. Straitlaced Julian, scaling walls?

She covered her mouth to keep from giggling, watching in growing awe as he lifted himself even higher, got one foot onto the ledge, then jumped inside. He straightened slowly, unfolding to that impressive height. She waited for him to stalk her, to say how angry he was, to show—something. But he did none of those things, only looked at her.

"It was a joke," she said, spreading her hands.

"I know."

Was he even capable of being angry, of losing control, of doing something reckless? Of course, he had followed her from London, but he'd probably say he was doing the logical thing, protecting her.

Slowly he walked toward her. "You did not consider the ramifications of your 'joke.' This is one of the worst inns I've ever stayed in. The stables are deplorable. Who knows whom the innkeeper might have been alerted to intercept a woman traveling alone."

She sighed uneasily, uncertain of his mood. "You're right. I'm sorry."

He looked down her body. "Where's the tub?"

"I appreciate that you thought of sending one up," she said, feeling more confused by the minute.

"I'll hide when it arrives," he said, then arched a brow, a smile playing about his mouth. "Unless you want the establishment to think you sleep with your manservant."

She returned his smile, determined to show him that she could play along with his teasing.

"Are you still hungry?" he asked.

She shook her head.

"Then I think you should answer some questions while we wait." He sat down in the room's only chair.

"About what?" she asked, trying to show that she was unconcerned.

"Before we reach Manchester, I'd like to know more about the artist, Roger Eastfield, and the painting you posed for."

And then he pulled her onto his knee. Rebecca felt a surge of trepidation and uncertainty—and excitement.

Chapter 12

Julian enjoyed the curve of Rebecca's hips on his thigh, the way she pressed her knees together where they touched his other leg. Her back was as straight as a girl fresh from finishing school, as if she didn't dare lean into him. He found it amusing that one moment she asked for a kiss, and the next she seemed uncertain about his intentions—off balance. That was the best place to keep her. How else would she learn how to handle herself in the intimate world of scandal she now inhabited?

"I *could* sit on the bed," she said calmly.

"And what would be the enjoyment in that?"

He let his arm circle her back, resting his hand on her hip. He put the other hand on her knee, which became the focus of her widening eyes.

He waited to speak until she met his gaze.

"I assume Eastfield painted your portrait within the last year?" Julian asked.

She blinked as if she'd forgotten the reason for their discussion. "At the end of the holidays."

"You weren't in Cambridgeshire?"

She shook her head. "We wanted to give my brother and his wife more time alone together, so we spent Christmas in London."

"Ah yes, they'd been separated while he was in India, presumed dead." With his fingers, he caressed her knee slowly, almost absently. "Do you know how long Eastfield had been in London?"

"No, I didn't ask. I only knew he'd been in France for several years."

"Where he could have fled because he'd stolen the jewel."

"But if he'd done so, why hadn't he sold it?" she asked, meeting his gaze again as if at last she were more caught up in their conversation than his nearness. "Wouldn't greed have been his only reason for the crime?"

"Perhaps he found its notoriety made it difficult to sell."

"In France?"

"One must still know the right people to insure that the diamond's sale remains hidden."

"I don't think he knew the right people—I don't believe he stole the jewel. It was tossed in a box with other pieces, tangled together, as if he were convinced it was paste. And why else would he let me take it?"

"To put something else in motion, perhaps."

"To put something in motion? I don't know what you mean. He felt compelled to sell the *painting* for money, not the jewel."

He frowned thoughtfully, even as he tucked a stray curl behind her ear. "Very true. So how long did the actual painting take?"

She gave him a faint smile, touching her hair as if to find anything else out of place. "What does that have to do with the Scandalous Lady? Or are you back to the wager now? Perhaps you and your friends will compare our stories, see who's making a mistake."

It was easier to talk about Roger Eastfield than think dispassionately about that painting. It haunted him, the dark background, the candles that gave her body a sensual glow. He kept picturing himself there at her side as she displayed herself only for him. But right now he had to remember the diamond, and finding the truth, even as he continued to unsettle Rebecca by stroking her hip.

"I want you to talk freely of the artist," he said, his voice smooth. "You may say something that will unexpectedly help."

Her face was a study in patience and amusement, and he was impressed at her success in ignoring his touches.

"Very well," she said. "The painting took several weeks of twice-weekly visits."

"Then you spent much time with him. What did you talk about?"

"He did not wish to be interrupted by idle chatter. He mostly said, 'Tilt your chin. Arch your back.' " Her tone had grown dry.

Had she realized that her words were themselves a tease? Or did she think him so unaffected by memories of the nude painting? If he shifted her just a bit, she'd know how aroused he was becoming.

To distract himself, he said, "I've come to think of you as a woman who has difficulty *not* talking."

"I don't think that's a compliment. Talking implies ease, and I was not feeling that way."

"Did you regret the decision, Rebecca? You could have stopped at any time."

"I finish things I start," she said. "Julian, this is a useless line of questioning. The painting is already hanging on a wall for all to see."

Since she hadn't clarified her regrets, he wondered if she truly had none at all? That amazed and intrigued him, but it was not yet time to explore that part of her. "How did you meet Eastfield?"

"Through my sister, Susanna. They were introduced at a showing of his work in London. They corresponded and occasionally met to discuss their projects, and I happened to be with her once. He expressed an interest in painting me."

Something unpleasant seemed to twist in his gut as he imagined her with Eastfield. Was this jealousy, this dark intensity that was part anger, part desire? How unexpected. "And you just agreed?"

"No, I gave it some thought and researched his work. He asked several more times."

"And then your longing for adventure overcame you," he said in a soft voice.

She lowered her eyes, dark lashes fanning her cheeks. Was she blushing? Had she wanted to be nude for the artist alone? Jealousy was a rush of untamed emotion that swelled him, crawling into his mind.

"I'm surprised he had to ask more than once," Julian said, "considering how much you longed to be free of constraint."

"You disapprove," she said slowly, studying him. "Why . . . you're as much a prude as a little old spinster."

A prude? He found himself amused, surprised that she could draw such an incorrect conclusion. "That's a mistaken assumption, Rebecca. You are not the common young Society miss, and that intrigues me."

They stared at each other, eyes locked together in heat until there was a soft knock on the door.

"Mrs. Lambe?" called a woman's voice. "I've brought yer bath."

Rebecca broke their shared gaze and jumped to her feet. "Just a moment!"

Then she folded her arms across her chest and stared at him, arching a brow. He debated rolling under the bed, but considering the unclean state of the establishment, that seemed unwise. He went back to the window and boosted himself up onto the ledge.

Rebecca followed him, her expression growing concerned as she whispered, "What do you think you're doing?"

"Keeping your reputation pure. When I'm outside, close the shutters." He gripped the ledge, then swung himself down and hung from it. He was only one floor off the ground, and he didn't even think he'd break a leg if he fell.

She leaned out the window with a gasp.

He looked up at her. "I'd appreciate if you'd hurry."

She withdrew quickly and closed the shutters. He hung immobile, hoping that no one would see him against the dark building in the faint moonlight. There were few guests, and the stables behind him looked unused.

He could hear little of what was going on inside Rebecca's room. If he were lucky, several servants would be bringing buckets to fill the tub, hurrying the process. Time crept by, and his shoulders began to ache, along with his fingers. At last the shutters opened.

"You can come in," she called.

When he dropped back into the bedroom, he rubbed his fingers and found himself staring at the bathing tub.

It wasn't large, and she would not be able to totally submerge herself in it and hide her body from him.

A cold sweat broke out on the back of his neck. She was a virgin, he reminded himself.

Or was she?

But there she was, oblivious of his thoughts, staring at the tub with a longing that looked almost sexual. He could have groaned.

"I have to bathe," she said, eyes flashing with amusement as she looked at him.

Did she understand how she affected a man? Perhaps he should see how she reacted to a small test. In a low, husky voice, he said, "If you're so proud of your modeling, then you should have no problem undressing in front of me, because I've seen everything you have." Then he sat down in the only chair and crossed his arms over his chest, facing the bathing tub.

She blinked at him, her face slowly flushing, but she made no answer. Challenging Rebecca seemed to fire her reckless spirit, and his bold invitation hung between them, crackling in the room like a rising storm.

He saw the moment she made up her mind, the way her hazel eyes glittered and her mouth turned mutinous and daring. Everything inside him clenched, as if he was caught unmoving in a vise, and his brain seeming to lose all higher functioning. His groin won the battle over the rest of his body.

She lifted her hands to her hair and began to remove

the pins. Sable brown curls slowly cascaded about her shoulders, one at a time. He clenched his sweating hands into fists.

She tugged the laces at her throat, loosening them, and slowly her bodice opened wider. He could see a glimpse of white chemise beneath.

A fine trembling began inside him, disturbing his usual calm. Did she *want* him to throw her down on the bed and take her? She wasn't going to have what she wanted, because that would go against the rules he lived by. No bedding virgins. And she *was* a virgin; he could tell simply by the way she'd sat all tense on his knee, as if that were almost as intimate as her nude modeling.

She lifted the hem of her gown and began to pull it up. His eyes were fixed on her black boots, then her trim ankles covered in black stockings. The gown kept moving higher, up and over her head, blocking her face for a moment. And then it was gone. The chemise was plain and serviceable, but it was worn by Rebecca, hinting at all the rounded curves he'd seen displayed to their best advantage in the painting. Her breasts hung heavy within the bodice, and he could see when they hardened in arousal.

His mouth was dry, and to his surprise, it took everything in him not to throw himself from the chair and on top of her.

Rebecca did not think she'd ever felt so overheated in her life. She wanted to look away, pretend she'd not gotten herself into this fix, but Julian's pale gray eyes held her like a butterfly pinned to a display. And she was definitely on display, feeling fluttery and trapped—and excited, far too excited than could be good for her.

He'd annoyed and angered her, and this had been the result: her pride had demanded she not back down, when in truth, she should have fled—or demanded he do so.

But she hadn't, and now she'd taken off her gown, and only wore her chemise. Thankfully, it was not her own fine, sheer garment, but she was still almost naked. If only she hadn't felt the need to prove that she was the model once and for all. She was certain her sister and cousin were working just as hard to convince the other two men of the same thing—but hopefully in a tamer manner.

Would she really do this—and could he really expect her to? She had thought him staid, competent, calculating—and then he'd pulled her onto his knee and caressed her the whole time he interrogated her. Was it a calculated ploy on his part to unbalance her, to persuade her to speak the truth? She didn't know what to think about him.

But he said nothing, only watched her with shadowed eyes that made her feel even hotter. He wasn't looking at her face. He was waiting for her to reveal more.

Would she stop disrobing? Could she? Or was this a dream she'd had of inspiring a man's desire, something she'd worried that after her last illness she might never have a chance to experience?

Just a little bit farther, she told herself. Just to see what he'd do, how she could prove to him that he was as human as everyone else.

Her boots were next, and she had a wild thought of propping her foot on the chair right beside him. But that was far too daring, so she sank onto the bed, reaching down to unlace her boots. The bodice gaped dangerously, and she lowered her head to hide it.

Had he made a noise? What had he seen?

After removing each boot, she set them aside on the floor. She stared into his eyes as she slid the chemise higher to reach the garter just below her knee.

His gaze moved leisurely between her face and what she was doing with her hands. She rolled her stocking down, letting the chemise remain folded at her knees, out of the way. Her lower leg looked so bare and white, and soon the other matched it.

There wasn't much left to remove, she realized, feeling the first shiver of panic. She rose to her feet, letting the chemise skirt fall back down to cover her drawers.

She had thought the room cold, but now it was so hot that she was perspiring. Or was that nervousness? For all of her bravery, she did not know how far she could go with this, without him thinking that she wanted—

But she didn't stop. She gathered the chemise skirt forward, reaching beneath it to unlace the back of her drawers, letting the majority of the skirt hang low in front of her. She drew the drawers down, feeling a draft of air on her backside. The linen garment puddled at her feet and she stepped out of it.

Julian's gaze rose from her feet all the way up her body. She paused, knowing they both realized that only one garment separated her from complete nudity.

How could she possibly compete with Roger's overly generous interpretation of the female form? Did she want to see the answer in Julian's eyes—perhaps the disappointment?

But she was trapped, made helpless by her own longings and the desire in his eyes, desire for her, not a painting, not a memory.

She reached for the hem of her chemise and began to lift it.

"Stop!" he said, his voice harsh and sounding unlike his own.

She did so, gazing at him helplessly, for she fought the very real need to finish what she'd started, to understand everything that happened between a man and a woman.

He came so quickly to his feet that as her head tipped back to look up at him, she fell back onto the bed. He leaned over her, hands braced on either side of her head. She couldn't breathe, could barely think. His body was so massive that he could crush her if he wished. Had she driven him past gentlemanly restraint? Did he mean to—

"Did he touch you, Rebecca?" Julian asked in a hoarse voice.

"Who?" She sounded dazed and unlike herself.

"Eastfield."

"I—"

He put his big hand on her hip, his fingers wrapped around it, curling against her backside. Her chemise seemed like no shield at all. Her breathing grew faint and labored as she stared wide-eyed at his intent features.

His hand slowly moved up her body, not quite pulling her garment with it. She gasped, feeling his palm against her ribs, his thumb rising between her breasts. Her heart pounded, blood thundered in her ears.

Julian put a knee on the bed at her side, looming even more above her. "Did he pose you, guide you with his hands? Tell me the truth, Rebecca."

She opened her mouth, wanting to be flippant, to tease. But instead the truth came out. "He never touched me, not like—"

Words failed her as his hand moved a bit more, almost cupping the underside of her breast. She arched, her eyelids fluttering, the heat of arousal almost more than she could bear. She wanted to whimper, to beg for more.

"You don't have to prove something to every man who demands it of you," he said gently. "Not to the artists of the world, and not to me. You can make the choice that is right for you. Never forget that."

Then he leaned above her and pressed his lips to her cheek, just beside her mouth. She could feel the rough stubble of his bearded face rasp her skin, and a lock of his hair brushed her forehead.

"Now bathe," he whispered, "and I'll return shortly to take my own turn in the bath."

And then he strode from the room. She closed her eyes, shaking the bed with her trembling, and waited to feel relieved, as a proper girl should. But all she felt was regret, and an aching need that she had no way to understand or assuage.

An hour later, Julian stood outside the door to their lodgings. Surely enough time had passed. He'd nursed a beer in the taproom below, and no one had spoken to him. He imagined that his frown had kept them all away.

He'd gone too fast, too far with Rebecca. He hadn't meant to—and that's what bothered him. *He* was supposed to be the one in control, and yet it had almost deserted him.

And he would suffer for it, he thought with strained amusement.

Yet . . . he was enjoying this game they played together. He didn't have to take things to their final conclusion with Rebecca. She wanted to be kissed—perhaps she even wanted more. She needed to learn that such curiosity would get her into trouble.

But if he introduced her to the ways of pleasure, she would no longer be vulnerable. He'd give her another, more intimate, taste of adventure, enough to sate her and keep her from further ruin.

She didn't have to fear him, for although his control might be shaky, it was still sound.

He couldn't stand out here much longer—he'd already made certain no one saw him coming up the stairs. He should have returned through the window, he thought, but hadn't relished the climb again.

He knocked softly on the door. "Mrs. Lambe? Might I have a word with you?" He would have preferred silence, but he wanted her to know that it was he.

When she called for him to enter, he did so quickly and silently, then came to a halt. She stood before the hearth, combing through her long hair. She was wearing a clean chemise, and a shawl demurely about her shoulders. They had not purchased nightclothes—and he was secretly glad they didn't have enough money for the expense. Spread out across the chair and table were clothes she'd washed out—including his own.

"You didn't have to wash my clothing, Rebecca, but I thank you."

She nodded, studying him even as she continued to

work on her hair by the heat of the coal fire. She looked very aware of what they'd begun, but as if she wouldn't stop it. He was relieved.

He glanced at the bathing tub with its thin film of soap on the surface. "How were your abrasions?"

She seemed surprised that he remembered. "Since I didn't wear a corset, they've begun healing well."

"No redness or pus?"

She stopped combing and eyed him. "You are talking to a woman who knows every sign of infection."

"Of course." He shrugged out of his coat and began to unbutton the collar of his shirt. Those hazel eyes watched him. He almost warned her to turn away, then decided to see what she'd do. "You're not going down to the taproom, as I just did. An evening gathering in such a place is not fit for a lady."

She hesitated, then turned to the hearth and continued drying her hair. He almost sighed his disappointment.

"Should we not send for clean water?" she asked doubtfully.

"I will make do." He quickly disrobed and sank into the now tepid water, which barely came to his waist. The chilliness added even more incentive to wash quickly—as if he needed incentive. Especially since his knees were so bent as to be almost uncomfortable. The tub wasn't made for a man of his size.

She said, "While you were gone, I wrote a letter to my aunt."

"We'll post it in the morning. We have time, since the second wagon will leave closer to noon."

"Are you certain you don't mind the delay?"

"What choice do we have? If we remain with the same wagon, under the same names, all the way to Manchester, we're far more likely to be found, if someone is asking questions."

"Perhaps they're doing what we are—following the artist. He made no secret of his journey."

"I've thought of that," he said, not revealing his worry. "But we must be cautious rather than hurry. And why would they care about the artist, when they know you have the jewel?"

"I could have left it behind."

"That would have put your family in danger. They know you didn't do that. Why else would you flee?"

He heard her sigh. "I guess I should go to bed—"

She obviously forgot herself, for she turned around while he was still in the tub. He arched a brow, wearing a knowing smile and nothing else. She gave a squeak before turning her back again and covering her mouth. Her shoulders started to shake.

"My near nudity is amusing?" he asked dryly.

She shook her head and gasped out, "I had no idea how tiny that bathing tub was until I saw—" Laughter erupted from her, and it took a minute before at last she wiped her eyes. "Sorry." She crawled beneath the covers and turned her back.

But she was not laughing when he came to bed. She rolled over and looked up at him. They'd played a tantalizing game not two hours ago, and she'd removed most of her clothing for him. She was only wearing a chemise even now, and he, only his drawers.

Staring at his bare chest, she pulled the covers back. "I think this bed is larger than the last. I will try not to attach myself to you in my sleep."

He sat down on the edge. Something skittered in the corner of the room.

She gasped. "Get your feet off the floor!"

Now it was his turn to laugh as he followed her wishes. Unlike the previous night, he was able to lie on his back, one arm pillowed behind his head. She lay beside him.

"Good night, Julian." Her voice was soft, almost tentative.

"Good night, Rebecca." He could smell the scent of her, of clean, plain soap mixed with a scent that was all her own. He wanted to pull her against him, show her the pleasure he could give.

But he wanted it too much.

Chapter 13

I n the morning, Mrs. Lambe's manservant Tusser was dutifully awaiting her in the taproom so they could have breakfast together.

"And how was yer accommodation in the stables, Tusser?" Rebecca asked.

"Very good, ma'am," Julian answered, sliding into a seat opposite her. "Thank ye for allowin' me to share this meal with ye."

She almost giggled. She hadn't been giggling earlier that morning, when once again she'd awakened to find herself wrapped around Julian. They'd both been wearing far less clothing, and she'd been able to feel the long, smooth muscles of his torso and hips, and the bare flesh of his feet meeting hers. Her face had been pressed to his back, and she swore she could yet taste the salt of his skin. She'd been embarrassed, he'd been amused, content to linger at her side. When he'd come up on his elbow and leaned over her, she'd embarrassed herself even more by fleeing.

What was wrong with her?

His playacting as her servant eased some of the tension between them, but not all. Sleeping night after night with a man made her far too aware of him. She'd never spent so much time with a person who wasn't family, and to her dismay, she enjoyed it. She didn't want to feel this way, not when she had such grand plans to travel, once she'd convinced her mother she didn't want to marry immediately. She reminded herself that she wouldn't be lonely, that she'd have servants, and even friends with whom she would stop to visit.

But this intimacy called to her in a wicked fashion. She needed to find a way to keep her distance. Marriage was the easiest story to tell the other wagon passengers, one that allowed them to be alone together without suspicion. But surely there were other stories they could use . . .

After breakfast, Julian commanded her to remain in their room while he walked back to the other inn to reserve a spot on the next wagon. She agreed, not needing to leave when she could use the services of a maid to flesh out her plan. She had to part with one of the precious coins in her possession, but it was worth it. The thought of the coming freedom was a heady incentive.

The maid was obviously enjoying the activities of the eccentric widow. She returned before Julian did, bringing the new garments, so Rebecca had time to quickly change.

She was the very image of a boy by the time he returned, hair pulled up in her cap, linen shirt, breeches and boots. A well-patched jacket disguised her feminine curves. She heard his discreet knock—"Mrs. Lambe, may I come in?"—and tried to position herself to look young and masculine. She ended up standing with her hands on her hips, cap pulled low over her eyes.

He came to a halt, then slowly shut the door behind him. Though he was smiling, he shook his head. "Rebecca, you aren't going anywhere dressed like that. You're reminding me of the first night I met you—and even then, I knew you were a woman."

"We don't always have to pretend to be married, you know. If I'm your younger brother, no one will think—"

"You aren't my younger brother," he said, advancing on her.

She backed up until her legs hit the bed, her heart fluttering with excitement. "What do you think you're doing? You cannot stop me if I choose to wear this."

"Oh, you think not?" He tossed her cap aside. "Though your hair is pinned up, one stiff breeze and you would have lost the cap and your disguise."

"I'll hold on to it."

She tried to pass him, and he grabbed her arm and

tugged the jacket sleeve off. Indignantly, she held on to the garment, only to be easily spun about. He tossed the jacket onto the chair.

"You can't be wearing a chemise under that shirt," he said.

His voice sounded gruff, deeper, and it incited a strange shiver inside her, one that she was beginning to recognize too well. She did *not* want to desire him, did *not* want to enjoy this little game of his dominance over her. She tried to run past him, but he caught her easily and set her on the bed as if she truly were a small child. He began to peel her boots off. She pushed at him, but it was like attempting to move a mountain. She tried to kick free of his hold, but he only gripped her legs under one massive arm and held her still while he finished with her feet.

"Julian!" she hissed his name and squirmed, but she couldn't move.

And then she felt his hands at her waist, loosening her rope belt. Something deep inside her mind went to mush, and she almost relaxed, almost let him do anything he wanted to her.

But did she want him to know he had that kind of power over her?

So she continued to struggle, even as he pulled the loose breeches down her thighs, revealing the fine, lacy drawers that she'd worn beneath her skirts when she left London.

He went still, then looked up at her from beneath hooded eyes.

She tried to buck him off with her hips. "I only have two pairs!" she cried.

Holding her down, he got the pants off her. She boxed his ears, a trick she'd seen little boys perform on each other. Wincing, he leaned across her body and pinned both her arms wide.

They were both breathing heavily in the sudden silence. She realized that he stood between her thighs, pressed hip to hip. His position over her meant that his chest brushed hers, although he did not lower his weight totally on to her. Oh, he didn't need to do that, not when she could feel every detail of how different they were made against the most private part of her body.

And then she felt that male part of him swell, right against her, and the sensation was so startling, so forbidden, so deliciously pleasurable that she moaned. She suddenly wanted to distract them both.

She licked her dry lips. "You don't want me to have any amusement at all, Julian."

She kept expecting him to move, but he didn't. He just continued to look down at her with an unreadable expression on his face. He could have been as impassive, as unemotional as stone—but he wasn't, for she felt the evidence against her. She was positively warm down there, with an achy feeling of fullness that was so new and so compelling. His garments and hers still separated them, and she suddenly wished there was nothing at all.

"This has nothing to do with depriving you, Rebecca," he said, an almost lazy rhythm to his speech.

She tensed even more. "Try to convince me of that."

"But if you go around dressed as a boy, it will still be obvious to others that I'm attracted to you—and then I'd be labeled a deviant."

They remained silent for a moment, the sounds of their breathing like engines in the quiet room.

"You're attracted to me?" she finally said.

His smile was as seductive as sin. "You can't tell?"

She lifted her head off the bed and kissed him. She knew it would last but a moment, fully expecting that Julian, so conscious of his place in Society even though he liked to tease her, would pull away to protect her sensibilities. In that brief moment, she tried to memorize the wonder that blossomed inside her because his lips were soft while the rest of him was so hard.

Then with a groan, he came down on top of her, releasing her arms even as he gathered her to him and deepened the kiss. At once she lost any semblance of control. This was no gentle suitor's kiss. No, he slanted his mouth across hers, all heat and demand, forcing her mouth open, commanding that she accept his invasion when she'd never imagined such a thing.

His tongue was subtle seduction, sweeping into her

mouth, exploring. She heard herself moan again, and this time he answered with a groan of stark need that thrilled her. She let herself touch him, felt the hard muscles of his back, the incredible width of his shoulders. He seemed carved of marble, yet so warm and responsive to the touch. Her legs moved restlessly, clasping his hips as if with a will of their own. Between her thighs, he moved against her, rolling into her, pressing his erection in a way that made her shudder. She gasped against his mouth, then rocked her hips instinctively, searching for more.

He suddenly lifted himself off her body. She clung to him with her hands, needing him to show her an end to this terrible, consuming passion that rose within her like wildfire, burning out of control.

"Julian!" she cried out. "Please don't stop."

And then he was on her again, kissing her face and her neck, trailing his moist mouth and licking with his tongue, even as his hips merged with hers. He rocked against her slowly, over and over, and again she felt a swelling of emotion, of powerful pleasure that she'd never imagined. She made incoherent sounds, urging him on, caressing him, kissing his hair as he bent to kiss his way down the narrow opening at the top of her shirt. His cheek brushed her breast, and she shuddered with a new stab of fierce pleasure. He turned his head and caught her nipple into his mouth through her garments.

She bit her lip to keep from screaming at the shocking new sensations that coursed through her body. She could only move helplessly beneath him, arching against his mouth, thrusting her hips ever harder into his. She was hot and needy, spiraling ever higher, desperate for whatever came next.

And what came next suddenly consumed her until she was a shuddering, clinging cat. If she'd have had claws, she would have attached herself to him and never let go, not if he could make her feel *this* wonderful, so aware of her body and what it could do.

He suddenly rose up above her on his hands and knees. His face was a mask of itself, hard and grimacing, even as he hung his head and struggled to breathe.

She had the most wonderful need to lie still and let this languid sensation draw away her very bones. But not Julian. He seemed stiff, almost as if he were in pain. Surely if he'd felt what she just did, he wouldn't be so . . .

And then she realized that she'd been selfish. She'd taken every ounce of pleasure he could give her, but he hadn't had the same in return. Did a man need to be inside her to feel such release? She knew something of what was expected on a wedding night, for her mother had never wanted her to be ignorant.

"Julian?"

She touched his shoulder, and he pushed away from her and collapsed on his back on the bed. He flung an arm across his face and lay still, his chest rising and falling like a blacksmith's bellows. She came up on her elbow and looked down his body, where she could still see the ridge of his erection, which had given her such pleasure.

She touched his chest, and felt the tremor within him.

"Julian." She said his name as a caress, and watched in amazement as he shuddered. "You didn't . . ." She didn't know how to say the words. "I felt . . . but you didn't."

In a guttural whisper, he said, "It is better this way."

Confused, she inched closer until she could lean over him, though she still couldn't see his face. "I never imagined how you could make me feel. I want to do the same for you."

"No." He rose swiftly to his feet.

She sat up. The coarse shirt she wore barely covered her thighs, and her feminine drawers seemed provocatively on display. She almost wanted to hide herself, but Julian was watching her hungrily.

"Rebecca, you did nothing wrong. You enjoyed the wonder that is pleasure. I wanted that for you—perhaps not so soon," he added ruefully.

"I don't understand. I felt . . . a culmination"—now she felt truly hot with embarrassment—"but you didn't."

His grin was strained, yet genuine. "No, I didn't. A man doesn't have to finish the deed to enjoy himself. Don't ever forget that."

"But—"

"Dress yourself, Rebecca—but not in those garments, please."

For one moment, she almost refused, but he seemed strung as tightly as a violin. She decided to put her boy's clothing in the portmanteau. Perhaps she'd find another chance to use them.

She wasn't going to forget how he'd made her feel, how she wanted to experience more. She would take her time, conquering him slowly. When she put her mind to something, she achieved it. And she wanted him.

Passion was a new world to her, but he didn't know that. He thought her a nude model; did he believe she'd given herself to someone else, if not Roger? He'd never specifically asked.

Yet he must still want to protect her, even if she had no virtue left to protect. She thought it a sweet sentiment, but inconvenient on this grand adventure she was allowing herself. Perhaps he would eventually succumb, if she didn't let him know the truth of her virginity.

Suddenly, the day seemed even more full of promise. They were eluding villains, tracking down the history of a stolen jewel—and now she was learning the mysteries of what went on between men and women. Her life had never been more exciting.

* * *

The wagon rolled on into the early evening, and Julian bore Rebecca's weight with satisfaction. She'd fallen asleep, head bobbing, body swaying. He'd pulled her against him, and with a sigh she'd relaxed, her body slumped beneath his shoulder, her arm draped across his hips.

The other passengers—a group of five Irish brothers on their way to Manchester to look for factory work— smiled and elbowed each other at Rebecca's antics, but said nothing. There was nothing to say; Rebecca and Julian were supposedly married.

With every sleepy sigh she gave, he relived the sounds of her passion, her desperation for orgasm, the sensitivity of her body to every caress. And then his imagination would take him further, stripping her of her garments. She would arch like she had in the painting, then spread her thighs to welcome him in.

But no, that wasn't part of his plan. He'd tried to leave her after the kiss, wanting to take things slowly with her. But when she'd clung to him, when she'd begged, refusal seemed impossible. He almost lost himself with her, had stopped just in time. It might have been one of the hardest things he'd ever done, and he didn't like feeling so overwhelmed by mere foreplay.

At the inn that night, he decided to slow things down. They would be together for a few more days yet, and he enjoyed the sense of anticipation. He lay down at her side, but did not continue where they'd left off. To his surprise, it was far more difficult than he'd imagined, and that annoyed him. He was used to not sleeping—his mind was always difficult to shut down each night, and this time with Rebecca proved no different. She seemed confused, even hurt, which he regretted, but she was yet too uncertain to question him.

The following night, they stayed in a small village, where the only room to rent was above an alehouse. Their fellow passengers had been local and didn't need lodgings, leaving the small cramped room to Julian and Rebecca. They could hear the shouts and singing from below them, and they shared a glance of understanding that they might not sleep well that night.

The room contained only a broken chest of drawers and a bed. He'd be next to her again all night.

There were no meals served to their room; he had to go down to the taproom to order food. He waited, seated in a wooden settle in the corner; it had a high back that he could lean his head on and appear to be dozing. But he never forgot that men were looking for them; his eyes constantly scanned the room.

Next to him, stew bubbled in a cauldron hung over the fire; the smell made his stomach growl. At several tables, men talked and laughed over their beer, and two others played darts at a board hung on the far wall.

With his eyes half closed, Julian watched it all. No

one came near him but the barmaid who brought his beer. At times like this, it was always good to look like he was the kind of man who started fights. Never had his size helped him more. He found he liked being anonymous, after years of people giving him second looks or talking in whispers about the scandals that had plagued his family.

A young lad came in from the hall, looking for his father perhaps, to drag him home after a day's work. Julian half smiled at the thought. The boy's eyes lingered over the crowd, then landed on him.

And then Julian recognized Rebecca. He didn't let himself stiffen or betray his sudden worry. He saw her take a breath and boldly stride toward him. Gone was the graceful walk of a lady. But he didn't care that she might look the part. She'd disobeyed him, and that was dangerous.

She stopped near the cauldron and sniffed. "I'm hungry, George. You were takin' too long."

Boldly, she plopped herself down on the settle beside him and let her gaze roam the crowd with interest. He crossed his arms over his chest and glared at her, but she gave him no notice.

"So this is an alehouse," she said quietly. "Not much different than the public dining room of that last inn we stayed at."

"Women aren't allowed."

She shrugged. "I don't look like a woman."

He leaned toward her, trying to be menacing. "You know I told you—"

"I know what you told me. But you are not my master and—"

The barmaid approached, her curly hair coming undone down her back. She pushed a strand behind her ear and smiled tiredly at Rebecca. "Do ye want somethin', lad?"

Rebecca said, "A beer, please," at the same time Julian said, "He'll take cider."

Rebecca grimaced, but didn't contradict him.

"That's the last thing I need is you drunk," Julian said quietly when the barmaid had left.

"Afraid I'll take advantage of you again?" she asked, giving him a sly smile from beneath the lowered brim of her cap.

He thought about her eager and yearning beneath him. But if she wanted to keep bringing the topic up, then he would oblige her and maybe learn something about her in the process. "Take advantage of me?" he echoed after drinking another swallow of beer. "Is that something you learned how to do with Roger Eastfield?"

He saw her smile falter. "I certainly did not take advantage of him. He asked me to pose and I did."

He nodded, scratching his bristly chin as he studied her. She avoided meeting his eyes, but nodded to the barmaid when she set down the cider. Rebecca took a gulp, then coughed. Cider served in an alehouse had its own punch, mild though it might be.

"I've been considering your reasons for doing the painting," he said.

She frowned. "I told you my reasons."

"I've come up with more."

"If you feel the need to rehash this again, that must not be your first beer."

He smiled. "I think you spent your whole life feeling frail. That painting—and Eastfield's interest—showed you as otherwise. And you liked it."

She rolled her eyes and took a smaller sip of her cider.

"Did you feel angry at being frail?" he asked.

"What are you talking about?" she asked sharply.

"Or angry at your mother perhaps, for making you feel that way."

"Nothing was my mother's fault. But if we're going to talk mothers, then I warn you, yours is fair game."

"So you don't blame your mother?"

"Blame her? For my childhood? She doted on me, nursed me through everything."

But she wasn't meeting his eyes until she narrowed hers to regard him. "So you seem fixated on my mother. Does that mean you blame yours for something, and think everyone should?"

"Blame my mother? Our reduced circumstances were hardly her fault."

"No? Then what was?"

"You're changing the subject. I think you did the painting to prove something. And now you insist on traveling with me for the same reason."

"I'm not quite sure how daring to pose nude and this journey are related."

" 'Daring' being the operative word." He lowered his voice even more. "You're daring a lot here, aren't you? Daring someone to catch us together, daring two villains to succeed against you, daring to wear that . . . item around your neck instead of allowing me to keep it safe."

She met his gaze boldly, took a healthy swallow of her cider, and said, "I like to be daring—unlike you."

Chapter 14

Rebecca knew she risked much—and not just by provoking Julian in an alehouse.

But he eyed her almost lazily and said, "I do not need to be daring. I think through every situation and make the proper response—unlike you."

A proper response? She wanted *some* kind of response, after two days of being held at arm's length. He'd given her the most wondrous, transformational pleasure, but had denied himself, then denied her the chance to relive the moment. Had he wanted to escape her?

Or escape himself?

After her anger and hurt at his rejection had faded, she realized his feelings were more about him. He was not a man to lose control. Yet he'd lost almost every bit of it, holding on by a fingernail to reason, enough to push her away before the final act.

Did he regret their abrupt ending as much as she did? She had barely been able to sleep last night, thinking about what he'd done to her, how he'd made her feel—

and that was with their clothing on! She had fantasies night and day of nothing between them, just warm damp flesh sliding against each other.

Tonight he would sleep at her side again; she welcomed the challenge—the dare. She would not be so acquiescent to his mercurial decisions.

"You've lost the power of speech?" he said dryly. "I find that hard to believe."

"We're in too public a place for me to tell you what I think of your claim that you always make the proper response," she said sweetly.

With one glance, she could see his contemplative look, and knew that he, too, was remembering what had happened between them.

She swallowed another mouthful of cider, feeling braver by the moment. "But then again, perhaps kissing me *was* the proper response."

He gave a faint smile. "Speak quietly."

"Or was the proper response totally ignoring me, and it just took you a while to remember that?"

"I'm not ignoring you, I'm protecting you."

"Protecting me from *you*?" she asked in disbelief. "Except for the wager over the painting, I've long since stopped fearing your motives."

He downed his beer and nodded for another.

"Or do *you* worry over your motives, George?" she asked softly.

"You're speaking in riddles—Lionel."

She chuckled.

He peered into her half-empty tankard. "We need to get some food into you."

"I'm fine." She looked about. "So what does one do in an alehouse besides drink?" She focused on the men grouped in a corner. "They must be playing darts. I've never watched a game."

She flung herself away from the settle before he could stop her. He swore softly as he followed, forced to stand at her back while she studied the game. He was like a mountain of doom towering behind her, and she enjoyed every moment of it. She ate hot stew by the fire, drank more cider, and even convinced Julian to let her throw a few darts when no one was at the board. All in all, it was an enjoyable evening compared to sitting primly with needlework while the men had all the fun.

When they returned to their room at last, she fell back on the bed, even as the room seemed to whirl slowly about her. She laughed at the sensation.

"You're drunk," he said as he came to stand above her.

Did his smile hide disappointment? She wondered why.

Flinging her arms wide, she said, "I've never been drunk before. I'm determined to experience everything— George. See, I remembered your name!" She giggled.

He rolled his eyes. "Go to sleep, Lionel."

After pulling off her breeches and jacket, she pretended to sleep, because he must want that, but instead she rolled on her side and watched him undress. He glanced over his shoulder at her once, but she closed her eyes and remained motionless. She didn't open them again until she heard water poured into a basin. She should feel guilty for watching such a private moment, but she didn't. Her mind felt strangely overheated, her conscience submerged.

Julian was wearing only his trousers as he washed himself, and she pouted with disappointment. How was she ever supposed to learn about men? But she could not be disappointed at the sight of his skin wetly gleaming by candlelight. He looked rough and dark and far too masculine with his face covered in several days' growth of beard. She felt restless and achy just looking at him. She wanted to experience even more of the passion she'd glimpsed, but she could not force him to show her.

At last he came to sit down on the edge of the bed to remove his trousers. Foolish man, he'd donned a shirt, but she still snuggled against his broad back.

"You're overdressed," she murmured.

She could see his profile as he glanced back over his shoulder.

"You'll have an aching head in the morning," he said.

"Don't sound so satisfied."

"Believe me, I'm not." He punched his pillow into shape beneath his head.

"I'm not so innocent that I don't know the double meaning of your words."

He laughed.

She snaked her arm about his waist, surprised his body became tense, even as his laughter seemed choked. "Are you frightened of me, Julian?" she whispered, pressing herself against him.

"Go to sleep, Rebecca," he said.

She gave an exaggerated sigh, even as she tucked her thighs behind his. "You're so warm," she murmured.

He didn't answer.

She settled into a sulky silence, and at last fell asleep.

By late afternoon, they reached Manchester, and Julian felt a surge of satisfaction and anticipation. The town was much like London, large and sprawling, with a pall of smoke hanging over everything. The factories lined the canals and rivers, belching smoke and steam from their tall stacks. Seated beside him in the wagon, Rebecca, wearing a gown instead of breeches, thank God, looked solemnly at the crowds that teemed in the busy streets. Workers coming home from the factories watched out for desperate little boys picking pockets. Women filled their baskets with groceries from the market stalls.

Rebecca received more than one second glance from men walking or riding beside them. He saw her tug her bonnet a little closer about her face. It was difficult to hide her beauty, even though she looked smudged and weary from the travel.

The public wagon deposited them at an inn near the Bridgewater Canal before supper. Julian was too eager to find what they'd come all this way to find: Roger Eastfield, and the mystery of how he'd acquired the Scandalous Lady. Julian thought Rebecca seemed a bit quiet through it all, which made him curious. But there would be time to discover why.

Or would there? If Eastfield answered the questions to Julian's satisfaction, and they didn't encounter the jewel thieves, he would have to return her to London. Would she go willingly?

And why did he feel as if his life would be so much . . . less, without her to amuse—and bedevil—him? He had so much more he wanted to show her, to prepare her for the not-so-proper life she'd chosen.

The innkeeper knew little of Manchester's art community, but did know of the Royal Manchester Institution on Mosley Street.

"Paintin' pictures is a waste of time," the innkeeper told Julian and Rebecca, frowning at them from beneath his bald head, "and the Institution is a waste of taxpayer's hard-earned money."

"I'm lookin' for my cousin," Rebecca said apologetically. "He's an artist—how else can I begin to find him?"

The innkeeper snorted, but was persuaded to give them directions.

Out on the busy street, Julian said, "It's too far to walk. We'll have to hire a hackney. And that will leave us precious few coins for tonight."

She slid her hand into his arm. "Should we wait until tomorrow? We can earn money then."

He frowned at her. "*We* will be doing no such thing." He looked down the street to where the wharves along the canal streamed with cargo. "I can't sit here and wait. Perhaps we can learn something at this institution."

It took over an hour to reach the Royal Manchester Institution in heavy traffic, but they were in luck. Artists from all over the city sold their wares outside the impressive multi-columned building. With just a few questions, they found that many people wanted to talk about the growing fame of Manchester's native son, Roger Eastfield. Soon, they even learned the name of the street his mother lived on, and the fact that Roger was still in town.

"The directions put it only a half hour's walk from here," Julian said, tamping down his eagerness.

"But if we're out after dark . . ."

He looked down, surprised by her hesitation. "Don't you want to know the truth at last?"

"I do, but we aren't the only ones who know I wore the diamond in the painting."

"More than enough reason to get to Eastfield and

warn him," he said grimly. "And I'll protect you along the way." A growing feeling of urgency could not be denied.

She seemed unconvinced, but nodded her acceptance of his plan.

Twilight began to overtake the streets as they walked. At least they were in a more middle-class neighborhood, where little gardens lined alleys behind small houses.

Someone brushed by them on a run, and Julian braced himself to deal with a pickpocket, but it was a grown man, respectably dressed, clutching his hat to his head. Soon two children passed them as well, followed by a woman, who didn't yell at them to stop.

"What is going on?" Rebecca asked in confusion.

Before Julian could answer, someone shouted, "Fire!"

And then Julian's sense of unease changed into fatalism. "Hurry!" he said to Rebecca. As he gripped her arm, he forced her to increase her pace to match his.

To the north, the darkening sky began to give way to a pale, unnatural brightness.

"Oh my," Rebecca breathed. "You don't think—"

She broke off, saying nothing else, even as they both began to run. At the end of the corner, they saw a growing crowd of people gathered across the street from a two-story home. Smoke poured out of the windows, but they could not yet see fire. The fire brigade hadn't yet arrived to combat it.

No one seemed to know if anyone was inside, but all agreed that this was the Eastfield home. Rebecca stared up at it in dismay.

"Follow me!" Julian said, pulling her away and down the next alley.

She didn't question him when he reached the garden behind the threatened home. The gate was unlocked, and they were able to approach the rear entrance. Julian flung the door back and dark smoke billowed out, rumbling like an old man's belch.

Rebecca grabbed his arm. "What do you think you're doing? You can't go in there!"

"I must." He pulled the scarf from around his neck, dipped it in the small fountain, and tied it around his neck, ready to pull it up over his mouth and nose.

Her eyes were wide with terror. "You could be killed! We have the jewel—what more do you need?"

"People could be trapped, Rebecca."

She opened her mouth, but nothing came out, even as she clutched her hands together. Frantically, she seemed to search the back of the house. "Look in the windows first!"

"No time." He gripped her upper arms and gave her a little shake. "Stay here—promise me!"

Somewhere in the distance, they heard the clang of a fire engine, then the shouts of the crowd at the front of the building and the growing din of a house about to die.

"I—I promise," she cried, then flung herself against him.

He cupped her head to tilt her face to his and kissed her roughly, passionately. The wetness of her tears touched him, created the first open wound of tenderness for her. And then he pushed her away, pulled the wet scarf over his lower face and ran inside.

Immediately he ducked low as the smoke rose in a haze, getting trapped up at the ceiling. Somewhere he could hear the crackle of flames, but he couldn't see fire yet. He almost wished he could, for the lack of light made maneuvering difficult. Blindly, he ran with his arms forward to protect himself from running into furniture.

"Eastfield!" he shouted, but his voice seemed swallowed by the dull roar of fire, closer and closer to him.

Then he stumbled over a body lying on the floor. Using his hands, he could tell it was a woman dressed in plain clothing, perhaps a servant. She was already unresponsive. Dead from the fire?

But he felt the stickiness of blood on her forehead. She'd been injured—but the house had not yet begun to come down around them, although it groaned in protest at the blazing siege.

Had this woman been deliberately harmed? If so, that meant the fire wasn't an accident.

He left her behind, heading to the front of the house, hoping that someone would be in the lower rooms, for he didn't know if he could make it up to the first floor.

When he reached the front hall, flames flickered around the edges of an open doorway. Heat wafted out at him in waves, making the skin of his hands and face feel seared. On the far wall, fiery draperies framed the front windows in which glass was starting to pop. The flames had traveled over the ceiling, licking toward the hall—and Julian—like the grasping hands of the devil.

There were two more bodies on the carpeted floor.

Hunched over, he raced into the room and dropped to his knees. The man stared sightless up at the ceiling, flames glistening in his lifeless eyes. He, too, had suffered a fatal wound to his head. There was nothing that Julian could do.

Next to the dead man lay a gray-haired woman, her body half covering his as if she'd clutched him in grief. Then she groaned, coughing feebly. Julian didn't hesitate—he scooped her into his arms and started to run back the way he'd come. The front entrance was surely closer, but the flames from the parlor had already reached it.

His eyes streamed tears, his lungs began to burn with the smoke that seeped through the wet scarf. He heard a crash behind him, felt a wave of blown heat, but he didn't look over his shoulder. He vaulted over the dead servant, his eyes straining for the rear entrance.

And then he was out into the garden, the dark, cold sky of night above him, lit from behind by the fire.

"Julian!" Rebecca screamed his name, her voice full of relief and tears.

Dazed, he let her guide him to the back of the garden, away from the dangerous home being consumed.

"Set her here," Rebecca said, gesturing to a bench.

He did so, even as his protesting lungs began to cough. He tore the scarf from his face, then braced his hands on his thighs, coughing and coughing until he thought his lungs would burst. He vaguely watched Rebecca on her knees beside the old woman. She was holding the woman's head to the side while she, too, coughed weakly. The sound rattled in the woman's lungs in a way that didn't bode well.

When at last her body seemed to wilt as the onslaught of coughing weakened, the old woman murmured, "Roger . . . Roger . . ."

Rebecca looked questioningly at him over her shoulder, and Julian pressed his lips together grimly as he shook his head.

"I am so sorry about your son, Mrs. Eastfield," she murmured. "But you must be quiet now and gather your strength."

Mrs. Eastfield pushed at her soothing hands. "For what? There's nothing . . . left. I was . . . already dying, but I never thought . . . that my poor boy would leave this earth before I." She closed her eyes and wept silent tears, her body shaking.

"The flames didn't kill Roger," Julian said as he knelt beside Rebecca. "Something else did."

Rebecca gasped as she searched his face, but didn't interfere.

"Murdered," the old woman said, her voice raspy. "Murdered . . . right in front of me. Oh God . . ." She started coughing again.

The sounds of a clanging siren had grown louder, the roar of the fire beginning to compete for attention. But no one came back into the garden. Julian knew the firemen would be most concerned with keeping the fire from spreading to the houses on each side.

"She needs help," Rebecca said urgently. "We can find out about Roger later."

"There won't be a 'later,' " he murmured.

Mrs. Eastfield lifted her head. "Roger? . . . Did you know my son?"

Rebecca took Julian's wet scarf and tried to dab at the old woman's sooty face, but she pushed her away.

Rebecca sighed. "I knew him in London, Mrs. Eastfield. He was a gifted artist."

"Then you . . . should know. You can tell . . . the police. My son was . . . murdered."

"You can tell them yourself," Rebecca said gently.

"No! I . . . I'm dying. I have been for a long time. I need you to know . . . what happened!"

The old woman flailed, agitated, setting off her

coughing again, as Julian met Rebecca's frightened, sad, eyes.

"We'll listen," he said, putting a hand on Mrs. Eastfield's bony shoulder. "Tell us what you can."

They fetched water from the well in the rear of the garden, propped the woman on Julian's folded coat, and after several sips she began her halting story.

"Three men burst in . . . demanding he tell them about a necklace, a diamond. Roger . . . Roger said he didn't know what they were talking about, but . . . they hit him"—she gave a weak sob—"and he admitted that he'd had it. Said it was paste—paste! But they didn't believe him . . . and at last, even I believed that it was . . . priceless. But poor Roger had lent it . . . to one of his models. Oh God, they hit him again. The man . . . in charge . . . said it was his, that Roger had only been hired to paint his wife . . . and said my boy had stolen it."

Julian exchanged a quick glance with Rebecca. A tear tracked through the dirt on her face as she stared down at the fading old woman.

"Roger . . . wasn't a thief! Oh God, they kept hitting him, and . . . at last he admitted the man's wife had given him the jewel. The man . . . wouldn't believe it . . . and Roger was forced to say he'd been . . . intimate with the woman. She said . . . she was bored with the diamond. I never saw such . . . fury and hatred . . . in a man. He refused to believe the words, said his wife told him Roger had stolen it . . . and he hit my boy, hit him hard with a vase. He didn't move again . . . my poor boy . . ."

Her next cough was far weaker, and she couldn't keep her eyes open. Every breath was a gasping effort.

Rebecca was openly crying. "Mrs. Eastfield, you must rest."

"Too late," she moaned, her head rolling back and forth. "Too late. They didn't care . . . about me. I clutched my boy even as they set fire to my home to . . . hide what they'd done."

"Do you know who they were?" Julian asked urgently.

She shuddered, her body arching. "Windebank," she whispered. "They called him . . . Windebank. He said . . . he was going . . . home. Oh, Roger—Roger—" Then she collapsed back onto the bench and became still.

In that moment of silence that cocooned them, they both stared at the woman's body. Rebecca sniffled and rubbed at her eyes. Julian felt frozen, stunned, telling himself to think logically, calmly, even as a rising tide of fury seemed to choke him.

"Julian?" Rebecca said, shaking his arm. "What is it? Do you know that name?"

"My uncle," he said between clenched teeth. "He's my uncle."

Chapter 15

S till on her knees, Rebecca gaped up at Julian, his expression harsh and forbidding. With his dark features and heavy brows, the width of his shoulders, he looked like a man to be feared. But she didn't fear him.

She was angry with herself, had stood outside a burning building and let him take all the risk, wondering if she'd ever see him again. He'd coddled her, as she'd allowed everyone in her family to do for her entire life. A person of action would make her own choices. Instead of proving that she could be his partner, she'd wrung her hands and waited while terror and helplessness choked her.

Now he faced a revelation that might be worse to him than the danger of a burning building. An ache of worry and sympathy tied a knot beneath her breastbone. He finally had a connection to the theft of the diamond— and it was within his family.

Had his own uncle stolen the Scandalous Lady?

Before she could speak, she heard a crash at the back of the garden near the alley. Julian came swiftly to his feet and began to run. The growing fire lit the night, throwing wild shadows against the garden wall. A tall bush shuddered back and forth, although there was no wind.

Rising, she watched in amazement as Julian flung himself toward the bush. It bore his weight, and he swiftly scaled it so that he could look over the wall. He froze, suspended, and she thought he might throw himself over and leave. But instead, he lowered himself back to the ground and returned to her.

"What did you see?" she cried.

"A man at the far end of the alley. Running *away* from the fire. It would have been useless to chase him."

"Why would you have even considered it?" she asked.

"I think he was left to watch for the fire, to make certain no one escaped alive. He also could have been ordered to look for us."

She swallowed heavily and shuddered. "On orders from—Windebank?"

Julian shrugged and said nothing.

She looked down at the poor dead woman. "We must do something for her."

"It's too late to help her, Rebecca."

"But—"

"They'll think she crawled out of the fire only to die. We can't involve ourselves. Can you imagine the questions?"

"But we have some of the answers! It was all about this—" She broke off, putting a hand to the hidden jewel at her throat. It almost seemed to burn her, as if men killing for it made it evil.

"Windebank will soon know we were here. We can't waste time, or he'll find some way to elude punishment. And do you want the world to know of our involvement—together?"

"It isn't about us, or some foolish notion of impropriety!" she cried, rocking back in outrage.

"I don't want it to be about our deaths either!"

She stared up at him, with no way to counter such a truth. She watched in shock as he knelt down and gently lifted Mrs. Eastfield's head so that he could retrieve his coat.

"No one can know we were here," he murmured, looking at Rebecca with his piercing gray eyes. "Come with me."

She didn't hesitate—what would be the point? Climbing to her feet stiffly, slowly, she didn't protest when he took her arm and half lifted her. He grabbed their portmanteau, and they went out through the garden gate to walk several blocks away from the fire.

"Where will we go?" she asked at last. His face was so forbidding that she wished to distract him—for the moment. But they would soon have to discuss what they'd learned. He needed to talk about it, though she sensed he wouldn't want to.

"We can't afford the inn where the wagon left us," he said.

"Can there be any place worse than that?" she asked with faint sarcasm.

He nodded. "A lodging house in a poorer section of the town."

"Will it have food?"

At last he seemed to really see her. "No. We'll look for a tavern after we make arrangements for the night."

As the last gray of twilight faded, they found a lodging house where Rebecca saw a truth she'd never imagined before. Each floor was one open room, and people of both sexes, even children, slept wherever they could, on pallets and bedding or even on straw. Though the windows and doors were open, the smell made her nauseous. Several candles guttered on broken crates, and she could see more than one child stare at her listlessly.

"I'm sorry," Julian said in a low voice. "We have barely enough coins to eat."

"Don't apologize. It isn't your fault." She clutched his arm when a rat boldly scurried past them. "Can we find a tavern before we sleep?"

"Of course. But first I have to clean off this soot."

He paid a halfpenny for some rags and a basin, and drew up water from the well in the middle of the courtyard shared by all the surrounding tenements. He washed his face as best he could, then she took the rag from him and searched for the last smudges he'd missed. He watched her, his face so close to hers, those opaque eyes revealing nothing. One eyebrow seemed singed at the end, and he had several red patches on his hands and face. He'd come so close to being seriously injured.

"I can't wear this filthy shirt," he said, and pulled it over his head.

She felt flushed with embarrassment that he should be half clothed so openly, but of course anyone here who saw him thus would be suitably wary before challenging him. She bit her lip and said nothing as he pulled out his only fresh shirt from their sack. How could she clean them while staying in such a place?

At last he put his arm around her and she welcomed his strength and protection as they left the lodging house. She felt abashed that in all her dreams of grand adventures, she never imagined what some people had to live with every day, with never a hope to escape. And what did *she* want to escape . . . parties where she ate the best food, wore the most expensive clothing? She wanted to bury her face against him so she wouldn't have to confront the truth about herself.

To her surprise, a nearby tavern proved half decent, and several cleanly dressed women were sitting among the men, eating. When Julian would have taken any table, Rebecca asked the barkeep for one in the back, where they could have privacy. Again, they sat in a settle, whose high wooden back protected their conversation from the table behind them. In front of them was the hearth with its coal grate empty on the warm spring evening. The room was large and noisy enough that people across the room would never be able to hear them—not that anyone looked their way.

As they awaited their order of mutton and boiled potatoes, she kept near him, her hand still wrapped about his arm. His gaze seemed unfocused, his expression impassive.

"Julian?"

He blinked several times before looking down at her.

"Windebank is your uncle?" She felt him stiffen. "No, you can't keep quiet now. This involves me, too. And if this man knows we're aware of his crimes, and we're in danger, I should know everything." When he was still silent, a muscle working in his jaw, she softly added, "You would feel better if you spoke about it. Tell me, Julian. I want to help."

He took a deep breath and let it out slowly. "I don't even know where to begin."

"Are you certain Windebank is your uncle?"

"The name is rare. And he had more access to the diamond than most. But I never suspected—never imagined he would steal it."

"Is he your mother's brother?"

"No. His wife, Lady Florence, is sister to my father, making her the daughter of an earl. She always thought highly of herself, and is rather melodramatic. I can see her having an affair."

"But apparently Windebank couldn't."

"Harold Windebank," he murmured. "He's a gentleman without title, and I remember being surprised that my aunt, so self-important, had not married a nobleman."

"Perhaps she loved him."

"Not enough, apparently." His voice was grim.

"You are certain they stole the Scandalous Lady?"

"How else would they have gotten it? The hue and cry was great, since the jewel was bestowed so openly by a grateful maharajah. If Windebank had 'accidentally' found it, he would surely have returned it. And the police never did have proof that someone broke into the house to take it."

"Did your father ever mention a belief that it was stolen by a family member?"

"No, he . . ."

She watched as Julian's face turned ashen.

"Julian? What is it?"

He cleared his throat, but his voice was still hoarse, and she knew it wasn't because of the smoke he'd inhaled.

"My father was humiliated by the accusation that he'd

sold such a precious gift for his own benefit. A darkness of the mind seemed to come down over him. It didn't seem to matter to him that soon I would turn eighteen, and I would inherit enough to save the earldom."

Worry coalesced inside her at the pain in his voice, and she almost didn't want to know what happened next.

"He died," Julian said impassively. "We were hosting a hunt during the weekend celebration of my birthday. Everyone was there, including my uncle." His face seemed to twist as he said the words. "They found my father's body. He'd gone off alone, chasing the deer. It looked like he tripped climbing over a fence, discharging his gun."

"It was an accident," she murmured.

"Everyone said that to our faces," he said bitterly. "But he was an expert huntsman, and knew our land from childhood. He would have never made so foolish a mistake. I knew what no one would say—he'd killed himself."

She gasped. "Oh, Julian!"

"I never said those words aloud, but others in Society did. They assumed Father killed himself out of guilt over the scandal of the missing diamond, and what he'd allowed the earldom to come to."

She touched her hand to the jewel hidden beneath her gown. It seemed cursed, the source of so much bloodshed.

"I was just so angry with him, too angry to grieve. I thought it cowardly for him to leave us rather than help resurrect the earldom." He bowed his head, and rubbed his face with one hand. "I believed the worst of him, Rebecca, even though it didn't make sense. I was inheriting money; everything would have been better. I didn't understand why he would commit suicide . . . but maybe he didn't. Maybe he discovered the truth about who stole the jewel, and to silence him, Uncle Harold killed him."

He had a spasm of coughing then, and she patted his back and kept her arm around him, though she couldn't reach far.

"I blamed him," he said at last, his voice rough, "when all along I should have been looking for his murderer."

"Stop this," she said firmly. "Are you a god, all-knowing, all-powerful, that you should have been able to figure everything out? Why would you even suspect your uncle capable of such a thing? Only now do you know he's a murderer of innocents."

"I should have known," he said too quietly.

"And I think you're being arrogant to assume so much. You were eighteen!"

"This eighteen-year-old saved an earldom."

She was shocked. "You really *do* think you can fix anything, don't you? As if everything should rightly rest on your shoulders. Oh, Julian, how can you hold yourself to heights you would never expect from another?"

Their mutton arrived then, and he began to eat, his face back to that impassive mask that kept her out. She could think of nothing else to say that would make a difference. He needed to let all of this sort out inside him, to come to peace with this new revelation that changed his past.

He was a man who didn't like to make mistakes, who controlled everything around him. And in this, he'd had no control except over his emotions, and he thought even those had failed him. What must it be like to believe the worst of your father, and then have it all shown to be wrong?

As they walked back to the lodging house, Julian stared at the decrepit building and came to a decision. He pulled her to a stop beneath a gaslight before they reached the open door, where people lingered on the stoop.

"After I earn money tomorrow, I'm sending you home."

She rolled her eyes, which only irritated him more.

"Take the necklace and keep it safe," he insisted. "Keep yourself safe."

"Julian, I have a very good reason why I will disobey you."

"Rebecca—"

"I listened to you, now you can listen to me. How

do you even know if I will be safe? Your uncle knows I have the jewel, and now he'll surely think there's a chance I know what he did in that house to those poor people."

"Your brother will—"

"My brother is not in London, and neither is the duke."

"Then you'll go the Metropolitan Police."

"And tell them what? 'Officer, I have this rare diamond which has been stolen and now several people are dead because of it.' Julian, they could just as easily believe I'm the murderer."

"They would never—"

"I posed for a nude portrait. Will they think I'm an innocent Society miss? Even you don't believe that of me."

He winced, wondering if he'd hurt her. If only she didn't make sense.

"And I don't want to leave you," she added softly, slipping her arm into his and leaning her head against his shoulder.

He didn't know what to say to that.

"You're suffering, Julian."

"That is ridiculous."

"You've discovered things about your family you never imagined possible. You shouldn't be alone right now."

He thought of the days they had spent together, the

fascinating revelations of her personality as if he'd peeled back each petal of a blossom. She made him crazy; she made him laugh; she made him ache with lust. She confused the hell out of him. Did he want that distraction right now?

But Rebecca was right—he couldn't risk sending her back. He trusted himself to protect her more than he trusted anyone else.

But what if he failed?

That gave him pause, but he thrust the bleak, unsettling feeling away. He would not fail. And it was a mark of his confusion that he would even momentarily consider it.

"Very well, you may remain," he said at last.

She looked up at him, wearing a satisfied grin. "So what do we do next?"

"We attempt to get a good night's sleep."

She glanced away from him, her expression resolute and brave. She'd never faced such a place in her life, and he could not make it better for her.

"And then what?" she asked. "I imagine you wish to confront your uncle. Is his country estate far?"

"A trip of many days, with our money problems. But we'll get there."

"And then you'll have the truth."

"And justice," he added meaningfully.

He put his arm around her and frowned his menace as they approached the lodging house. One man stepped out of their way, and another hesitated before doing the same. And then Julian and Rebecca were inside, looking for the pallet that had been promised to them.

Rebecca said nothing when she saw the heaped bedding and the narrow pallet that they would both sleep on.

"It's off the floor," she said, giving him a grateful smile.

He was certain she was remembering the rat they'd seen earlier.

Much as he was usually a man who slept little, who worked late each evening, he felt exhausted. They went to bed fully clothed, Rebecca at his back near the wall, their portmanteau on the pallet between their feet.

But others did not sleep. Even as Rebecca curled against his back, sharing her warmth, he found his eyes would not close. In the gloom and the guttering candles scattered through the large room, he could see people moving about, especially the children. Their little voices were high-pitched, and they should be frightened, but the hopelessness was the worst. It made him angry with their parents.

Rebecca felt the stiffness in his body. For all she thought he would surely sleep soundly, he did not seem to be able to relax.

"Julian?" she murmured.

He looked over his shoulder.

"Is something wrong?"

In the gloom, she saw the trace of a wry smile.

"What could be wrong?"

"Such sarcasm, sir." She snuggled closer, tightening her hold about his waist, glad his shirt didn't smell of the fire. It smelled of him, and she was startled at how much she enjoyed that. "If nothing is wrong, then you must relax and sleep. What good will you be to me tomorrow?"

She meant to make him chuckle, but he didn't.

A baby started to wail, and as his mother tried to hush him, her next oldest child echoed the baby. They could barely be a year apart, and she had several other young children beside them.

"I don't understand why they keep having children in such conditions," he said in a low voice. "Good God, I've known about the ways to prevent conception since I was fourteen. And it's not that grave an expense."

She came up on her elbow and stared down at him. "Really? I had no idea."

"If only my mother—" He broke off, muttering something, but she didn't catch the words. If there was more light, she wondered if she'd see a flush of red in his face. It was a frank conversation. Had he thought his mother should have had fewer children?

She found herself brushing the dark hair back from his face, the better to see his expression. He inhaled swiftly, but didn't stop her. "I feel compassion for these women," she murmured, continuing to stroke his soft hair. "They probably had no choice. For me, the hardest part is hearing people cough."

He glanced back at her, eyes narrowed. "Of course! And here I bring you to such a place, knowing you're susceptible—"

"No, you misunderstand me. I don't fear for myself. I learned long ago that I have no control over my health. But I had my parents to care for me, to try to heal me. All these poor people can do is endure."

He said nothing, and she at last lowered her head back to the folded clothing they'd used as pillows.

"You are a good woman, Rebecca," he murmured.

Smiling, she hugged him tighter.

She thought sleep would come easily after the day they'd had, and truly, the noise of so many people didn't bother her—until she heard a man's moan, one of pleasure rather than pain. Surely she was imagining it, she thought in shock and embarrassment. A baby still cried, people still talked in low voices, a drunk bawled something out in the courtyard—and a woman moaned in response.

Without thinking, she whispered, "Is that—" She broke off, regretting even speaking of such an intimate thing to Julian.

"It is. This is their home, after all."

She buried her face between his shoulder blades, burning with mortification. She covered her ears, and he must have realized what she did, for his body shook with laughter. She hit him on the shoulder. How dare he feel amusement when something so painfully private was going on not ten feet away! In her world, if a man was caught even kissing a woman, the shock and scandal were grounds for an immediate marriage.

The liaison became even louder, and she heard a rhythmic thumping. Julian wasn't laughing now; he seemed just as tense as she.

And she was pressed up against him. It seemed wrong to touch him, but there was nowhere for her to go.

When she thought it might surely go on forever, at last the man gave a groan, and the thumping died away.

She heaved a sigh and let her hands fall from her ears. It hadn't helped much anyway.

What caused the thumping? she wondered, even as she fell asleep.

At noon, Rebecca found a spot of shade at the fish market, sitting on a rock that overlooked the canal and the many barges that served the people and the industry of Manchester. She could just see Julian, an open box of fish balanced on his shoulder, as he disembarked from a barge and went into a warehouse.

She tried to put aside her feelings of guilt, knowing he would be upset with her. He was unloading fish to earn them traveling money. But she felt so useless, wishing to somehow contribute. When she'd expressed her feelings before dawn as they drank coffee and ate bread huddled around a movable coffee stall, he'd scoffed at her.

She had learned so much today. When they'd left the lodging house, others were just coming home from their night work at the factories, taking the pallets newly vacated by the day workers, a way to save money that had her shuddering. Watching Julian unload fish for hours on end made her feel even more thankful that her family had been able to support themselves with tenants cultivating the land.

Julian never seemed to tire. And he looked for her every few trips he took between the warehouse and the barge. She learned quickly not to linger too long in the stalls, examining the wares offered for sale, knowing that Julian counted on being able to see her, to watch over her. If she had her choice, she would have spent time salivating over the oranges and lemons, but the price proved out of their reach.

When he took his luncheon break, they shared ham sandwiches and cider. He ate steadily, hungrily, and she wished she had more to offer him, for he must be starving after working hard for so many hours. She offered half of hers, but he refused it.

At last he sat back, leaning against the boulder she'd perched on most of the morning.

"I imagine you've been bored silly," he murmured, eyes closed.

"You might think so, but I wasn't. There is so much to see. And I feel positively unencumbered without a chaperone."

"What a grand adventure," he said, sarcasm laced through his words.

"It truly is," she insisted, "even if you are too single-minded to see it as so."

"I am keeping many thoughts in my head. The one that amuses me the most is the look on your face when candles were lit this morn, and you could see everyone who'd occupied our room at the lodging house. Your blush rivaled the reddest sunset."

She groaned and closed her eyes. "I wish you wouldn't bring it up. My ears—not to mention my sensibilities—will never be the same."

He gave a low chuckle. "I must admit, I never thought to share such an experience with you."

"How can you imagine sharing such an experience with anyone?" she demanded.

He looked at her from beneath half-closed eyelids. "I can imagine it."

Her breath caught.

"And now you're blushing again."

"Oh, just go to sleep. I'll wake you when I see the other men returning to work."

"I certainly won't be sleeping," he said, even though his eyes were closed again.

"Aren't you exhausted?"

He shrugged. "You may be surprised to know that I've worked just as hard in the fields and barns of my home."

She wasn't surprised at all. "I imagine the servants appreciated your assistance."

"I was learning, so I felt the benefit as much as they did."

"And with your help, they agreed to stay, although they weren't being paid much."

He closed his eyes again. Another topic he wouldn't wish to discuss. Didn't he want her to think well of him? Or perhaps he was used to doing everything out of sight, being shown little gratitude. She hoped that wasn't true. Then she remembered the troubles he'd been having with his younger brothers. Obviously they didn't appreciate him.

"Did you unload fish another time in your life?"

He smiled. "No, this is a new skill to add to my repertoire."

They sat in silence for several minutes, and he twitched as he dozed off. She liked looking at him, at his skin already darkening in the sun beneath his unruly black hair. His broken nose above his heavily whiskered jaw made these people think he was one of them. He was at home in many worlds, and she wanted to learn to feel the same.

At last she shook his shoulder, and he came awake with an abrupt start.

"Sorry. The other men are returning to work."

He nodded, got to his feet, and gave her a last look. "You will be all right here?"

"No one bothers me. I'm certain your uncle thinks we fled Manchester immediately. And he would never think to look for us here."

His smile was faint. "True. But don't relax your vigilance."

"I won't."

He suddenly leaned down and pressed a kiss to her cheek. She held still in surprise and pleasure as he whispered, "I look forward to spending another night in your arms with all of our new friends."

She made a face that sent him off with a laugh, but her own amusement faded more quickly. She prayed they would only spend one more night in that lodging house, for if she had to listen to all the moaning and thumping again and again, she was going to demand that Julian explain it all in detail.

He wouldn't be laughing then.

Chapter 16

Julian walked at Rebecca's side as they returned to the lodging house, feeling tired and sore but satisfied. He looked down at her and jingled the coins in his pocket. She grinned and stuck her hand in, startling and pleasing him.

"Ooh, feel all that wealth," she said, bumping against him as they walked.

The feel of her hand against his thigh was making him forget his aching muscles, but she seemed oblivious.

She looked up at the overcast sky as a light misting rain continued to dampen their clothing. "Maybe the rain will rid us both of the stench of fish."

"I was the one who carted them around all day," he protested.

"And I wandered in the midst of the fish stalls. Trust me, I didn't pick up this odor just from you."

He laughed and hefted the wrapped package in his other hand. "But it will taste good cooked, I imagine."

"Do you cook?" she asked. "Because I never have.

Oh, wait, of course you do! You surely spent time in the kitchens as you grew up."

He smiled. "As a matter of fact . . ."

"Then you can cook for me."

"I provided the food, I'm your guard. I imagine I can be your cook, too."

Slyly she said, "I think I like this arrangement."

At the lodging house, they commandeered a coal grate and grilled the fish he'd received from his temporary employer. There was more than enough to share, and soon Rebecca moved among the children, offering the plain fish as if it were a feast. And the children treated it as such, although they respectfully waited for their turn. More than one child was sniffling and coughing, and Julian wanted to pull Rebecca away. But that had been her childhood, always kept away from others, and he knew she would no longer accept such treatment. But he understood her parents' fears.

When the food was gone, and people began to settle in for the night, he saw Rebecca's hesitation. He took her hand, and when she gave him a puzzled look, he gestured with his head toward the door. She grinned and followed his lead. He led her outside into the courtyard, and they sat down on two crates. Out of his pocket, he brought a small wrapped package and handed it to her. She gave him a curious look even as she untied the string.

She gasped and her face lit up. "A tart!"

"Strawberry," he said, "I'm sorry if it got a bit crushed."

"Oh, it will taste the same," she said, taking her first bite. Her eyes closed with bliss.

He felt hungry for more than food as he watched her. "I never imagined giving such a gift to a woman."

She chuckled and caught crumbs from her cheek with the back of her hand. "And I never imagined how I would appreciate such a hard-earned gift. But thank you so much." She broke off a piece. "Take some."

"No, it's yours. I'm enjoying watching you eat."

With determination, she leaned forward and put the piece to his mouth. "Take a bite," she insisted.

At last he did, his gaze locking with hers as his lips brushed her fingers.

She paused and blushed. "I must taste like fish," she said awkwardly.

He chewed and swallowed. "I don't mind."

Tension and anticipation for their next private moment simmered between them once more. He remembered the way they'd kissed, the feeling of her in his arms, her face lost in pleasure beneath him. It had been three days since that stolen moment, three days where he told himself he'd regained control. And then each night they lay entwined, as they would again tonight. And he would awaken every time she moved against him. He'd see the painting in his mind, and imagine her stretched out on his bed like that, just for him. Lately, his thoughts seemed uncontrollable, something he'd never imagined would happen to him.

He cleared his throat. "So what would your family think if they knew what you were doing?"

Her laughter was more like a snort. "Because it's me, I imagine they'd be surprised. But I'm a Leland through my father, and a Cabot through my mother. I think it would be more surprising if I *didn't* find some kind of trouble." She eyed him with amused suspicions. "Don't tell me you don't know what my family's done."

He folded his arms over his chest, deciding not to tell her that he knew much about her family through his search for a suitable wife. "I know your brother was thought dead until he returned—that's quite a story."

"Oh, believe me, that was minor on the scale of scandal. That was simply a joyous miracle."

"Are you trying to say you can compete with *my* family scandals?" he asked with feigned astonishment. "We're talking a stolen priceless diamond, a thieving uncle—"

"You didn't hear about my father caught up in a grave-robbing scheme?"

He blinked at her.

She smiled. "As an anatomy professor, he paid men to bring him the corpses of prisoners, all very legal. He didn't know that asking for a female made them steal her from a grave."

"That must have been difficult to bear."

"It happened before I was born, but it harmed my parents' marriage for many years. My mother was quite humiliated. But surely you heard that my uncle, the duke, made a common Spanish girl his duchess."

"I did know that."

"The present duke married a female journalist who was investigating him by pretending to be someone else! Another cousin won the right to court his eventual wife in a card game with her mother. And my aunt was suspected of murdering her husband so she could claim credit for a symphony he'd supposedly written. And my grandfather—"

"Enough! I cannot believe I'm admitting this, but I think your family is far more scandalous than mine. My association with you might very well be harming my reputation as we speak."

"You were seen flirting with me by much of feminine Society." She fluttered her lashes. "And if they knew what we've done since . . ."

He gave her a slow, intimate smile. She watched him, moistening her lips, driving him to distraction.

"But don't you see, Julian," she said, "my family is full of scandal, but none of it happened to me. I was always ill, confined to my bed. My family's exploits might as well have been fictional stories I read in a book."

"And now you have your own adventure. Surely you'll be more than able to hold your head up when, in your old age, you and your cousins reminisce about your frivolous youth." He cocked his head. "Will you tell them someday about the painting?"

A strange expression passed over her face, and she straightened. "That might be asking for too much understanding, don't you think?"

"Your family seems accepting of artists—there's your sister's study of dissections, and didn't you just say an uncle composed music?"

"And I have a cousin who plays the violin. But none of them took their clothing off." She ate the last crumb of her strawberry tart and sighed. "Oh, Julian, that was simply delicious. Thank you for the treat."

They remained silent for a moment, listening to the sounds of overcrowded humanity, from crying children to squabbling adults. At last they could put off sleep no longer and they went inside, where the smells and the sounds assaulted the senses.

"We leave Manchester tomorrow," he said firmly.

"Thank God."

Julian assumed he would be tired enough to fall asleep quickly. But when Rebecca was safely asleep behind him, and he'd just begun to doze off, regardless of the crying baby, Rebecca coughed.

He frowned but didn't open his eyes. Anyone could cough. Who knew what was floating in the air in an industrial city like Manchester?

Just as he relaxed, she coughed again—and again.

He looked over his shoulder. "Rebecca?" he murmured.

"My throat is simply scratchy," she said, then was overcome by a long fit of coughing.

She moved away from him, closer to the wall, as if she didn't want to disturb him. Julian felt helpless, so he fell back on his instincts, rolling over and hushing her protests as he reversed her position as well. He folded his body around hers to comfort her so she would not be afraid, his hips behind hers so she could share his warmth.

"Relax," he murmured, stroking her arm and down her hip.

She was faintly trembling, but at last the cough died away. He tried not to think what illnesses she'd been exposed to here—how he hadn't protected her.

"It was nothing," she said briskly. "I thought I inhaled a piece of your hair. After all, I was trapped between you and the wall."

"So would you rather face my back or the wall?" he asked, struggling to sound amused.

"I can't exactly see the wall, but I imagine it might be a sight better than the filthy shirt you're wearing."

He chuckled, continuing to stroke her body. "It is difficult to bathe or wash clothing here."

"Believe me, I'm looking forward to both those things tomorrow. And Julian?"

"Yes?"

"You must remember that I've stopped living my life in constant worry. I won't live like that again."

They were silent several minutes, and she gave a contented sigh. By not thinking about her risk of illness, he found himself feeling the softness of her hair against his cheek, the long lean slope of her back, and the way her ass cradled him sensually. He kept imagining the caresses he could show her, the expressions on her vivid face as she experienced unimagined pleasures.

No, don't think about that tonight, he told himself, but it was too late. If Rebecca noticed that he was aroused, she did not mention it. He should stop caressing her, but that might be even more obvious.

"I can hear the gears in your mind turning," she said, tilting her head to look back at him.

He came up on one elbow, the better to see her face. "What do you mean?"

"You're thinking too much. I swear that my throat was only irritated."

"Prove it to me," he whispered, leaning down to kiss her.

Her lips were as soft as he remembered, and he wanted to moan with the pleasure that flooded through him. But he restrained himself. He kissed her gently, parting her lips more with each kiss, until he could enter her mouth, stroking, exploring, tasting strawberry tart.

At last he lifted his head. "You're a bold vixen. I guess I can no longer be surprised you'd pose nude."

Again, he let his hand slide appreciatively over her hip.

Hesitantly, she asked, "Are you . . . disappointed in me compared to the painting?"

He gave her an astonished look. "How could I be disappointed?"

"Roger made me look so . . . provocative. I never thought of myself that way. And I could understand if you agreed with me."

"He captured your spirit perfectly," he said, nuzzling behind her ear, "as far as I can see. Which hasn't been all that far."

Her sensual chuckle made him give her another deep, drugging kiss. He lifted his head, taking a deep breath, struggling to find a distraction. Hoarsely, he said, "You know I've already won."

"The wager?" she replied faintly, inching her body until she lay on her back to look up at him.

"Of course. My proof is the diamond."

He traced its outline beneath her bodice, and could tell she held her breath.

"I could have *borrowed* the necklace."

"An excellent try, but I don't believe that. But tell me, why did you and your cousin and sister all feel the need to proclaim yourself the model?"

"We've always been close, being raised in the same home. When Elizabeth and I were still in the school-room, we used to analyze how we would have handled the scandals of our relatives. Susanna overheard us, and being older, she decided that the best way to not get into trouble was to swear a pact that the three of us would always protect each other, always help each other avoid scandal."

"*You* swore to this?"

"I was much younger," she said with a laugh. "I was wistful even imagining that I could ever come close to a delicious scandal, but I wanted to go along with Susanna and Elizabeth, to pretend I was just like them."

"But now you've created your very own scandal. Do you have a plan for what will happen if Society finds out about your connection to the painting? Not that they would through myself or my friends," he added. "But there are always those who delight in overhearing conversations that they shouldn't."

"I will not care," she said, tilting her chin, her smile delightfully wicked. "I will not be in London. I will be traveling. And my parents are well used to handling scandal."

"You would leave such a thing to them?"

"Did we not have to bear some of the burden of our parents' scandal? It is only fitting that they return the favor."

"How generous of you."

She laughed, then covered her mouth. "Good night, Julian."

She was smiling as she turned away from him, but

she gave a little squirm with her hips that made him shudder. She was learning far too quickly.

Julian was not sorry to see Manchester fade behind them. The wagon jerked and shuddered on the uneven road, but where once that had annoyed him, he no longer minded it, for every turn of the wheels took them toward fresh country air. Rebecca would not have to breathe in the foul smells of the slums.

Although his uncle lived in Lincolnshire, Julian had felt it wise to travel north for a day. His uncle's men, who were most certainly looking for them, would probably watch the roads east of Manchester, in the direction of Windebank's home, or south, if they thought Julian and Rebecca meant to flee to London.

Before dinner, he and Rebecca left the wagon in the countryside, as if they were close to home, and allowed it to go on to the next village without them. They'd decided to camp out of doors for the first night, the better to confuse their pursuers.

Rebecca put her hands on her hips as she looked into the distance. The Lancashire moorlands rose high above the valley of the river, with flat tops of endless grasslands dotted with flocks of sheep. Though some might think the scenery bleak, she looked serene and satisfied.

"Let's find the most private place on the river," she

said, beginning to walk to where the trees clustered at the banks. "I cannot wait to bathe!"

He could not imagine another woman of his acquaintance so at ease in the countryside, or thrilled at the prospect of a cold bath in an unfamiliar river. His admiration for Rebecca only grew the more he knew her. Perhaps he needed to add another accomplishment to his "perfect wife" list: the ability to adapt.

They walked in peaceful silence for little more than a half hour, listening to the birds as the sun sank low in the sky, the clouds around it beginning to take on a tinge of pink and orange. At last they found a secluded bend in the river, with trees forming a canopy and shelter.

"This will do," Rebecca said. "Can you help me unhook my gown?"

He'd been anticipating such a request all day, but had to be practical. "Wouldn't you prefer to eat first?"

"We'll lose the light too soon, and I don't fancy bathing in the darkness." She shivered. "I won't know what's coming at me."

She presented her slim back, and he whispered into her hair, "Perhaps it will only be me."

She laughed, but also gave a little shudder that satisfied him. To his surprise, his hands trembled once or twice as he worked with the tiny hooks and eyes on the back of her bodice.

"You brought the soap and towels left over from the

last inn?" she asked as she stepped away and began to pull the gown forward and down to her waist.

"Yes."

He could barely get the word out. All he could think was that she wanted his touch—she wanted her adventure. What would he give her? Where should he draw the line? It would all depend on how much passion he could tolerate without taking what a woman prized.

She was already down to her chemise—the sturdy linen one, he saw with regret, rather than the sheer confection that was her own. She left her gown in a heap on a rock.

"I'll wash our clothing later," she said, even as she seated herself to reach beneath the skirt of her chemise to remove her boots, garters, and stockings. She gave him a saucy smile. "The drawers are next."

"It will be cold fast here on the edges of the moor," he said, openly leering until she blushed. "I'll start a fire."

"Afraid to bathe with me?"

Her eyes were lively with humor as she slid her drawers off from beneath her chemise.

"Not afraid at all," he said with meaning. "But if I join you in the water right now, you won't get any bathing done and we won't have a fire."

Her smile faded and her expression smoldered with interest. The faced each other for a long moment, until at last she went to the portmanteau and rooted around in it for the wrapped bit of soap. With a sigh, he began to gather pieces of wood along the pebble-strewn embankment, watching openly as she stepped into the shallow water and shuddered.

"It's cold!" she gasped.

"You expected otherwise in late spring?"

"But . . ." Her shoulders slumped. "I had so been looking forward to a bath."

"Then you'll have to look forward to simply being clean."

She straightened. "You're right. And that is definitely worth it."

She waded out a bit farther, the water coming up to her knees. The river wasn't wide, so it could hardly be that deep, but he'd grown used to always watching out for her.

"Can you swim?" he asked.

She shook her head and spread her hands. "They didn't allow me to ride a horse. Can you imagine them allowing me in a cold pond?"

"Then be careful. Only go in as deep as your thighs. Deeper than that, and you could easily lose your balance. The current seems mild, but one never knows. Perhaps I should explore the riverbed first—"

"Julian, you are taking good care of me, never fear. And I promise to obey, so you will not have to prove what a capable swimmer you probably are. Aren't you?"

"I am."

"Of course. Now go on about your chores, and I'll get to mine later."

After he piled the sticks and small logs at the base of the trees, he began to work on sparking a fire in several tufts of dried grass. When at last a small blaze crackled, he glanced at Rebecca. Dragonflies danced about her as the sunlight sparkled in the river and reflected off her smooth skin. She was rubbing a soapy facecloth along her arms with determined vigor. Her expression was intent and serious, rather than one of enjoyment, which made him curious.

When the fire was burning steadily, he stripped down to his drawers and waded into the water near her. She glanced at him, her gaze roaming his bare chest. He sank up to his waist quickly, shuddering as the cold tried to dampen the lust she inspired by simply looking at him,

And then she went back to scrubbing herself—this time her legs—as if all the dirt in the world coated her.

"Easy," he said. "You'll take off your skin with the dirt."

"I'm not certain I'll ever feel clean again," she murmured.

There was something in her voice that concerned him, so he moved closer, kneeling to keep himself used to the cold water.

"Rebecca?" he said softly.

She didn't seem to hear him, only continued to scrub as she said, "The smells of that place, the sadness of those children with nothing to look forward to except illness and death . . ."

"They won't all be ill," he said, realizing how close she felt to the subject. "And some will make good lives for themselves."

She closed her eyes, sitting in the water to scrub her torso beneath the chemise. "I know how they feel—so helpless, so pessimistic, as if nothing can ever be better. And then . . . and then it's too easy to become angry."

"Angry with what?" he asked gently.

"With—God! With everything that keeps you trapped in a frail body, with death hovering like a nightly demon. Childhood should be full of games and exploration and wonder. But they have no childhood at all."

"As you didn't."

She glanced at him almost angrily. "That's not true, not compared to those poor children in Manchester."

"But you have a right to feel cheated out of what your brother and sister took for granted, health and vitality and freedom."

He thought her lower lip trembled a moment before she worried it with her teeth. "It bothers me so much when I see that the past still affects so much of my life."

He felt uncomfortably close to her conclusion. "But remember, we also learn from the past. It can affect us in good ways."

Yet she continued to frown. "But am I basing every decision I make on the past? And is that any way to live?"

She looked so upset that he found himself moving toward her, taking the facecloth and soap from her hand. Kneeling in water up to his waist, he cupped her face in one hand and began to wash it.

"Let it go, Rebecca," he murmured.

He worked gently on her delicate skin, her nose and cheeks pink from the sun. As the crickets increased their rhythm, evening birdsong showered the land, and water gurgled all around them, she gradually relaxed beneath his hands. He worked his way down her neck and behind her ears. With a faint sigh, she leaned her head forward, letting him minister to the back of her neck and her shoulders. She felt so slim and fragile beneath his hands, but he knew how great her strength truly was; she was strong in spirit, which had allowed her to conquer illness, when others might have given up.

Another important wifely attribute: courage. He'd never thought it important before now, before Rebecca.

He began to pull the pins from her hair, then transferred them to her. She stiffened but said nothing, even as lengths of brown curls began to fall about her shoulders. She leaned back on her hands, the pins fisted in one, tilted her head back and let the mass fall into the water, spreading out about her like a halo as the water tugged at it.

Her eyes were open now, and she watched him intently. After tucking the facecloth into the waistband of his drawers, he held the soap in one hand and soaked her hair with the other. She had so much of it, but it felt sinfully good. He didn't remember paying attention to a woman's hair before. For some reason, simply bathing Rebecca seemed more intimate than his focused and intense experiences with other women.

At last he began to work the lather into her hair. Still she watched him, eyes half closed yet so alert. It made him feel hot and aroused, even in a chilly river.

At last she had to close her eyes against the suds, since she had to tip her head forward so that he could reach the ends of her hair. Then he rubbed her scalp gently with his fingers until she moaned.

His body tightened with need. "Time to rinse," he said hoarsely.

She leaned back, trying to drop to her elbows, but that would have taken her too far under. He held her to him instead, arms about her shoulders, and dipped her back.

"Trust me," he whispered.

"I do."

Swallowing a sudden knot in his throat, he let the

moving water work its way through her hair. She must have realized that he still held the soap in his other hand, for she lifted up her arms and began to rub her fingers back and forth through her hair.

And it was then that he noticed that her wet chemise was translucent across her breasts. He could see the darkness of her nipples, tight points from the cold water. Staring at them, transfixed, he remembered how he'd briefly taken them in his mouth through her clothing.

He could lose himself in her. He wanted to taste her bare flesh. It would take so little to free the laces at her neck, to part her neckline and follow the deep line of her cleavage down into oblivion.

Chapter 17

Rebecca felt boneless with pleasure, bent backward in Julian's arms. The water wasn't even cold anymore, only briskly refreshing as it filtered away the last of the filth and stench of the Manchester lodging house. The current tugged at her hair and she moved her fingers through the curls, searching for the last of the suds.

He had gently bathed her face and neck, and the feeling had been indescribably pleasurable. Her skin was alive, so very sensitive, aching with the arousal and tenderness his touch inspired.

But now as he held her, he said nothing. His incredible stillness made her open her eyes at last in curiosity. And then it was her turn to hold her breath. Since she was bent backward over his arm, her chest was high in the air—right beneath Julian's face. And he was looking down at her breasts, his expression raw and tense and focused.

Would he touch her? Would he share the pleasure they each craved?

Then right near shore, a frog croaked loudly and plopped into the water.

Julian gave a start, then looked back at her face. They stared at each other for a long moment, and the amused expression he often wore had been replaced by something almost . . . solemn.

"Don't you understand that I want to make love with you, Julian?" she whispered.

His answering smile was full of regret. "I won't do that, but I will show you more of what you long for, what to expect."

"But—" she began.

But he strangled her confusion by lowering his head and planting a kiss between her breasts. She gasped, and her mind threatened to turn right off, although she fought it. She needed to understand what he was talking about.

But he was loosening the laces of her chemise, drawing the fabric down, baring more and more of her flesh. His mouth followed, and then his tongue, as he licked his way up the curve of her breast. The chemise caught at the peak, then came free, baring her nipples to him. With the flat of his tongue he licked the hard point, and then the other, as if he had to choose between two pieces of plump, ripe fruit and could not decide. And everything he did made passion suffuse like hot chocolate through her body as the swirling water tugged at her in a subtle caress.

But he wouldn't make love to her, she thought, gasping, pleasure trying to drown out her thoughts. He wanted to give to her, and expected nothing else. That did not seem like any other man she'd been warned against.

Though it was the hardest thing she'd ever done, she put her hands on his shoulders. "Stop," she said weakly, then with more force. "Stop!"

He lifted his head. "Don't make me stop, not when you taste like the sweetest—"

She covered his mouth with her hand, already shuddering. "Julian, I don't want this if you won't finish it."

He frowned, his face damp with river water, the gray of his eyes suddenly obscured. "Rebecca—"

"What did you mean by saying you'd show me what to expect?" she demanded.

"Surely that is obvious," he said, his gaze drifting back to her chest.

She pulled the chemise back up, even though she had to tug because it was so wet. He let her go then, his expression confused.

"Explain it to me," she insisted.

"Rebecca, I am experienced, and you are not. You need to know about the world you've chosen to enter."

Her eyes narrowed. "I think I'm in the same world I've always been."

He lifted one eyebrow as he sank back onto his heels in the water. "Really? Don't you realize that by posing nude, you've gone outside the bounds of Society, taken yourself into a world where rules are broken, where restraint is gone?"

"Restraint?"

"How else would you expect men to act toward you, once you devote your life to living as you choose?"

"I—"

"I've decided to show you what to expect, so you'll know how far to go with a man, and when it is wise to stop."

Her stomach seemed to roil with confusion. She suddenly couldn't imagine doing such things with other men, but that wasn't the point. "You've decided? For me? What do you know about my choices?"

"Only what I see," he answered calmly, "and what you've explained to me."

Her confusion merged into hot anger and a twinge of hurt that she didn't want to feel. "It is not up to you to decide what I need. You don't even know how many men I've been with."

"If that were true, you wouldn't be so anxious to experience something you already had."

"But I haven't with you! I have spent night after night against your body. Not everyone has your superior powers of restraint."

"I am hardly superior. It's taken every last bit of my control to keep from touching you. I never imagined it would be so difficult."

He spoke lightly, but she sensed that his tone was forced. She couldn't even feel triumphant that the plans he made for her were not going as he expected.

"You are a man who cannot live in the moment," she continued. "You need a plan for everything—how did I not see that you had a plan for me? You won't allow me to be an equal and have my say where my own life is concerned."

"Let you have your own say?" he shot back, his expression stunned. "I'm the fool who allowed you to continue on this dangerous journey simply because you wanted to. What more 'say' do you wish?"

He was right of course, but only about the journey. "You exert your control every moment you can, including this idea that you're so above me in experience and sophistication that you can't treat me as a real woman. Perhaps you're the one who's afraid to go past the rules, the boundaries you've set yourself as a man of the world. You wouldn't like being so vulnerable then. You've spent your life controlling everything, including your own family. No wonder your brothers are rebelling!"

He stiffened.

"Well, you cannot be in command of me! I want to make love to you. What is so wrong with that?"

"Because you're a virgin, and I don't deflower innocents."

"Deflower? What a pretty word you've used. Perhaps

it lets you ignore the truth. You're hiding the reality of two people giving themselves to each other, of revealing every vulnerability. Oh, that's right—you don't have any."

They were both still crouched in the water, she sitting, he kneeling. Now he rose up above her, so tall, so imposing. Water sluiced down the contours of his body, reflecting the light of the dying sun in each rivulet. His drawers clung indecently, outlining the part of him that she wanted to take inside her. He seemed more than ready. Even their heated argument aroused him. She felt a pang of lust so strong that the muscles deep within her body clenched. Why was he denying what they both obviously wanted? All for the sake of the control he'd wrapped around himself all his life?

He bent over her and pointed a finger in her face. "Maybe you haven't been honest with yourself or me."

"How much more honest can I be?" Outraged, she came to her feet, not missing the way his hot gaze dropped down her body before he mastered his vaunted control.

Narrow-eyed, he said, "Sex means marriage in your world. You talk about living a different sort of life, but maybe you want to marry me."

"Are you not listening?" she cried.

"Why else would you continue this insistence that I bed you?"

"That is ridiculous. You're the one who watched me bathe, who washed my hair, who looks at me as if you might eat me right up!"

His nostrils actually flared. "I am only a man," he ground out, "and I want you. My control around you is shaky at best."

That caused a delightful little zing of triumph. "You cannot possibly be admitting you're fallible, that you're as human as all the rest of us."

Ignoring her interruption, he continued, "But I know what happens when a woman is ruined—when a family is ruined. How will you feel when you cannot take back your foolish whim? How will you feel when your disregard of the consequences of your wildness means you can never marry?"

Did an actual growl emerge from his throat as he stomped away from her? It was primitive—and thrilling. She wanted him to throw her to the ground and have his way with her.

"I don't want marriage!" she cried. "As if I would ever consent to something so confining." Her parents suffered for years with their mistrust of each other. Even though they were happy now, they'd wasted so much time. She didn't want to be like that.

But she had a momentary image that startled her, of coming home to his bed every night. It felt warm and safe.

How could she want to be safe?

"You didn't bathe," she called to him, her words saucy and defiant.

He came to a stop in the shallow water, and she could see his longing to storm away from her. But they'd been too filthy for too many days. He spun around and waded toward her. She expected to see anger, confusion— something. Instead his expression betrayed nothing of his feelings, only that faint amusement that infuriated her. But she had just as much control as he, and she wouldn't reveal any more of her inner self. He reached out an open hand for the soap.

"I'm not done yet." She rubbed both hands in the soap, handed it to him, then sank into the water to wash her most private flesh.

It was obvious that he knew what she was doing. And he watched her, even as he rubbed his soapy hands all over his upper body. A thrilling shiver made the very blood in her veins run hot and fierce.

And when he sank into the water, taking the soap beneath the surface, she knew just where he was washing. And she wished his hands were soaping her again.

But not if he expected her to be the only one to succumb to the twin dangers of vulnerability and passion.

They remained silent, doing the chores that needed to be done. Julian collected as much firewood as possible, knowing how cold the night would get, while Rebecca washed their garments in the river. The light continued to fade, even as the insects picked up their chorus. An owl gave a hoot as it awoke, but Julian could enjoy none of it. He was still too annoyed.

He was a man who was used to manipulating the emotions of others. He was always the cooler head, able to negotiate logically and calmly while others let their emotions sway them.

Why could he not treat Rebecca the same way? She was a woman who wanted something that was bad for her. He thought he'd found a way to help her protect herself.

But perhaps he should be protecting her from him. When she'd given him a hot glare as she washed between her thighs, he almost dove on top of her. Even as she crouched to wash his clothing, he was full of savage lust, as if they were two primitive people, alone in the world. The feelings were overwhelming and unfamiliar to him.

He reminded himself that he was in the right, that they should not consummate their unusual relationship. How could she not see that?

She spread their garments over bushes and rocks near the fire, even as he finished piling the last of the wood and knelt down. She came to sit down across the fire from him, rather than at his side. That almost made him smile, but he wasn't yet ready to forgive her.

Silently, he unwrapped the meat pies he'd bought that

afternoon and reached across the fire to hand her one.

"Thank you," she said coolly.

They ate in silence, passing back and forth a bottle of cider.

"Have you ever slept out of doors before?" he finally asked, almost expecting her to ignore him.

"No."

"I did when I was younger. Several times I went out with the shepherds as they moved the sheep to different pasture. When the lambs are born, a shepherd has to remain nearby at all times so none are lost."

"Hmm." She didn't look at him.

He lay down in the grass and covered himself with a dry shirt.

"I'll be sleeping over here," she said.

"Very well."

"I wouldn't want to risk your virtue."

He chuckled, and by the frown on her face, he knew she didn't appreciate it. She flounced onto her side and pulled her third gown over her shoulders.

It suddenly seemed a long time since he'd slept alone, but that was a foolish thought. He would go back to sleeping alone when this was done, back to his daily routine and his search for a wife, back to his businesses and estates, which surely needed him.

And his life seemed dull in comparison to sleeping outside, on the run with Rebecca Leland.

The last of the sun was gone and the night noises

came to life. There was the hoot of an owl, of course, and sheep bleating quietly on the moor. Crickets chirped and frogs croaked as if competing against each other.

Then something in the wooded copse along the river gave a yelping bark.

Rebecca bolted upright. "What was that?"

"I don't know. It could be a fox, it could be a wild dog."

"A wild dog?" Her eyes glittered as she looked about. Insects hovered about her head and she swatted at them.

Then he heard a growling, grunting noise that he suspected might be a badger, but she didn't bother to ask. She simply rose to her feet, walked around to his side of the fire, then lay down between him and it, covering herself with her gown again and leaving six inches of space between them.

He grinned into the darkness, but didn't approach her.

Although sleep came quickly, he came awake too soon, and by the look of the rising half-moon, it couldn't have been more than two hours later. The ground was cold and damp beneath him. Her body blocked most of the heat of the fire, and behind him there was nothing to warm his frozen ass. He rose to add more logs to the fire, and saw that she was watching him. He lay back down and put himself flush against her.

"I could hear your teeth chattering," she said. "I wondered when you'd surrender."

He thought she smothered a laugh, but he didn't care. It was all he could do to control his shivering until the warmth of her body began to penetrate the depth of his bones. He'd almost drifted back to sleep, content, when she spoke.

"This isn't over between us," she murmured. "I'll have what I want."

"Even if it means losing everything you have?"

She didn't answer.

The next day was a miserable one, wet and windy. Julian was surprised that Rebecca actually murmured aloud her longing for an enclosed carriage. Then she seemed embarrassed at what she'd revealed and became even more cross. They'd accepted a ride from a farmer taking jugs of milk into the nearest village, where they paid for a public wagon for the rest of the afternoon. Through it all the sky poured rain, water streaming down crevices from the tops of the moors until he thought for certain that the roads would flood.

It was almost dark before they reached the village of Dewsbury in the West Riding. They were cold and wet, and he saw Rebecca's expression of gratitude when he registered at the humble inn where the wagon left off its passengers.

The maid who showed them to their room was heavily pregnant and seemed miserable, although polite. She attempted to add more coals to the grate, but Julian gently steered her aside and completed the task.

"Me thanks, sir," the woman said, grimacing.

"Perhaps ye shouldn't be on your feet," Rebecca said.

"I'm just feelin' a mite poorly. Pay me no mind. Shall I bring ye some dinner?"

"We'll come down to the taproom," Julian said.

She gave him a grateful smile.

None of their garments were completely dry, so they hung the worst across chairs by the hearth. Julian turned his back on Rebecca as he took off his sodden clothing, all the way down to his drawers.

"Your drawers are soaked, too," Rebecca said.

"You've watched me bathe, and now you have no problem watching me undress?"

"I'm not watching; I'm changing. I simply know everything about you, Julian, and I know you wouldn't want to offend my delicate female sensibilities by taking off all your clothing in the same room. Don't worry, I will not throw myself at you."

He sighed and removed his drawers and replaced them with ones only slightly damp.

At last they were ready to descend to the taproom. Since it seemed to be the only eating establishment in the village, there were other women present. Rebecca probably would not have cared one way or another, but

Julian didn't want to draw any attention their way.

To his surprise, the same pregnant maid was serving dinner, with no one else to help her. He left her as much extra coin as he could spare, knowing he wouldn't have enough for another night in an inn. Rebecca saw what he did and nodded.

"We'll make more money," she said with conviction.

"Your faith sustains me," he said dryly.

She only shrugged, and he found he missed her smile. He wondered how long she would remain angry with him.

But perhaps it was better this way. They were growing too familiar with one another; he was learning her every expression, the exuberant way she moved her body, her joy in every new day. It was more and more difficult to think of himself apart from her.

And it was she who was pushing him away, after all. She did not want to be married, much as he was beginning to think no other woman had ever suited him in such an easy way. Ever since he'd brought up the subject of marriage, he couldn't quite seem to keep it far from his thoughts. They desired each other, he found her pleasant to converse with, and they each came from an appropriate family. She fit his criterion in almost every way. He had hoped to find a wife whose family was not so steeped in scandal, but how could he complain about that? Marriage would be satisfying to them both.

But she didn't want to be married to someone like him. And for a moment, he understood what she meant. He was already thinking of marriage as a logical step, but she, as a female, would see it much more emotionally. He believed there was no reason for strong emotion; one was only distracted by it.

When they returned to their room, Julian stripped down to his shirt and drawers and practically fell into bed. Rebecca's mouth seemed to quirk at his behavior, but she said nothing. She could not have slept well on the cold ground either. And the long, wet day had surely exhausted them both.

After blowing out the candle, she crawled beneath the covers, and this time, when she kept space between their bodies, he honored her wishes.

Julian came awake suddenly, as if from far too heavy a sleep. He lay still, knowing that something was wrong. And then he realized that Rebecca was not at his side.

He opened his eyes, but knew before looking that she wasn't in the room at all. A feeling of dread seemed to curdle in his stomach. How had he slept through . . . whatever had happened? He swung his legs off the side of his bed, pulled his trousers on quickly, and was buttoning the front flap when the door opened and Rebecca walked in. She carried a covered tray, which she set on the small table.

Then she smiled at him, even as he scowled.

"Where have you been?" he demanded.

She shut the door. "Perhaps you should lower your voice, so people don't assume you're one of those husbands."

He put his hands on his hips and waited.

She sighed, her gaze frankly roaming his bare chest. And passion too easily surged to life inside him. He tried to ignore it.

And then he realized she was wearing an apron about her waist. She grinned and jingled coins that nestled in the apron pocket.

He raised his eyebrows. "How did you come across money?"

"I worked for it."

He took a deep, furious breath.

"Remember the ill maid?" she quickly said, raising both hands. "I went down to buy bread for our breakfast, and saw that she was again working alone. I offered to take her place, and she agreed very quickly."

"You waited on customers?" he demanded.

"It is not difficult with such a limited menu." Her smile was full of satisfaction and pride. "I was very good at it, and people left me generous tips."

He didn't know what to stay. He was bothered by the fact that she'd worked for money, something that no gentlewoman should do. But then again, it wouldn't be the first time she'd flaunted Society's expectations.

She came to him then and put her hands on his chest as she leaned into him. He took a sharp breath and felt his reasoning power drastically decrease.

"I want to care and provide for you," he said roughly.

Her smile faded and she seemed to search his gaze. "That is very sweet of you, but I feel like I contribute nothing to this partnership. I am demanding of your time and attention—and demanding of you sexually." She tilted her head flirtatiously.

He took her upper arms and gave her a little shake. "You could have been abused."

"By farmers and peddlers?"

"By men who do not know how to treat a lady."

"But I'm not a lady today. I haven't been one for a week now."

"It doesn't matter what others believe, only what you believe about yourself."

"Very well, then I'm a lady. But I'm very good at concealing it when necessary. Even you must admit that."

He grunted.

"Prepare yourself, Julian. I'm going to work again this evening."

He stiffened. "What?"

"The poor girl needs more rest. And I've already committed myself, so you cannot change my mind. We'll have to delay our travel another day."

"Rebecca, this is inappropriate and dangerous."

"And I disagree."

He opened his mouth to continue his protests, then closed it. He knew better than to forbid her. And then he realized how his own past was still affecting him. He found himself wanting to protect Rebecca too much—as his father had done to his mother. Julian used to blame his father for that, for his mother hadn't seemed to realize the true depths of their financial problems. She'd been so blissfully ignorant she'd sent Julian off to school, not knowing they didn't have the money to pay for it. And she'd kept having children.

That was another thing he used to blame his father for. But now Julian understood better. It was so difficult to let Rebecca risk herself. He wanted to hold her to him, to protect her against the world.

But all he did was sigh. "Very well, you may fulfill your commitment. But I will be there the entire time."

Her eyes opened wide, as if she hadn't believed he would acquiesce so easily. "Thank you, Julian. I am glad you could listen to reason. Now let us eat our breakfast."

He caught her arm before she could turn away. "This is the last time you commit to something without discussing it with me first."

"I would gladly discuss everything with you, Julian, if only you weren't so set in your ways."

He flung his hands wide. "*This* is set in my ways?"

"This is about your restoring your family honor, and you know it. It's more important to you than anything else."

"That's not true," he said. *You're important to me.* But he didn't say the words as she went to seat herself at the table.

Chapter 18

They spent the rest of the morning and early afternoon in their bedchamber. Rebecca would have given anything to explore the village, but she understood Julian's reluctance. He didn't want them on display any more than was necessary. She could almost hear him grinding his teeth as he looked out the window.

For several hours, she'd gone over their clothing and made sewing repairs after borrowing supplies from the grateful maid. But Rebecca's gaze often drifted to Julian's broad back. Never in her life had she spent so much time alone with a man not related to her. Now she knew why it was so forbidden—it brought out one's wicked nature, for she was dwelling on the other things they could be doing alone in a room with a bed.

But he was being so stubborn, resisting succumbing to temptation. He wanted to show her pleasure, he wanted her—but he wouldn't follow through. He had a strict personal code he believed in, that he'd learned by surviving crises that might have destroyed another man. She admired him.

But that didn't mean she had given up trying to change his mind.

Late that afternoon, he followed her down to the tap-room, a hulking presence at her back. Unshaven and intimidating, he caused more than one man to look at him twice and then back slowly away. This was another thing that didn't offend her—she was secretly thrilled that he felt so protective—as long as he didn't act on it too restrictively. And so far he hadn't. She was beginning to think he was a little less controlling than she'd accused him of.

Once in the taproom, she saw him study every table and chair, even leaned into the room next door, where the barkeep kept the beer and ale kegs. Home-cured bacon and dried vegetables hung from hooks in the ceiling, and she smiled as he ducked to avoid them. At last, he settled at a table in the far corner, where he could see everything that was going on. She sighed in relief even as she tied on a fresh apron.

Soon she was too busy to think about Julian. The five tables were full of hungry people, and she did her best to serve them from the limited menu offered. She was surprised to find that her arms were sore from the morning spent carrying trays and pitchers. Her back soon ached from all the bending, but it was a satisfying feeling of usefulness.

Every time she looked at Julian, he was watching her with dark, hooded eyes. He signaled her whenever he wanted another beer, and as far as she was concerned, he had a few too many. But he did not seem inebriated, only watched her with more and more of a frown, as if he could no longer control his true feelings of unhappiness. He didn't like what she was doing, but he hadn't tried to stop her. She was grateful.

She noticed almost immediately that the evening patrons were a different species. In the morning, men had been on their way to their employment and customers of the inn were about to depart on the rest of their journey. Women, although a minority, had been present.

But in the evening, she was the only woman moving between boisterous men. They were anxious to relax after a long day of work, hear the local gossip, and have a good time competing at the dartboard, or at chess or checkers. And part of their enjoyment was staring at her, more openly than any man—except Julian—had done before.

She gave Julian more of her attention than she gave the others, of course. Every time she brought him a drink, she made certain to lean over him, pressing her breast into his shoulder, smiling into his face. He watched her warily, but did not protest, for after all, he was playing the part of her husband. This was the kind of flirtation not seen on ballroom floors, where using a fan was an art to snare a man's attention. This was bawdy and sensual, tactile and so alluring. In London, a woman might never know if a man was interested unless he came to call, sitting so properly across from her, discussing the weather. Such limited interaction was supposed to tell her everything?

No, she knew Julian's every earthy thought, the way his gaze raked down her body, the way he put an arm around her waist when she brought him a tankard. His actions said "mine" and she thrilled to it, even if it was only temporary, she reminded herself. A faint sensation of sadness moved through her, and she told herself every adventure had to come to an end. There was no use mourning this one before it was even finished.

She knew Julian was watching over her, and he made her feel . . . safe. Much as she had longed to deny wanting to feel that way, it gave her a freedom to move at ease among these rough strangers.

She tried to take the extra attention from the patrons in the spirit it was meant—they simply wanted to enjoy themselves, and she was a fresh face. She pushed away the occasional roving hand, felt a pinch on her backside once. She glanced hastily at Julian, but the offense had happened on the far side of a table where he couldn't see. She breathed a sigh of relief.

"I knew ye'd like that," said the mustachioed man who'd pinched her, erupting in guffaws with his mates.

She held back his tankard of beer. "Now ye don't

want me to go spillin' this in your lap, do ye?"

"She's a feisty one, Wilfred," another said as he took off his cap and tried to plaster down his curly red hair. "Why don't ye show us how ye dance?"

She felt Julian come up behind her even before the men's eyes grew wide. His hand came down to rest heavily on her shoulder.

"My wife doesn't dance." His voice was low and threatening—dangerous. Never in her life had she imagined that the man she'd first seen across a ballroom could speak like that. It was far too thrilling.

Wilfred raised both hands, "O' course, o' course. No harm meant."

With a menacing glare, Julian went back to his seat. She came to him eventually when there was a lull in her duties.

"I could deal with Wilfred," she said quietly.

"And I think you're wrong." He folded his arms across his chest and frowned at her. "His kind feel entitled to do as they wish."

"And you know that from one exchange in a taproom?" she said doubtfully.

"I do. I don't suppose you can water his drink."

She smiled. "No, I can't."

"Stay on the far side of the table from him."

"I'll try."

The next time she approached Julian's nemesis, he and the other men were pounding the table as they roared over a joke. They ordered more beer, and when she returned with it, Wilfred caught her about the waist before she could dart away. She'd played the humming-bird all evening as she flitted among the men, but of course she had to be grabbed by this man.

"Dance for us, Lucy me girl," he said, giving her a squeeze. "Dora is too big with child to give us any entertainment."

She smiled and pushed at his arm. "Not tonight, gents. I dance for no one."

"But me," came a deep voice behind her.

She winced, turning to see Julian striding toward them, his expression dark and ugly. She tried to meet him partway, but Wilfred still had her by the hips. She frowned a warning at the man, but he wasn't paying attention. Egged on by his friends, he rose to his feet. He didn't look unsteady. And although he was thinner, he was only a bit shorter than Julian.

"Now, boys," she began.

But Julian moved her aside as if she were as light as a child.

"Get 'im, Wilfred," one of the group grumbled.

The Earl of Parkhurst was in a confrontation in a taproom? Because someone had touched her? It didn't seem possible. He was a rational man who used words to settle his affairs and defeat his business opponents.

"I suggest ye leave your hands off me wife," Julian said, stepping close to stare the man down.

Now he was using intimidation, instead of words.

"Ye 'suggest,' do ye?" Wilfred shot back. "How polite o' ye. 'Tis a shame I won't be listenin' to yer suggestion."

The barkeep came out of an adjoining room, wiping his hands on his apron. He was an older man, with bags under his eyes and thinning hair, and he regarded Wilfred with resignation.

"Now stop this, boys," he said.

Julian turned toward the barkeep, and Wilfred took his chance, popping Julian in the face. Rebecca gasped, but Julian only took a step back with the force. She would not have thought it possible for his expression to darken more, but it did, and he bared his teeth in a fierce grin.

She covered her mouth, afraid that he would see how utterly thrilled she was that he was fighting for her.

The barkeep said, "Wilfred, not again! Ye broke a table last time."

"Not this time." Julian picked him up by the lapels of his jacket and carried the squirming man outside.

As everyone emptied out of the taproom to follow the men, Rebecca tagged along, feeling almost giddy at such a display of Julian's strength. She wanted to feel that strength at her command.

The barkeep was beside her, and he shook his head as they walked. "Wilfred just can't keep his hands off my girls," he said. "My apologies, Lucy. Hope yer husband doesn't take the brunt of it."

"Does he look like he will?" she asked.

But really, she shouldn't be exuberant. Maybe Julian didn't know how to fight at all. He was a businessman, a nobleman.

He launched himself at Wilfred, punching him in the stomach, and then when Wilfred bent over, punching him in the face for good measure. Two blows, and Wilfred was flat on his back, moaning.

Julian was a fighter. She sighed with happiness.

"Hope this teaches ye a lesson, Wilfred," the barkeep said, shaking his head as he turned to go back inside.

The crowd muttered with disappointment, and someone took a bucket of water from the horse trough to dump in Wilfred's face.

Rebecca rushed to Julian, who stood looking down at his opponent, hands on his hips. "Are you all right, Ernest?"

"I'm fine." He took her arm and propelled her back inside.

When he would have bypassed the taproom, she dug in her heels. "I made a commitment. I have to finish."

He looked at the clock on the mantel, then said to the lingering barkeep, "How much longer?"

The baggy eyes narrowed as if he had a hard time seeing at the distance. " 'Nother hour."

"Very well," Julian said. "But if another man so much as bumps her—"

"Who would dare?" the barkeep said, eyeing the width of Julian's shoulders.

Julian resumed his place, and Rebecca glanced at him with interest as she continued to wait on the tables. She would have thought the fight would settle him down, now that all the patrons knew what he was capable of. But his gaze followed her from beneath lowered brows, and his mouth was grim. She did not sense anger directed toward her, but . . . she wasn't quite sure what she sensed.

After that, all of her customers were respectful, and the hour passed uneventfully. Most customers had gone home to their beds in anticipation of another day of work. And the ones who lingered were only finishing their beer. The barkeep gave her a nod, and Julian must have been waiting for such a signal, for he came immediately to his feet.

"Ye have my thanks, Lucy," the barkeep said. "Ye won't be charged for yer stay here tonight."

"Thank you!" she said brightly. She took Julian's arm. "I'm ready."

After spending her whole life hoping for a journey like this one, she had made it happen herself, running away from London and forcing Julian to keep her with him. She'd even earned money on which to survive. She had to make her own goals happen—and would do that again this night. Waiting for Julian Delane to see the truth of their relationship was useless. The reoccurrence of a fever last autumn had made her realize that nothing was certain. She was going to make love to him, just in case she didn't live long enough to ever have the chance again. The long wait was over.

They walked up the creaking wooden staircase, lit by the candle Julian had plucked from the counter in the hall. She kept her arm through his, and he felt stiff with tension. She would have to tread carefully, looking for a way to turn his anger into passion.

Once in their room, he placed the candleholder on the table as she shut the door and leaned against it. She didn't know how she was supposed to school her expression for a seduction, but she let herself look down his body and imagine touching it, seeing everything he'd kept hidden from her. Her limbs felt deliciously heavy, her heart sped up in anticipation. He would no longer deny her.

Before she could even walk to him, he gripped her arms, pulling her against him. Dumbfounded, she gaped up at him.

"You're mine," he said hoarsely.

And then he kissed her.

Rebecca could have swooned with the heat and need and relief those words inspired. And his kiss—! Strong and powerful, his tongue thrusting into her, one hand holding her head still, the other moving sensually down her back. He pulled her hips hard against him, his arousal saying everything words couldn't.

With joyous abandon, she wound her arms about his neck, running her hands through his thick, dark hair. She moaned as she met his tongue with her own, teasing and darting. He tasted of beer, and it was more erotic than she could have imagined. She pressed herself against him, as if her aching breasts could only find relief against his body.

He lifted his head, and she felt a momentary disorientation and even disappointment. Would he refuse her yet again?

Instead he turned her around and pressed her against the door while he began to unhook her gown. She tilted her head to the side, her cheek against the cool wood, eyes closed, enjoying every sensation. She moaned as he kissed her neck. She felt her garments loosen, and he nibbled at her bare shoulders.

He turned her about again, her back against the door, her loose bodice beginning to slide down her torso. They looked into each other's eyes as her garments caught on the peaks of her breasts—and then he tugged, revealing her bare flesh to him, set off by the beauty of the red diamond gracing her cleavage.

He dropped to his knees, murmuring her name even as he cupped her breasts, molding them, lifting them to his mouth. She cried out when he licked a path between them, pressing kisses up the valley to the very peak.

She held his head to her while he gave her nipple the gentlest kiss. Then he met her eyes from below, and she knew hers were wide with anticipation and yearning.

Then he took her nipple deep into his mouth and suckled. She gasped and shuddered, only the strength of his body keeping her standing there. Glorious pleasure seemed to be in every part of her at once, from her fingertips to the very depth of her belly. Then he moved to the other breast, pushing her dangerously to the edge with his tongue and lips, even as his fingers soothed and teased the first nipple.

She couldn't stop shaking, and felt as if the whole world was about to be revealed to her.

With one fell swoop, he pushed the rest of her garments off her hips and she was naked, but for her stockings and boots. He kept his hands on her hips, looking at her with the smoky light of desire in his gray eyes.

And then he lifted her off her feet and deposited her in bed. She sprawled there, naked and open to him, and felt almost embarrassed as she tried to bring her knees together.

"No," he said hoarsely, hands on her knees. And then he spread them wider. "Don't move."

And she didn't. She watched with pleased awe as he began to shed his clothing at what was surely a record pace.

"Can I not help?" she asked.

"Next time."

She could have laughed her delight. There would be a next time.

But her urge to laugh faded, as she was able to see more and more of his magnificent body. By candlelight, his muscles were sculpted in shadows, the ridges of his abdomen awe-inspiring. A dark, narrow streak of hair began just below his navel, leading her wide eyes downward as he removed his trousers, then undid the fastening of his drawers.

When his erection came free, she stared at it in amazement. She'd once snuck a peek at a book of her sister's anatomy sketches, but she was still unprepared for the sheer size. She felt a momentary qualm at the thought of such a thing fitting inside her.

Then he bent over her, bracing his body with one arm beside her shoulder, his face intent, his hand trembling as he ran the backs of his fingers down her belly. Something inside her went so soft and tender that he felt emotional at the thought of being with her.

"So beautiful," he whispered, leaning down to press a kiss just below her navel.

She shivered and jerked, her breath coming harder now, her anticipation bubbling over until she felt that every second's delay was torture.

"Julian, please," she whispered, her voice trembling. "Don't make me wait."

And then his fingers sifted through her pubic curls, and her limbs trembled.

He parted her and she moaned. He caressed and lingered and circled, until she was gasping his name.

"I can't wait," he said, his voice guttural.

"Then don't."

He pushed her farther onto the bed and stretched his body over hers. "This will hurt the first time."

Desperate not to give him a reason to stop, she said, "Oh, no, I've had many lovers."

His laugh was more of a grunt. He settled between her thighs, bracing himself so that he didn't crush her. Feeling awkward and unsure of what to do, she lifted her knees. She could feel the hardness of him probing at her, and although it should have been embarrassing, so intimate, this was Julian, giving himself to her at last. Just as she was thinking that this didn't hurt at all, he gave a hard thrust, and she gasped at the brief, burning pain.

He didn't move, his body held still above her, the faintest tremble in his arms. "Are you all right?"

She bit her lip and nodded. She wanted to feel all that rising passion again, all the heat and need building inside her. Surely this wasn't all—

And then he started to move, coming almost all the way out of her, and sliding back in, deep.

"Oooh," she said, understanding suffusing her. "This feels . . . oh—"

"Yes," he whispered, his thrusts increasing in pace.

He angled his hips against her, and the friction and

pressure set off an answering urgency inside her. She abandoned thought, knowing only he could give her what she wanted. She dragged his torso down to her, moving with him, against him, her arms around him. He met her open mouth with a deep, passionate kiss. As their bodies fused together below and above, she lost herself in the need that pounded through her. She made sounds she didn't know could come out of her throat, and he answered her wordlessly, bending to take her breast into his mouth.

She strained toward the ending that eluded her, gasping, going ever higher, feeling the terrible tense stillness rising and rising—until a burst of hot pleasure came over her in waves. She shuddered down through it, awed and grateful and so very satisfied. The world was a glorious place.

And then Julian rose up and increased his pace. All she could do was hold on.

Chapter 19

Julian felt mindless, beyond pleasure into a world of sensation he'd never felt before. The depths of Rebecca's body were hot and tight, as if made to give him pleasure. She didn't shy away from the earthiness, the sweat, the friction of two bodies rubbing against each other. She caressed and held and urged him on, looking for her own pleasure.

And when at last she took it, her face full of radiant, wondrous bliss, he let himself go, shuddering over her, thrusting over and over until pulling out of her at the last moment, his own climax cascading over him, sweeping away the last of his doubts and indecision.

He came down onto his elbows, not wanting to crush her into the bed. Yet the moist heat of her breasts enticed him. He couldn't seem to remember how to slow his breathing. His chest ached with the effort.

Still she touched him, torturing him with her hot, inquisitive fingers. When her thumbs rubbed gentle circles on his nipples, he groaned and moved against her thigh.

She smiled up at him. "At last I know what all the thumping was about when we were in the lodging house with all those other people."

He gave a hoarse laugh. "You knew they were having sex."

"But I didn't quite grasp what they were doing."

He collapsed at her side, his arm across her, his leg over her thighs.

"Holding me captive?" she murmured, her voice musical with amusement.

"It's not necessary?"

"No. There is certainly nothing to flee from."

After using his shirt to clean his seed from her thigh, he realized she was watching him almost uncertainly.

"Is something wrong?" he asked, letting his hands soothe her, cupping her breast.

She trembled, eyes half closing, even as she said, "I keep waiting for you to be angry."

"I won't," he said, holding still instead of distracting her. "Once I've made a decision, I never regret it."

She seemed to relax then in his arms, and her hands went back to caressing him, which he well appreciated. He sighed with pleasure.

"You say you won't marry, but it doesn't change the fact that you're mine, Rebecca."

A faint frown furrowed her brow, and he tried to smooth it away with his fingers.

"For now," she said.

He shrugged, not ready to destroy their peaceful contentment by arguing with her. She could think what she liked, but she'd been a virgin, and he'd taken her innocence. She could not deny the truth. Although he'd taken one precaution, there could still be a child. He would not spoil the mood by reminding her of that. But they would wed. He smiled and closed his eyes.

"You seem almost smug, Julian," she accused, her voice light. "Why is that?"

"You have not had other lovers."

"Hmm. Why does it matter one way or the other?"

"A man likes to know that no other man touched what is his."

"You're beginning to irritate me."

He opened one eye.

She was frowning.

"Why are you irritated?" he asked.

"Do not think this means you have any say in what I do, Julian."

He smiled. "Don't be irritated. When a man takes a virgin, he cannot help but look forward to all the delightful things he's going to teach her."

She bit her lip, but she could not hide the pleasure his words seemed to bring her. "Have you taken so many virgins, then?"

"You are my first."

"Was that your first fight earlier tonight?"

He propped his head on his arm, letting his fingers play on her belly.

"You're distracting me," she accused, even as she began to tremble.

"No, just unable to keep my hands off you. As for fighting, no, it was not my first. I studied boxing for many years, but I haven't had a real fight since reaching adulthood."

"Did you fight as a child?"

"Occasionally."

She stopped his caresses. "What reason could you possibly have for such behavior? You do not strike me as the kind who goes looking for a fight."

"But others are, and I am not the kind to back down."

"I've noticed that," she said dryly.

He chuckled.

"Did the other boys . . . tease you?"

He removed his hand from hers and continued his exploration of the damp under curve of her breast. "It was long ago, Rebecca."

"If they teased you because of your family's problems, that is just terrible. Where were . . . their parents?"

Her breathing started to hitch as his fingers climbed the hill of her breast.

"Children cannot always be under watchful eyes," he said. "But perhaps you don't know about that."

Her eyelids fluttered as he lazily circled her nipple, but she managed to say, "No, I didn't play with other children much. Who . . . taught you that fighting . . . doesn't solve problems?"

She wasn't distracted enough, so he bent down and breathed on her nipple. It puckered even more, and he felt the same sense of satisfaction he might equate with buying a company, strange as that seemed. He licked the tip of Rebecca's breast as if it were sweet candy. She moaned.

"Oh, yes. Can we do this again?" she whispered.

He was determined to take his time. He caressed and teased her breasts with his mouth and fingers until she was shivering and restless.

"Julian, please, I need—more!"

He laughed against her skin, letting his hand part her thighs and begin an exploration. She was soft and moist, and so very heated. He could barely keep himself from plunging inside. But she wanted to learn about everything, and he would teach her this.

He caressed the recesses of her body, dipping his fingers in and out of her, taking deep delight in her whimpers, and the way she clung to him. He watched her face when he gave her another orgasm, then pulled her on top of him until she straddled his hips. Her hair cascaded about both their bodies just as he'd fantasized.

She sat on him, a bit dazed, but her hazel eyes began to show her interest.

Her body cradled his erection and he arched his hips, even as he reached to play with her breasts.

"Oh!" she gasped. "Can we make love like this?"

He grinned. "See what you can do about it."

He let her figure out her position, exploring him with her squirming hips and then her bold fingers. He groaned.

She stopped. "That hurt?"

"Not a bit," he said hoarsely. "But the more you take your time, the sooner I'm going to take control."

"Oh, no you don't." She lifted herself and held his penis, trying to see how easily they could fit together.

When she had it just about right, he took her hips and pulled, settling himself deep within her. They both gasped.

"Oh, yes," she breathed, eyes closed, head thrown back.

The sight of her pleasure, and the way her hair parted about her breasts, was erotic and wild.

"Do I get to do all the moving?" she asked innocently.

He choked out a grunt of agreement even as she lifted herself. He came all the way out of her.

"Oops!" she said. "Sorry."

When he was inside her again, he took a shuddering breath. Soon she found the rhythm and began to tease him with her movements. She leaned forward to lick his nipples, and he arched into her with desperation.

She moved his hands away from her hips. "Don't rush me, Julian. It's my turn to explore."

Never had he been with a woman who cared so much for his pleasure, who wanted to know everything about him. He felt like the luckiest man on the earth as she pleasured him until he was shaking and arching his hips desperately. At last she began to lift herself up and down, her eyes shining as she watched him.

He lost himself almost immediately, shuddering and groaning when he pulled out of her to empty everything inside him. Again, he used his shirt to clean up, while she watched him speculatively, but asked no questions. At last he went slack beneath her, arms wide, eyes closed.

She giggled and leaned down over his chest to snuggle against him. "That was fun. Am I supposed to get off now?"

Without thinking, he mumbled, "Don't leave me."

She went silent, and regretting the words, he cracked open his eyelids to see her pensive expression.

"I'm not leaving the room," she said at last.

"You'd better not," he said with relief, hoping she didn't read more into his words than he'd meant to show her this soon.

*   *   *

In the morning, a bathing tub was sent up at dawn, a gesture of thanks from the maid, Dora. Rebecca watched the kitchen boys troop past a scowling Julian, who wore only his trousers, rendering him sufficiently intimidating. She was still in bed, the covers up to her chin. But she didn't care how many people saw her nearly naked, as long as they were bringing hot water.

When they'd gone, she was in the tub before he'd barely closed the door. She gave a delighted sigh, wishing it were deep enough that she could totally submerge herself.

She expected Julian to busy himself, but instead he pulled up a chair as if her bath was the main entertainment of his day. His interest made her blush. She was naked and he was nearly so; she was surprised to feel a little discomfited, but she thought that was only natural.

She used a facecloth and dripped water across her upper body. "I was never allowed to linger in a bath as a child. It makes me feel decadent."

"Then feel decadent quickly, because we must leave."

"But you'll need a bath—"

"I'll use yours."

She grinned at him, enjoying the intimacy. He didn't grin back. She gave an exaggerated pout. "It's back to the jewel again, isn't it?"

His eyes dropped down to her breasts, between which the Scandalous Lady hung, glinting light. "I want to confront my uncle, yes. The sooner it is done, the sooner I can concentrate on you."

She quickly scrubbed herself. When her hair was soapy, Julian was waiting with the rinse bucket.

Rebecca reluctantly rose from the bath, and he was there to wrap her in a towel. She dried herself slowly as she watched him bathe. Just looking at him gave her such pleasure. His body was so different from hers, so large and hairy and masculine. Yet not too large at the moment, she thought smugly, feeling worldly with her new knowledge of men.

"Let me erase that pleased look on your face," he said as he rose from the tub to dry himself, "by saying that you could have cost us much with your insistence on being a maid."

"Is that an 'I told you so'?" she said, frowning with irritation.

He shrugged. "Take it as you will. But things could have turned out very differently. What if they'd all attacked me, and I'd been unable to protect you?"

"I would have managed," she said stiffly. "I might even have saved you. Julian, just because we have slept together, I do not suddenly plan to become cowed into behaving as the obedient, respectful woman you seem to want. I am a real woman, with my own ideas, not some doll you can pose."

He dropped the towel and came toward her where she sat on the bed. She leaned back to look up at him, a little intimidated, a lot aroused by his nudity. She thought he might be angry, but his expression was playful.

"A doll I can pose?" he echoed, pushing her shoulder until she was forced to lie back on the bed.

He tried to take away her towel, but she found herself clutching it to her, feeling uneasy as a shaft of sunlight lit her body.

"I want to see you pose again," he whispered, ignoring the towel, but taking her arms up over her head. "In the painting, your back was arched. I remember each brushstroke as if I'd watched it painted."

She squirmed now, not enjoying the sensation of being compared to a work of art. "You know that was Roger's vision, very idealized. I'm not a fantasy woman."

"Are you saying you aren't the model?"

"Of course not! But it wasn't real! I was just a body to him, not a real person. How can I even begin to measure up?"

"It isn't a contest," he said, sliding the towel off her belly. He gently adjusted the jewel until it rested between her breasts.

She held her breath, frozen, wanting him to touch her again, yet feeling uneasy about . . . everything else.

With a sigh, he straightened. She could not mistake

his arousal now, but he turned away and reached for his clean drawers.

"Julian, I must warn you," she said, after sitting up and pulling her chemise over her head. She tossed her hair, tried to be flippant, but spoke seriously. "Don't fall in love with me."

He gave her a casual glance over his shoulder even as he continued to pull up his trousers.

She was irritated by his nonchalance. "We don't have a future together, because I probably don't have one. I'll enjoy whatever life is given to me, and I want more than to be a subservient wife."

He faced her now, and she didn't like the tenderness that shone in his gray eyes.

"Rebecca, none of us ever knows what the future brings. Never assume yours will be short."

Her throat felt tight, but she forced herself to say, "And never assume you'll have what you want from me in the end."

Chapter 20

Rebecca put their awkward morning encounter out of her mind. Her optimism resurfaced once she cajoled the grateful maid into finding her fishhooks and string.

She saw Julian watching her in bemusement as they began their journey on the public wagon. But he didn't question her, and she felt cheerful and secretive, which lasted until Julian had them disembark from the wagon before it reached the final scheduled village.

Rebecca regretfully watched the wagon leave them behind. "No inn tonight?"

"After two nights of visibility, I don't think it's wise."

She sighed, but followed him up the stream he'd chosen. They'd left the moors behind, and were now traveling through the fertile vale of Yorkshire. Half walls of stone and hedges divided distant pastureland and farm fields, and in every direction she could see milling sheep.

She told herself to concentrate on the tasks necessary to sleep tonight, and most especially to eat. But always she was conscious of being alone with Julian, out in the countryside. She had to control a blush of excitement at the thought of making love outdoors.

Julian at last agreed to allow her to fish when he felt they were far enough away from the road. After he finished building their fire, she felt him standing behind her, watching.

"Have you never fished for your own meal before?" she asked over her shoulder. She sat on the bank of a stream, holding her string, gently pulling the hook through the water.

"Of course, but I must say I've never seen a woman put a worm on a hook."

"I have many talents." She winked up at him. "My brother taught me."

"In truth?" he asked, coming to sit beside her. "I'm surprised your parents allowed it."

She offered him his own string and hook. He proceeded to tie his to a stick and cast the hook out farther.

"They didn't know. My brother managed to sneak me out of the house away from my protective nanny. Did you do such things with your siblings?"

"My sisters are not as adventurous as you," he said, watching his pole rather than looking at her.

It gave her the chance to study him. "Then they were

as most of my friends, concerned about behaving like a proper young lady in hopes of attracting a proper gentleman."

He smiled. "Do not think ill of them. They were very conscious of our monetary status, and their lack of dowries."

She winced. "Of course. I did not mean to make light of their situation."

He looked down at her, his smile lazy. "I know you didn't. Luckily, they are two and four years younger than I, and by the time they were ready to look for husbands, I had money to offer on their behalf."

"What a good brother you are," she said, elbowing him.

They were distracted when Rebecca's line went taut, and she pulled a wriggling fish out of the water in triumph. She insisted on removing it from the hook herself, even though it wiggled terribly, and Julian laughed at her. She felt he'd been punished sufficiently when he missed a fish nibbling at his hook, and lost his worm as a result.

When at last they both had newly baited lines in the water, she said, "Your sisters surely appreciate your efforts, but I imagine your brothers are far too carefree to admit they're grateful."

He shrugged, and for the first time he didn't seem tense when she brought up the subject of his brothers.

"They're young," he said.

She gave an exaggerated gasp. "I have not heard you make excuses for them before."

"I am attempting to give their age more consideration."

"They will make their own mistakes, as surely you did."

He arched an eyebrow. "I certainly never made mistakes." But there was a faint smile on his mouth.

"It's difficult to be so perfect. Perhaps you wistfully envy your brothers because they're younger, with less responsibilities."

He rolled his eyes and looked back at his pole, which she could see suddenly bow beneath the furious tugging of a fish. He expertly kept it on the line, then pulled it in.

"My brothers surely envy me, Rebecca," he chided her.

"I'm not so sure about that. They seem to be enjoying themselves, which you must wish for eighteen-year-olds—but that's just my opinion."

She sent him a sweet smile, and was glad when he suddenly seemed to focus on her mouth. For a long moment, she felt more aware of him than anything she'd ever experienced before. He knew her in ways she hadn't imagined offering to a man, and it was a little frightening.

But then he shook himself and went right back to the business of fishing. After all, he was a provider, she thought with bemusement.

Later, he was teaching her to clean a fish—a subject she'd avoided in her youth—when he suddenly stopped and lifted his head.

When she opened her mouth to question him, he put a finger near his lips, and she obediently remained silent. After several long minutes, where all she heard was the gentle gurgling of the stream and the croaking of frogs, she cocked her head at Julian.

"I thought I heard something," he said.

"A badger?"

Now that she knew what it was, she would not let herself become so disturbed by the sounds of the countryside.

But he didn't answer, only took their fish back to the fire, and laid them out on flat rocks he lined up near the flames.

Rebecca felt subdued as she waited for her dinner and watched Julian. He seemed tense, far too alert, and she knew he was still concerned about what he thought he'd heard. She gave him his solitude, letting him think and listen rather than pestering him with questions.

She, too, was thinking of Windebank's thugs, the men who'd come after her. They'd killed Roger Eastfield and his mother after all. To get their hands on the Scandalous Lady they might do worse.

But she and Julian had taken such pains to hide their journey, traveling north first, and now using public wagons. They'd constantly used different names.

But the man lurking outside the Eastfield home the night of the fire would have told Windebank that Julian and Rebecca had been in Manchester, that they'd talked to Mrs. Eastfield. Windebank would have to assume they knew of his part in these crimes. It put them in even more danger.

"Rebecca," Julian murmured, setting down a second fillet uneaten, "do not panic, but I believe someone is quietly approaching."

She tensed, straining to listen, but heard nothing except the wind and the rising chorus of crickets. The sun had set, and in the sky was the last gray of daylight. "I assume you don't mean a friendly shepherd," she responded through barely moving lips.

He briefly shook his head.

She should be panicked and frightened—but it was hard to be so when she had Julian to defend her. "What do you intend to do?"

"I will wait until they commit to a course of action. We can slip into the woods beside the stream."

"That is surely too cautious. I think we should challenge them."

He closed his eyes briefly, as if he were struggling to control himself. "We don't know how many there are, and you are not able to fight at my side."

"I still have the knife I used to gut the fish."

"And someone might very well take it away and use it on you. Now, casually walk with me toward the stream to wash our hands. When we squat, we'll be below the embankment, out of sight. We'll crawl into the copse of trees and then evaluate the situation."

She nodded, although regretted her agreement when it came time to stand. She felt so exposed. Would someone simply shoot them? Her back twitched all the way down to the stream.

Before she could even squat, she heard the sound of running feet. Whirling, she saw Julian knock over the first man before he could reach Rebecca. The man gasped and clutched his throat, where Julian's fist had slammed.

She was a liability to him, she knew. Without warning anyone—Julian and the second thug were occupied grappling with each other—she dove into the copse of trees where Julian had first wanted her to go.

He probably expected her to run as far away as possible, but she couldn't leave him alone. So she crouched in the underbrush between the trees and tried to keep as still as possible. She could just make out the fighting, covering her mouth instead of gasping when the first man rose behind Julian's unguarded back.

But as if he had a second pair of eyes, he drove his elbow backward, catching the first man off guard and sending him to the ground. The second man raised a knife—she stifled a scream—but Julian caught his wrist and twisted hard. The knife dropped. She heard the audible sound of a bone cracking, and the man's high-pitched scream as he collapsed.

The first man rose up again, and in his hands was the knife.

"Julian!" she shrieked.

He caught the knife, and guided its momentum as it swung about and imbedded in the villain's chest. The man crumpled to the ground.

She gaped at the scene as Julian stood over the still body of his attacker. Then he looked up as he realized the one with the broken arm had gotten away, and even now was riding off on one horse, and leading another.

They could have used a horse, she thought, feeling distant and rather off balance. Julian had almost been stabbed, she realized with a sick feeling of horror. What would have happened if he'd been injured? She would have had to find him help—with little money and no true knowledge of where they were. She was vulnerable in a way she hadn't felt since childhood.

"Rebecca!" Julian was almost running as he skirted the edge of the stream.

"I'm here!" she cried, emerging from the undergrowth.

He caught her hard against him, lifting her off her feet.

"I didn't see where you'd gone," he said gruffly

against her ear. "One moment you were beside me, and the next . . ."

His voice faded off. She winced as her ribs seemed to creak, and he set her down.

"I did as you wanted, escaping into the copse of trees."

He lifted his head to look down at her, his gaze searching as if he thought she might be wounded. "And why ever would I assume you'd done what I asked?"

"Well, what else did you think, that I abandoned you in a panic?" she asked, affronted.

"I don't know what I thought. I'm the one who panicked."

Mollified, she smoothed her hand down his crumpled lapel. "Well, that is . . . understandable, then. I just didn't want to distract you when you had to confront two men. Are you all right?"

He nodded. "A bruise or two."

"For a man who doesn't fight, you are getting too much practice."

He nodded, but his gaze followed along the stream, the way the injured man had disappeared. With the approach of night, they could no longer see far at all.

"I was foolish to engage in that fight last night," he said ruefully. "It made us too visible. I should have controlled myself."

"We'll share the blame. I was so determined to prove

that I could help support us, when I should have remained out of sight."

"We've both learned a lesson, then," he said. "As for my uncle, I can't decide if he was trying to have us captured or killed."

She shuddered, glad he was holding her, for she suddenly felt chilled in the near darkness.

"Are you certain they were from your uncle?"

He nodded. "They didn't demand anything, they just attacked."

"Why would he kill us? He cannot even be certain we still have the diamond."

"Maybe he'd prefer the loss of the jewel to the loss of his freedom when this whole sordid scandal comes to life."

"He's done too much for the Scandalous Lady, Julian. He won't abandon it so easily." She reached beneath the collar of her gown and lifted out the fine gold chain and, hanging from it, the red, heart-shaped diamond, which caught the light of the dying fire. She stood on tiptoes and placed it around his neck. "You wear this. You can protect it more than I."

His lips quirked in a half smile. "You trust me with it after all this?"

She smiled. "Roger would have wanted it returned if he'd known it was stolen. I trust you, Julian."

He searched her eyes, and in that moment of silent

communication, she knew her words were the truth.

"I'll take care of the body," he said at last as he tucked the necklace beneath his shirt.

"We can take care of it together. I don't particularly want to be alone just now."

He nodded, and in the next half hour, they gathered rocks and piled them over the body, hoping to keep animals away. When they were done, Rebecca washed her hands in the stream, scrubbing hard with their small piece of soap.

Firelight faded behind her, and she turned in surprise to see him kicking dirt onto it.

"We can't stay here," he said, handing her a piece of cooked fish. "Eat up, for you'll need your strength. We need to walk at least an hour or so, in case the other villain brings reinforcements."

Traveling in the dark was far different than she'd imagined. Once she'd thought it would be mysterious and exciting. Now she found herself stumbling over rocks or depressions in the grass. She held Julian's hand, wishing that clouds weren't obscuring the last quarter of the moon.

At last he decided to make a temporary camp at the base of a half wall built of rock. He wouldn't build another fire, so she was grateful that the wall kept the wind off them. They lay in damp grass, and he wanted to keep her behind him, closest to the uneven wall, but she wanted to feel his arms about her. He acquiesced, and she gradually relaxed enough to grow sleepy.

And to think, she'd hoped to be making love again this night, instead of escaping a pair of murderers.

Julian awoke at dawn, his body stiff and cold and damp—except where Rebecca huddled against him. He sighed, tightening his hold about her, and then could have groaned when she unconsciously wiggled her hips deeper into the bend of his.

This was not how he'd planned to spend his second intimate night with Rebecca. But her safety was more important than anything else.

Once again, he wished she would return to London, but knew she would not go. He was taking her closer and closer to danger, and for the first time, he felt nervous about his ability to protect her.

"What are you thinking?" she asked quietly. "You seem tense."

"I'm planning what we will do when we reach my uncle's estate. It will only be a few more days."

"Then do we knock on the door and say we've come for the truth?"

He knew she was trying to lighten his mood, but he couldn't even offer a chuckle. "I have a friend who used to be a detective at Scotland Yard in London, but is now the chief constable in Lincoln, not far from my uncle's estate. He'll be able to help us, and discreetly, too."

"I'm glad, Julian. That makes me feel better." She

sighed. "Standing will probably make me feel better, too. I'm terribly stiff."

"I can hardly remember how my bed at home feels," he admitted as they both slowly sat up.

The bed would not be lonely, he thought, determined that Rebecca would be joining him there permanently.

The dawn sky was overcast, predicting more rain. Everything he wore was already damp. After a meal of cold fish from the night before, they began to walk east, rather than south toward the road they'd been on the night before. A gracious farmer gave them a ride on the back of his cart for most of the morning until they reached the nearest village. Due to Rebecca's bedraggled, tired appearance, another farmer offered them a ride to the next village, where he said they could spend the night in a room above the alehouse.

But at dinnertime, when they reached the small village of Scotter, with its stone buildings around a central green, the alehouse was already full of boisterous, drunken men.

The farmer, a lean, sandy-haired man about Julian's own age, got down from the cart and looked between Rebecca and the alehouse, frowning as he twisted his cap in his hands.

"Ye can't stay there, Mrs. Hill," he said at last. "Won't be safe for a woman. My name is Stubbes. Ye can stay in me barn. Me wife would snatch the last of me hair if I left ye here."

Relieved, Julian nodded his appreciation. He hadn't planned to spend the night in the village anyway, and at least now he could keep Rebecca safe. "Mr. Stubbes, we accept your kind offer. Surely there's some way I can offer me help in return."

Mr. Stubbes scratched his bristly chin and looked Julian up and down. "There's a few chores ye can help with in the morn."

"I'm strong, sir."

"And I can help your wife, Mr. Stubbes," Rebecca added.

Julian thought that would be interesting to watch, but he was wise enough to say nothing aloud. Rebecca's life was quite different than the life of a farm wife.

It was another hour past the village before they reached the cottage. It was a small single-story stone building with a thatched roof. At the door, Mr. Stubbes introduced them to his wife, who was trying to put several children to bed. A small, plump woman with dark hair under her cap, she smiled at them graciously, although with distraction. Julian saw several children running behind her, gleefully avoiding the stairs to the loft.

"Mr. Stubbes," his wife said, "Please give them blankets. It can be so cold at night."

Julian saw Rebecca's look of relief.

"I've left stew in a cauldron over the fire," she continued. "Help yourselves while I see to the children."

They ate bowls of hot delicious stew, and Julian listened to the eldest daughter, who couldn't be more than twelve, try to settle down several of the younger children in the loft beneath the roof. The main floor was divided into two rooms, the kitchen and what must have been the bedroom of the farmer and his wife. There was another bed in the corner of the kitchen, where a boy of perhaps ten lay, watching them with sleepy eyes.

Soon Mr. Stubbes led them back to the barn, where goats and horses occupied the stalls. He left them the lantern and supplies and wished them a good night. When the big door closed behind him, Rebecca and Julian looked at each other.

"It already feels warmer in here," she said happily.

"Then up above must be even better." He settled a blanket over her shoulder. "Climb up the ladder, and I'll follow behind."

"You simply want to look up my skirts, sir," she said tossing her head.

She'd worn her hair pulled back in a simple ribbon, with her brown curls flowing down her back. He'd barely resisted threading his fingers through it all day, but now he wouldn't have to.

Unless she objected to being debauched in a barn loft. And a lady might. But she kept telling him she wasn't always a lady, so he had hope.

The hayloft was of course full of hay, but there were

several crates arranged near the wall in such a way that made it seem like the Stubbeses occasionally had guests. Julian unpacked their portmanteau and draped damp clothing over the crates and the railings that guarded them from falling below. Then he stood and watched with amusement as Rebecca used a pitchfork to spread the hay about and make a more comfortable mattress.

She glanced at him over her shoulder, eyebrows raised as if daring him to say something.

He lifted both hands and backed away. She spread a sheet over the mound of hay, then added several blankets, as well as two pillows.

"There," she said, brushing her hands together.

He came up behind her and began to unhook her gown.

She peered over the edge of the loft. "Are we certain he's gone?"

"You saw him leave. And the animals will certainly let us know when someone approaches."

Her shoulders relaxed under his hands. When she stepped away to continue disrobing, she kept her eyes on him as he removed his jacket. She wore an expression of eagerness and even hesitation, as if she didn't know what she was supposed to hope for.

He'd let her wonder, and then he'd amaze her.

They watched each other undress. She stopped at

her chemise, but he left all of his clothing behind. Her eyes widened as he approached, and without hesitation, she gathered up her chemise and pulled it off over her head.

He took her into his arms, and the heat of their flesh moved him. "You feel incredible."

"You feel ready," she whispered, her eyes wicked as she met his.

"But you're not." He began to walk her backward.

"Of course I'm ready," she said indignantly. "I've been thinking of nothing else all day—and all the day before, too!"

He gave a low laugh and lowered her to the blankets. She reached to pull him to her, but he held back, kneeling at her side.

"I was too eager the other night," he said ruefully.

"Too eager? We both were. And what is wrong with that?"

"I didn't take time to explore."

He could see her blush even by lamplight.

"Oh, that sounds . . . lovely."

"You simply lie there, darling, and let me kiss every inch of you."

He thought her smile briefly froze at his endearment—or was it because of his request?—but then she folded her hands behind her head, which brought her breasts into prominence. He swallowed hard. Her knees were casually bent, throwing shadows between her thighs. He had been with women who preferred the dark, and women who unabashedly displayed everything, for whom nothing was sacred.

Rebecca was somewhere in between, unashamed of her own body, yet innocent enough not to understand how he viewed her nudity. Was that why she'd posed for that painting?

She aroused and pleased him, and he wanted to show her so with every soft kiss. Her arms were long and delicate, the skin like silk. He let his tongue glide along the undersides of her breasts, never quite touching the peaks. He could hear her quick breathing, feel her restless movements. But he was taking his time.

He kissed a path down her torso, dipped his tongue into her navel, and continued on south, separating her thighs when she did not do so.

"Julian?"

He heard the hesitation in her voice. He knew she had no idea what he meant to do to her, and just imagining her excitement and response was almost too much for him. His fingers brushed her curls and she quivered and moaned. He parted her gently, held her gaze with his, lowered his head, and kissed her intimately.

Chapter 21

As Julian kissed between her thighs, Rebecca found herself shuddering, clutching the prickly blanket beneath her, her lips caught between her teeth to keep from moaning. She was filled with such pleasure she thought she would shatter with it. He spread her thighs farther, explored deeper, circling his tongue, nipping at her, taking her between his lips, delving even inside until she came apart, unable to control the way her body quivered and thrashed.

"Oh, Julian—"

She got nothing more out before he came down on top of her and thrust deep. There was no pain, only a sense of the deepest completion and satisfaction. They rocked together, and she tried to hold him with her arms and even her legs, wrapping herself about him, desperate to offer him the bliss he'd given to her.

This time she recognized the signs, knew that with his body's shudder he was pouring himself into her.

Pouring his seed, instead of pulling out of her.

That gave her pause, especially since he was so careful the first two times they'd made love. But she wouldn't think about it now—it was too late to worry. It must not be so easy to become pregnant, or there would be babies every nine months for a married couple.

And she wasn't married.

She liked the feeling of him on top of her, and was regretful when at last he slid to the side. He leaned to blow out the lantern, then pulled the blanket up over them both, holding her within the circle of his arms. She couldn't see his face in the dark, but she found herself tracing his features, lingering on his lips.

He nipped her fingers, suckling the tip of one. Even that made her tremble. She could not forget the things he'd just done to her with his mouth.

"Sleep," he said, laughter in his voice. "We'll have to arise well before dawn to help Farmer Stubbes."

"It's hard to turn my mind off, to forget what we just did . . . what you just did to me."

"Did you like it?" he whispered.

She felt him nuzzling behind her ear. "Surely you could tell what I thought, how it made me feel."

"I'm sure every animal below could tell."

She hit him in the arm, and he laughed and rolled onto his back, bringing her with him until she could snuggle against his side, her head on his shoulder.

"Is it always like this between men and women?" she asked softly.

"No. This is special."

Those words touched her in some way, made her feel tender and yearning toward this man who had a reputation as someone so logical and impassive.

"Surely you've seen the way some husbands and wives behave," he continued, "distant and bored. You cannot tell me they enjoy themselves in bed."

"But they do their duty," she murmured. "We're always taught that."

"So this is a duty?" he asked.

"Not with you."

He hugged her tight for a moment, and gradually they both relaxed. Sleep came with ease—for at his side, she experienced profound peace.

Four in the morning arrived swiftly, and the hours before breakfast were as full as many workdays. Rebecca wanted to prove to herself—and to Julian—that she was just as capable as he of showing gratitude to the Stubbeses for giving them a safe place to stay. While Julian worked with the farmer and his sons feeding the horses and hogs, she milked the cows along with Mrs. Stubbes and her daughters.

She'd seen Julian's brief, doubtful expression when she said she was capable of milking, yet after a few minutes her fingers did remember the task and soon she was working swiftly, cheerfully.

Afterward, the two of them were invited to breakfast

with the farmer, his wife and seven children, more children than she'd counted the night before.

This time she knew to watch Julian's face as several children doubled up on their stools to make room for the guests at the table. Although Julian came from a large family, in the past few days it had been very obvious that such broods made him uneasy. If he felt so again, she couldn't tell.

The men and boys went out to sow barley in the plowed fields, leaving Rebecca with Mrs. Stubbes. For a moment, Rebecca stood in the doorway and watched Julian walk away, head and shoulders taller than the other man. In the distance she could see sheep munching grass by the riverbed, and out in the cornfields were portable pens where Julian would next help drive the sheep so they could graze on the stubble. It was a peaceful scene, uncomplicated in many ways, dangerous in others, for one never knew what the weather would bring. But it seemed like a good place to raise children.

Rebecca spent a busy day with the gracious, chatty Mrs. Stubbes, helping wash the dishes and even doing some mending while the woman spun thread and took care of the chickens and dealt with her many children. She was teaching them their letters and numbers, which implied that there wasn't a school nearby for the children to attend.

The farmer and his wife depended only on each

other. Rebecca told herself that being married like this was so restrictive. But then weren't all women restricted in some ways? Yet she'd seen women of the lower classes doing things these last days that women of the *ton* were never allowed, from working to help with the family's expenses to even walking alone down a street.

Though she wanted to think Mrs. Stubbes's life was hard and unrewarding, there was a gentleness in the woman's eyes when she watched over her children, and an eager, happy expression when her husband returned from his long, exhausting day.

That night, when Rebecca and Julian were alone in the loft, she watched him sigh as he sat down in their makeshift bed to remove his boots.

"Tired?" she asked.

He smiled. "It's been many years since I did this sort of work. It feels good to be tired. I was glad to be of help."

"I know what you mean," she said, leaning against the open window. One by one the candles were blown out in the farmhouse, and darkness seemed to spread over the land.

"You worked hard. How did you know how to milk a cow?"

She laughed. "You are not the only one who can help the servants. I snuck off with a dairy maid when I was twelve, determined to see what cows were like up close. She put me to work, and my fingers ached so much I gained a new respect for how hard our servants worked."

"I hope your mother wasn't too upset."

"I never told her. I claimed my sore fingers were because she was making me work too much on my embroidery."

He laughed.

She strolled toward Julian, enjoying the way he regarded her body with bold appreciation. "You've said you're very tired," she murmured, kneeling down behind him and rubbing her hands over the hard muscles of his shoulders.

He turned and pounced, and she laughed as she found herself on her back in the hay.

"Not that tired," he said, then kissed her.

Much later, she fell asleep naked in his arms, satisfied and lazily content.

Several hours passed, and she came up from the depths of slumber, shivering. As she started to sit up, Julian rose on one elbow.

"Is something wrong?" he asked.

"I feel a draft from the open window," she murmured. "I'll close the shutters."

"Stay here," he said.

She knew he was being protective, but she accepted it drowsily. She felt the cold even more once he left her, and shivered for a few minutes.

When he didn't return, she glanced over to see the dark outline of him at the window.

"Julian?"

"I thought I heard something at the house, a child's cry. And there's a light on."

She got to her feet and slipped on a chemise. She brought a blanket to Julian and wrapped it about his shoulders.

He caught the ends to hold it about him as he smiled down at her in a distracted manner.

She stood at his side and stared at the light that glowed in the kitchen window. "Do you think this is unusual? They do have many children."

"But none still nursing, so no reason to be up." He hesitated. "I have a bad feeling about this. Mr. Stubbes mentioned to me that there's rumor of fever in a village north of here, and earlier I heard one of the young boys coughing."

She nodded, knowing that Julian watched her carefully. This news did not affect her in any alarming way. She'd spent her life constantly worried about illness, and she'd long since become immune to thoughts of it. What would happen, would happen. She could not affect it one way or another.

But she gripped the window frame and thought of the sweet farm family, with so many innocent children. "We should go to them."

He frowned at her. "I'll go."

"We'll both go. Julian," she added when he would have continued to protest, "I cannot insulate myself from life. I didn't become ill in that Manchester lodging house. I'm stronger than I used to be, healthier. I'll be fine. But I couldn't live with myself if we did nothing to help these generous people."

They dressed swiftly and went up to the house in the dark. When Julian knocked, Mr. Stubbes looked out a side window and opened the door. He wore his shirt untucked from his breeches, and his feet were bare.

"Excuse the interruption, Mr. Stubbes," Julian said, "but we noticed the light and—"

Rebecca, who saw his wife at the hearth holding a child, pushed past the two men. Mrs. Stubbes looked up, her hair down around her shoulders, her eyes betraying a glimpse of fear.

But she managed a smile. "Sorry I am to disturb ye, Mrs. Hill."

"Ye didn't," Rebecca said, coming closer. "I simply couldn't sleep."

Mrs. Stubbes held one of the boys in her arms. He couldn't have been any more than six, an age when he'd usually push his mother away. But now he laid in her arms coughing weakly, fingers at his throat, fighting to breathe.

"It came on so suddenly," she said, bewildered. "He coughed terribly loud, the poor mite. I thought . . . I thought . . ."

"I recognize the symptoms," Rebecca said, "I had it much as a child."

Mrs. Stubbes red-rimmed eyes went wide with sudden hope. "Do ye know what to do, Mrs. Hill? Since me own mother died when I was so young, I learned none of her secrets. The other children never had such a terrible cough."

"Do you have the herb coltsfoot?" she asked.

The woman shook her head, eyes filling.

Rebecca put her hand on the woman's shoulder. "It's all right. What about thyme?"

"Yes, in my garden! Or do ye want it dried?"

"Fresh would be best." Rebecca turned to Mr. Stubbes. "Could ye fetch us several plants? Leave the roots in the ground."

"Take Alice with you," Mrs. Stubbes said, motioning for her oldest daughter to come down from the loft. "She knows the kitchen garden well."

"And we'll boil water while we wait." Rebecca filled a cauldron with water from a jug, and hung it over the fire.

The boy started to cough again, and the terrible bark wasn't nearly as bad as the whistling sounds he made trying to breathe in enough air.

"Keep him calm," Rebecca murmured.

Mrs. Stubbes rocked and sang to him.

"Is there anything I can do?" Julian asked from behind her.

Rebecca turned to find him watching her closely from his place near the door, as if he didn't want to get in the way. She smiled. "Nothing. Only perhaps keep Mr. Stubbes company, should he need it."

Alice came in first, eagerly handing several stalks of the herb to Rebecca. While the two men talked softly in a corner, Rebecca boiled the thyme over the fire, instructing Mrs. Stubbes to hold the boy near the steam while the concoction was being made. She took some of the thyme and crushed it with a mortar and pestle, mixing in some hot water and forming a paste that she spread out on his chest. Once the rest of the thyme had boiled long enough, they allowed it to cool, then added some honey to sweeten the taste. The boy's breathing was noticeably better from the steam, and he was able to take sips of the cooling liquid.

The all sat together as the room grew hot from the steam. Their reward was the way the little boy's breathing began to ease, until at last a more natural sleep claimed him.

Mrs. Stubbes leaned down to kiss him, her tears falling into his hair. "Thank ye, Mrs. Hill," she said softly. "I will never forget yer kindness."

Rebecca felt hot with embarrassment. "Glad I am to help. Me own childhood was full of the same complaints. What I learned is provin' useful now."

"And it will be again, when ye have your own children."

Rebecca didn't want to look at Julian, but she couldn't seem to help it. She tried to smile shyly at him, as she thought a young wife should, but the image of children just seemed so . . . strange to her. She'd never thought about having them, since she hadn't wanted to marry. But suddenly, the thought of a dark-haired infant held to her breast was not so very terrible.

"You were marvelous."

In the hayloft, Rebecca lay safely within Julian's strong arms, smiling at the wonder in his voice. "I didn't invent the treatment, Julian. It was simply used on me so often that I memorized it."

"But your very demeanor calmed both of them. You were so competent, so convinced that the boy would be fine."

"It was what they needed to hear. The more frightened they were, the more tense their son would become."

He kissed the top of her head. "I still think you were marvelous."

"And I appreciate it." Her smile faded. "Julian, I am not a person to be admired when compared to the Stubbeses. They're alone in the world but for each other. They only have the work of their hands to provide for their whole family. In the face of their bravery, I feel very selfish."

He gave her a brief squeeze. "Rebecca—"

"No, listen to me. I go on and on about wanting my

life to be a great big adventure. My parents let me prattle on throughout childhood, and now you're doing the same, which is very kind of you. But I've been selfish, as if I should have everything I want, when there are so many people in the world who are simply lucky to survive."

"You are not selfish to want to do something with your life, Rebecca. A selfish woman wouldn't lead thugs away from London, endangering herself to keep her family safe."

"You're making my motives too pure," she insisted. "I also thought I was having a shockingly good time, never imagining the lengths these men would go to for a necklace, the murders they'd commit." She shuddered.

"So you're guilty of naiveté. You always want to see the best in people. I've spent so much of my life only seeing the worst in people, especially my parents."

"Julian—"

"No, let me finish. I never put myself in their place. I was angry with my father for his cowardice in abandoning us—and I had that all wrong, didn't I?—and angry with my mother for her blindness to the truth. But perhaps she was simply ignorant because my father wanted to keep her that way, to keep her safe and protected as much as he could."

"But what was your mother supposed to do to avoid having lots of children? She couldn't change her situation or deny your father his marital rights. And it would have shamed your father to show the world that they were close to penniless."

He sighed. "I know. And I know now how protective he felt toward her. He would never want to deny her children, even though there are ways to do so."

Other ways, she wondered? She almost asked him to tell her those methods, so that she would be prepared when they were together the next time. Or would he be hurt, thinking she planned to have a future lover? She couldn't imagine sharing herself so intimately with another man.

Did that mean she was falling in love with him?

The thought stunned her, and she didn't want to believe it could be true. She didn't want to think of it, or the implications for her future.

"Julian, don't you see that you've been living in a past you can't change? I'm trying to spend my life looking to the future."

"You don't think your love of adventure is a response to everything in your past?"

"Of course it is. Our pasts formed us both. But I can't live my life regretting everything that happened to me. I certainly won't regret what we've shared. Will you? Oh, wait, you never regret a decision once it's made."

She expected him to be angry at this conversation, but all he did was laugh and hold her tighter.

She fell asleep, but not for long, as a terrible nightmare about illness controlled her mind; only this time she wasn't the victim. It was Julian. Somehow he'd caught the Stubbes boy's illness, and he was the one coughing terribly, struggling to breathe. No remedy worked. His body became still, his breathing failed, and she started to scream—

Rebecca came awake on a gasp, realizing that tears streamed down her face. Her breathing was ragged, and although she told herself it was simply a dream, she couldn't shake the terror.

Julian murmured her name and tightened his hold on her. He was so blessedly cool to the touch, his breathing so calm, so even.

But still, she was caught up in the world of fright.

He came up on his elbow, and with gentle fingers combed her hair off her damp forehead. "What is it? You were tossing and turning."

"That little boy could have died," she found herself whispering. "I never imagined how a parent feels at such a time, the utter helplessness and fear. And what if it were you who'd been sick?"

He kissed her forehead. "So now you think of me as your child?"

"Do not make light of this! My whole adult life I've wanted to live in the way denied to me in childhood. But it wasn't just about me, and I never saw that. My illnesses caused my family terrible grief. I never understood the heartache and paralyzing fear. I thought of myself as some pure heroine of a book, without flaws, trod upon and rising from the ashes. But tonight, when I looked into Mrs. Stubbes's face, I could see my mother, and for the first time knew her fear. How self-centered was that?"

"All children are self-centered," he murmured, stroking her hair. "You only experienced one side of your childhood, as we all do. Surely we've learned as we've grown."

She nodded and tried to calm herself, but the dream was yet within her. Julian was well, thank God, but soon she meant to voluntarily part from him. Could she do it?

Whatever her questions of the night before, she knew one truth now: she was definitely in love with Julian. It seemed so . . . bizarre, almost frightening. She had never imagined such a thing for herself, and now suddenly she wanted to share a future with him?

But how could she give up striving to have a different sort of life? She didn't even know if he was capable of meeting her halfway, or if he even wanted to.

What would he think if she told him? Would he want to protect her even more? But . . . he'd already said she would be at his side when he went to the chief constable.

Or would he be awkward with her confession of love, because he might not feel the same way? Everything was so much more complicated now. She would have to give this new revelation more thought.

But her uncertainty did not stop her from snuggling back into his arms or accepting his comfort in the cold night.

She loved him.

Chapter 22

Well before dawn, Julian arose to dress. Dazed with sleep, Rebecca lay still for a moment, listening to the sounds of him moving in the dark, imagining what she couldn't see.

She loved him.

She groaned and rolled over.

"You should remain in bed—or in the hay—another hour," he said. "You worked hard last night. Everyone would understand. We won't leave until after the morning chores regardless. Mr. Stubbes has offered us a ride to the next village."

"And do you think Mrs. Stubbes yet lies abed?"

"But the sick child is her own."

"And I can help her. You meet Mr. Stubbes. I'll go into the house and see what I can do."

She felt his hands cup her face, and to her surprise, he gave her a fierce kiss. Would he call her "darling" again?

"Very well," he said. "I'll see you at breakfast."

And then he went down the ladder. She dressed slowly in the dark, feeling bemused and uncertain, then almost giddy with pleasure. Could a man like Julian fall in love with someone like her? Would it matter to her if he couldn't feel the same way? Or was he still fixated on his logical search for a wife?

She suppressed a groan even as she slowly descended the ladder. Outside she headed for the privy, fog swirling about her skirts in the early grayness of pre-dawn.

After she'd finished, she'd only taken two steps before someone grabbed her from behind, one hand on her mouth, another around her waist.

For a shocked moment she didn't even struggle, unable to believe what was happening.

And then she kicked back hard and connected with a shin.

"Fool, help me pick her up," the man hissed to someone else behind her.

Though she kicked frantically, another man caught her feet and lifted her off the ground so they could carry her between them.

She could say nothing, do nothing, although she continued to flail. But she was helpless.

They were Windebank's men, of course. She didn't need to see their faces to know that. Did they have Julian already? Would they hurt the helpless Stubbes family?

They were breathing harshly as they continued to carry her. It seemed to go on forever, but at last, looming out of the fog, she saw a black carriage.

Good God, hadn't she just wished for one to ride in?

The man carrying her feet reached to open the door, and she was able to kick him hard in the stomach. He let out a "whoof" of pain, but that didn't stop the two of them from throwing her onto the carriage floor.

She scrambled up to her hands and knees and felt the carriage rocking as one of them got in behind her. He shoved hard on her hips and she sprawled face-first onto the dirty floor.

The carriage jerked into motion.

Coming up onto her knees, she backed up against the far wall. Dawn had broken, and now she could see the face of the man holding her, the same face she'd confronted in a London carriage at the start of this fiasco.

He grabbed her by the front of her gown and shoved her backward onto the far bench. Wincing as her elbow slammed into the wooden seat, she pushed herself up into a sitting position.

"Where's the diamond?" he demanded.

"I don't have it."

"We'll see about that."

And then came the most humiliating moments of her life. Though she fought him and flailed, she was helpless to stop the vulgar way he searched her body, touching every part of her, even patting the length of her drawers, as if she'd sewn a hidden pocket.

He lingered too long at her breasts and between

her thighs, and for the first time she felt true terror. She was alone with him and he could do anything he wanted to her.

But at last he sat back on the far bench, and she pulled her skirts tight against her thighs as if to shield herself.

"I told you I didn't have it," she said, striving for bravery, but only hearing the quivering in her voice that matched the trembling in her limbs.

He shrugged. "Don't matter. Your bloke'll come for ye soon enough, and he'll have to hand the jewel over, or watch ye suffer."

Though it was difficult to swallow, and her eyes pricked with tears, Rebecca forced herself to hold his gaze with one of contempt.

After several hours of work, Julian and Mr. Stubbes entered the farmhouse, both of them freshly washed in cold well water. Mrs. Stubbes looked up from the table, where she and the children had been setting out plates and cups.

Julian could see the ill little boy propped up on the small bed near the hearth. He was well enough to look upset that he had to stay in bed, and that made Julian feel much better.

He grinned at Mrs. Stubbes. "Your husband tells me that your son slept well after the coughin' fit."

She nodded. "Thanks to yer wife, Mr. Hill. I felt terrible keepin' ye both awake on the night before yer long journey. Glad I am that she was able to sleep longer this morn."

His smile faded. "Sleep longer? We arose at the same time. She's not here with you?"

Mrs. Stubbes looked confused even as she shook her head. "No, I have not yet seen her. Perhaps she went back to the hayloft."

His stomach twisted with the first feelings of fear, true fear, that kind that was like sour nausea, panic, and desperation all rolled into one. He had never felt such a thing in his life. Perspiration broke out on his brow, in the palms of his hands.

"Would she have gone for a walk?" Mr. Stubbes asked.

Julian shook his head. "Would you please help me search for her?" he asked the farmer.

But he knew this was only a formality, something he had to do. Windebank's men had taken her, and might have several hours lead on him.

Rebecca, he thought, fierce with mourning and anger and guilt. They had been tracked down once, why had he not seen that it could happen again? Why hadn't he kept her with him every moment?

He hadn't protected her. He'd spent his entire life meticulously accounting for every outcome, building his reputation as a man who never made mistakes—who'd been determined never to be like his father.

And when it counted, when Rebecca's safety was at stake, he'd miscalculated. The only thing that granted him any kind of relief was knowing that his uncle wanted the Scandalous Lady—why else kidnap Rebecca? Windebank knew that Julian would follow wherever she was taken, and now Windebank had someone to use against him.

A diamond wasn't worth a person's life; Julian would gladly hand it over if he could have Rebecca back safe and sound. But he suspected it wouldn't be that easy, for his uncle obviously believed the jewel worth killing for. And Windebank must assume that both Julian and Rebecca knew his identity as the man behind the original theft, and now several murders.

It made Windebank desperate and dangerous.

Julian and Mr. Stubbes searched every outbuilding and the nearby grounds, even down by the river, in case she'd gone for a walk. But Julian didn't see any imprints of a woman's boots, and knew she hadn't been swept away by a river current.

Through it all, Mr. Stubbes watched him too closely. When they arrived back at the barn, Julian went up in the hayloft without a word, threw everything into his portmanteau, then climbed back down.

Mr. Stubbes stood looking at him, hands on his hips. "Ye seem to know what's happened to yer wife."

"I do. I thought I was protecting her, but I was wrong."

"Ye're leavin'."

"I know where they've taken her."

The farmer's sandy brows rose. "'Tis a kidnappin', then?"

Julian nodded.

"Yer wife and you were runnin' from it?"

It was only partially the truth, but Julian nodded again.

Mr. Stubbes narrowed his eyes and spoke softly. "Yer accent has changed, along with yer manner . . . milord."

Julian said nothing.

"Let me help ye," the farmer said earnestly.

"No. This is too dangerous. They won't hurt her; they're only trying to lure me to them. Forgive my words, but you mean nothing to them, and they might do worse to you."

"How will you follow them?"

Julian hesitated.

"Then take one of me horses."

"But you're plowing—"

"I can get by with one for several weeks. And I trust ye to return it sooner than that."

"I will, Stubbes, you have my promise."

Together they saddled the gelding, placing only the items Julian thought he would most need in one of the saddlebags. Mrs. Stubbes brought out a parcel of food and several stoppered bottles, packing them in the other bag. She watched Julian with a bit of awe now, so he assumed her husband must have told her of their conversation.

Julian swung up into the saddle. Several of the children stood at the door of the barn, watching him solemnly.

He looked down at the Stubbeses and gave them a grim smile. "I'll return as soon as I'm able with your horse."

"And with good news," Mrs. Stubbes insisted. "God keep you and yer wife safe, milord."

"Thank you—for everything."

Turning the animal about, he walked it past the children toward the barnyard before breaking into a trot. He wished desperately to gallop all the way, but there were still many miles to go, and he needed to conserve the horse's strength.

He needed to conserve his own strength as well. Now that Windebank had Rebecca, Julian's plan to go to the chief constable had to be abandoned. That would be the surest way to get her killed.

The thought of a life without her at his side seemed barren and worthless. She would be his wife; she was already his love. Somehow he would convince her that they were meant to be together.

But first he would have to face his uncle—and all his henchmen—and find a way to rescue Rebecca without any bloodshed.

Especially hers.

Chapter 23

Rebecca didn't know what she'd expected in the way of a prison. It certainly wasn't a scholarly library, complete with leather chairs, several writing desks, and wall after wall of books.

She was grateful to be alone after spending much of the day in a coach with a man who watched her as if he were only waiting for the signal to begin the feast.

What had Windebank promised him? she wondered with a shudder. To distract herself, she walked to the windows that overlooked a spacious park. It was a tranquil scene, with rolling fields of hedgerows and, off in the distance, plowed farmlands ready for the seed.

And yet it was her prison. She'd been dragged through empty halls and deposited here, with the door locked behind her. Her screams for help had been ignored. The windows wouldn't open—she'd already checked—so all she could do was wait, listen to her stomach growl, and try not to panic.

That was easier said than accomplished. This was

like a nightmare to her, helpless and dependent once
again after so many years of feeling that way. She
thought she'd triumphed over such emotions, but now
Windebank had so easily resurrected the fear. The walls
might be sumptuous, but they were closing in on her.
She stared at the poker in the stand beside the fireplace
and thought that if she were desperate enough, she
would use it as a weapon.

At last she heard the lock click. She faced the door,
head held high. An older man entered alone and shut
the door behind him. He was a lean man, with dark hair
graying at his temples, hollowed cheeks in front of mut-
tonchop sideburns, and bright, intelligent eyes.

"You must be Miss Leland," he said calmly, as if
she'd come for tea with his wife.

"And you must be Mr. Windebank."

His mouth lifted in half a smile. "My nephew spoke
of me, I see."

There was no point in pretending that she didn't
know why she was here. "It's hard not to speak of you,
when you've killed people." She couldn't believe such
words had come out of her mouth. But cowardly snivel-
ing would not impress such a man. All she could hope
to do was keep him interested in conversing with her
and pray for Julian's swift—and safe—arrival.

The lines in his forehead deepened. "To the point, I
see. A brave girl. Perhaps foolish."

She shrugged. "After what you've already done, I

know there's no point begging you to release me. You're using me to lure Julian. He won't be foolish enough to come alone."

"Of course he will, my dear. He knows what's at stake."

"My life?" She laughed. "I am a nuisance to him, sir. I forced him to bring me along. He's probably relieved he doesn't have to take care of me."

Windebank's smile was only faintly amused. "We both know that Parkhurst is a man who takes his responsibilities very seriously. He will not rest until you're safe. He'll do whatever is necessary," he added, his voice deepening.

She wanted to shiver again, but she held herself still.

"Although by the look of the clothing you're wearing," he sniffed distastefully, "he has not done his usual masterful job."

"Believe what you will. If you're so certain of success, then tell me the truth. Was this all worth it?" she asked, spreading her arms wide. "Chasing us, murdering people, all for a piece of jewelry?"

"You minimize its value, Miss Leland."

"Then tell me of it, sir. You've had it for much of these past ten years, I believe?"

He didn't answer, but the lines at his eyes deepened with amusement.

"You didn't sell it," she continued, "so for you, its

value was not in money. Ownership, then? Your wife couldn't wear it in public. Did you want it simply because your brother-in-law had it?"

"A foolish reason, Miss Leland."

She cocked her head, then casually sat down in a wingback chair. "Your wife had it, I believe, before she gave it away."

"It was stolen," he said, frost in his voice.

It was her turn to smile in what she hoped was a pitying manner. And when he stiffened, she thought she might have scored a point against him.

"Stolen? That's not what I hear, sir, and you heard it, too, directly from Roger Eastfield's mouth."

"He was lying."

"Or perhaps your wife was lying."

He took a step toward her, eyes blazing, then stopped. "She would never give the Scandalous Lady away. She prized it too much."

"So you stole it for her all those years ago."

"The earl didn't need it," Windebank said dismissively. "He wasn't going to sell it, although he damn well needed the money. Florence needed it more."

"She couldn't wear it," Rebecca protested.

"But she did, every single day. No one else had to see it as long as she knew it was there."

Rebecca felt a growing uneasiness. "That does not seem like normal behavior."

"It was normal—for her. The jewel calmed her. Once

I realized it had come to light again, I needed it back. *She* needed it back."

He was looking toward the window now, not at her, as if he were seeing something else.

"Why?" she asked softly.

At first, she didn't think he would answer. He wore a pensive, sad expression, and when at last he began to speak, it was as if the words simply tumbled out of him, unstoppable.

"It was damnedest thing how that diamond calmed her," he said. He sank down in a chair as if his bones were suddenly too heavy to hold up. "As long as she could touch it beneath the bodice of her gown, she seemed to be able to control herself." He grimaced. "My wife's mental state has not been healthy in a very long time."

Rebecca said nothing, only leaned forward with true interest.

"For many years she was capable of seeming quite normal. When we first married, I only noticed the occasional irrationality, and I put it down to the moods of the female mind."

Rebecca gritted her teeth to keep from telling him what she thought of that ridiculous idea.

"Gradually she began to tell me about the voices." His mouth twisted. "We had two children by then, and I believe her confession was a way to make certain I protected them from her. Because she wasn't herself when the voices told her what to do."

He didn't elaborate, and suddenly she didn't want all the details. Their sad life did not give him license to take the lives of others. But she did feel sorry for their children.

"From the moment the maharajah gave the diamond to Parkhurst, she was fixated on it. Finally I had to take it for her. It gave her a measure of peace that we all desperately needed."

"And it took away the peace of another family."

"Through events over which I had no control," he said tightly, not elaborating.

She must have made a sound of disgust, for suddenly he was standing over her, eyes blazing, and it took everything in her not to shrink back. Why hadn't she grabbed the poker when she had the chance?

"She threatened to kill herself if she didn't have it!" Windebank said. "Why keep the damned thing locked away, when it could give my family peace? If only Parkhurst hadn't—" He broke off, mastering his voice as he slowly straightened. "But that is the past."

Did he mean the old earl's death? Or was he referring to Julian?

"And what of the future?" she asked softly.

He regarded her with calm eyes. "I must protect my family, of course. My children need their mother."

"Their mother who might hurt them?" she asked with sarcasm.

"She'll soon have the diamond back, and things will be better." He sounded as if he were trying to convince himself of that. "But we can't safely hide it with the two of you aware of it."

She remained silent, although the need to shout, "What will you do to us?" fairly burst from her throat.

"It will look like an accident, of course," he continued, answering her silent question.

"Like the old earl's death?"

His eyes widened thoughtfully. "I imagine you heard that from Julian. His father always was a coward. No, my plan for the two of you is necessary. You disappeared from London quite suddenly, the both of you. It will be easy to make everyone see that you left together. Because of course, there are innocent witnesses who will swear to it."

She thought of the groom from the Madingley stables who'd driven with her to the train station. He'd noticed Julian following her. And there were countless train passengers, especially the Seymour family, who'd seen them together. Windebank was building an intricate lie using the truth as his foundation.

"You stopped here on your way north," he continued, watching her closely now. "You could hardly keep your excitement at bay. The two of you were off to Gretna Green for a romantic elopement."

He paused as if he expected her to say something, but she didn't, because the story worked so very well.

"Then a tragedy occurred," he said.

He didn't meet her eyes.

"Your rented carriage caught fire just as you were leaving the stables. We thought perhaps it was a faulty lantern, but we'll never know the truth. The two of you were terribly burned and couldn't be saved."

She let disgust and fury lance her gaze. "That will never work. Julian knows what you're capable of."

"Julian doesn't know how many men I have on the grounds waiting for him." He rose to his feet and calmly adjusted his waistcoat. "I'll let you know when he arrives."

And then he left her to her mounting fears.

Several hours passed, judging by the clock on the mantel and the setting sun. No one brought Rebecca food or water, and she knew Windebank didn't think it necessary to feed a person he meant to kill. She looked out the window, wringing her hands as darkness descended. Was Julian out there even now?

For the tenth time, she tried to open the window, but it had been nailed shut from the outside. Should she break one of the panes to escape, risk injuring herself? Then how would she be of any help to Julian?

Suddenly, she saw a flash of light out in the darkness, then heard a faint popping sound. Gunfire? She covered her mouth in horror. Would they truly fire at Julian, when Windebank wanted him alive to recover the jewel?

Once again she heard the door open behind her. She whirled, intending to tell Windebank what she thought about the stupid thieves he'd hired, but she came up short in surprise. A woman closed the door and leaned against it, taking her measure. Rebecca did the same. She was perhaps a decade or so older than Rebecca, with fine lines webbing out from her eyes and bracketing her mouth. Her blond hair was fashionably swept up, and her gown stylish enough to mark her as the mistress of the house.

The unstable mistress of the house. Did her husband know she was fraternizing with the prisoner?

"You must be Lady Florence Windebank," Rebecca said in a friendly manner.

"Do you have my necklace?"

No subtlety there. "I don't."

"But you wore it. I can tell."

Both her eyes and her voice were sly. Then she looked off to the side, head cocked, as if she were listening to someone else. Windebank had mentioned voices. What a sad way to live.

"I borrowed the necklace briefly, but now it's back with its rightful owner."

"It's called the Scandalous Lady. It's mine."

Should she simply go along with whatever the woman said?

Then Rebecca thought she could hear gunfire again in the distance, and she shuddered. No, this was her only opportunity to help Julian by creating a distraction.

"Do you remember Roger Eastfield?" Rebecca asked.

"He painted my picture." She spun about gracefully. "He said I looked lovely on canvas."

"I am sure you did, but I am his most recent model. I wore the Scandalous Lady in his painting."

Lady Florence's eyes narrowed the more Rebecca spoke.

"He said he never had a more beautiful model than me," Rebecca continued, smiling.

"That's not true," Lady Florence insisted. "Tell her it's not true."

The last was said as an aside to whomever she thought was listening. Rebecca felt a twinge of guilt for using the poor woman's illness—but Windebank was having his men shoot at Julian.

"Of course it's true," Rebecca continued, stalking toward the woman. "I am younger, prettier. The jewel hung between my breasts—Roger particularly liked that."

"Stop it!" Lady Florence screeched, hands fisted at her sides, body stiff.

"Lord Parkhurst is giving it to me, you know."

"You'll never have it!"

"Why? You didn't want it—you gave it away."

Letting loose a scream, Lady Florence rushed her, hands extended like claws. Rebecca put the sofa between them, then raced toward the door. It didn't open—obviously someone was in the hall, and had locked it behind the woman.

Even better, Rebecca realized. She let Lady Florence come at her, and the two of them slammed hard into the door. Rebecca belted out a good long scream, dodging the woman's gouging fingers, grappling with her wrists. She tried not to hurt Lady Florence, but the woman wouldn't be restrained.

Someone pounded on the door at her back and yelled, but she couldn't make out the words over Lady Florence's screeching. Rebecca flung herself sideways, dragging her opponent, and the door burst open.

"Stop this!" said a man's voice.

But it wasn't Windebank. It was the thief from the carriage. Rebecca bellowed again, and he scooped her off the floor, arm about her waist, holding her back against his front. But this only left her vulnerable to Lady Florence's attack. The woman came at her again, and Rebecca was forced to kick out.

Where was Windebank, and how long could she keep this up?

Chapter 24

In the darkness, Julian made it at last to the front entrance of the manor. He crouched beside a bush that grew just to the right of the door, breathing heavily. He felt his upper arm, but he didn't think it was bleeding too badly. A bullet had grazed him, but he'd made the man pay. It was a shame the pistol was already discharged, for he could have used it. He still carried it, hoping it would at least intimidate someone into making a mistake.

They were yet hunting him in the park, but he'd managed to elude them although several had fired at him. Windebank hadn't chosen them for their aim, thank God.

He reached for the front door and found it unlocked. Of course, Windebank wanted him to come in. There were probably other men inside, just waiting for him. They'd be covering every entrance, so there was no point in trying another.

Still crouched low, he opened the door and swung it

wide. Nothing happened. He dived in, rolling sideways, and slammed into a sideboard with a grunt. Still, nothing happened. The front hall was as richly decorated as he remembered, with doors off it leading into a drawing room and a music room. A hallway veered to the left, to another wing of the house.

And at last he heard something coming from that hallway. Could it be shouts? Bent low, he ran for the arched entrance and paused, peering around the corner. Most of the doors were closed, but at the end of the hall, where a library took up much of the wing, the door was open. The shouting came from within.

He could imagine that Windebank wouldn't want the servants as an audience for his crimes, but where were all the guards?

"Enough!"

This time the distant shout was a bellow, and he recognized his uncle's voice. Crouching low, Julian ran down the corridor, his back tense as he expected one of the doors to open. But that never happened. He reached the wall outside the library and kept his back to it, useless pistol in hand.

"Florence, she's goading you!" Windebank cried.

Julian could hear a grunt or two, then the crash of a vase.

"Go get help!" Windebank commanded.

Julian tensed, and a man rushed out. Julian used the pistol to hit him hard on the back of the head, and he went down. He recognized the face of the man who'd been following them since London, and felt a momentary satisfaction to see him lying still and bleeding.

Whatever was going on inside the library, no one seemed to have noticed what Julian had done. He dragged the man into the next room, a parlor, and locked him inside.

Back in the corridor, he could distinctly hear Windebank's exasperated voice. "Florence, the girl was only trying to get my attention. She's lying. Eastfield would never prefer her over you."

"I'm not lying."

Julian closed his eyes in relief as he heard Rebecca's calm voice. Much as he'd told himself that his uncle wouldn't dare harm her until he had the diamond, there was always a small part of him that had lived in fear.

Lady Florence gave an unearthly scream that made his hackles rise. It was the perfect distraction. He burst into the room. He only had a moment to take in the scene—Rebecca on the far side of the sofa, Windebank between her and the door, trying to calm his wife, who paced and muttered with agitation. Then Windebank saw him and pulled a dueling pistol from his coat pocket. He backed up against a desk, away from the door, but instead of aiming at Julian, he lined Rebecca up in his sights.

"No!" Julian shouted.

"You know I'll kill her now that you're here," Windebank said in a harried voice. "Put the pistol down and then don't move." His eyes darted about the room, lingering on his wife and Julian before returning to Rebecca.

Julian slowly lowered the pistol to the floor, then straightened. "I'm not moving. The same can't be said of your wife."

Lady Florence continued to pace and mutter, as if she had no idea that anything had changed. Julian could have easily reached her, but that would only give Windebank an excuse to shoot.

What was wrong with Lady Florence? Her face wore a confused, almost devious expression, and her lips continued to move rapidly as she carried on a silent conversation with herself. She didn't look at Julian or her husband, only darted the occasional furious glance at Rebecca. Now Julian remembered his uncle's words when he'd lingered in the hall, that Rebecca had been goading Lady Florence about Roger Eastfield. Was Lady Florence at the center of Windebank's lust for the diamond? And had it somehow unhinged her mind?

Windebank's eyes darted back and forth between the two women. His wife must be distracting him. Julian glanced at Rebecca, and she met his gaze, her expression serene. He wished he could somehow show her how grateful he was that she was alive, that she'd used her wits to help him—that he loved her, and she wasn't to take another risk again.

"Just give the diamond to me and the worst will be over," Windebank said, the gun unmoving on Rebecca.

"I don't believe you," Julian said.

"He plans to kill us," Rebecca said.

Windebank grimaced. "You don't have a choice. I have the gun."

"And two possible targets, but only one bullet. You shoot Rebecca, and you know I'll kill you—and if your wife happens to get in my way, it will be your fault."

Again, Windebank's gaze shot to Lady Florence. "None of this is her fault."

"Why not?"

"Because her mind is not what it once was."

"It's been this way for a long time," Rebecca said. "They've become masters at hiding it. Somehow the diamond helps keep her sane."

Windebank groaned. "Parkhurst wasn't selling it, the fool. It was just kept locked away. But around my wife's neck, it protected my family, kept our children safe, kept her mind whole."

"That's a lot to ask of a pretty rock," Julian said.

"It was for everyone's good!" Windebank insisted.

"But not for my father," Julian countered, suddenly furious. "You killed him to keep your secret."

"It was an accident!"

"I don't believe it! Or else you'd have spoken up from the beginning. It wasn't a suicide, it wasn't a hunting accident."

Windebank hesitated, and for a moment, the pistol trembled in his hand. "The old fool came at me, though he had ten years on me and I had a gun."

"He wanted what was his."

"Florence was his *sister*! But he still wouldn't listen. We struggled and the gun just . . . went off."

Julian almost winced as he imagined his father's death. He wondered if it were true, that Windebank's first murder was accidental rather than deliberate. He saw Rebecca's look of sympathy, but Lady Florence paid no attention to the recitation of her husband's sins. She mumbled and gestured and paced, providing a better distraction than Julian ever could.

"While you had the Scandalous Lady for years," Julian said, "you watched my father's memory soiled and you said nothing."

"He tarnished his own image long before he received the jewel!"

And that could not be disputed. But it was beside the point. If Julian's father would have lived, he could have helped turn around his own estate, would have made better choices—but that was the past, and since nothing could be changed, Julian wouldn't live there anymore.

The gun sagged a bit, but then Windebank steadied it on Rebecca. "I just wanted the diamond back. I was so desperate that it might help again, before my children could see and fear what their mother was hiding. I saw it on Miss Leland's neck at a ball, and then I saw it in the painting. I knew Eastfield was back in London. I had to know the truth of what he'd done with it. I could hardly go to Miss Leland's family and demand answers."

"I know Roger admitted to you that he'd had an affair with your wife, and that she'd given him the jewel."

"He lied!" Windebank shouted.

He was sweating now, his expression frantic. The gun wavered between Rebecca and Julian, for Windebank noticed that Lady Florence had stopped pacing, her body still, although she hadn't yet looked up.

"You tried to keep their affair hidden," Julian said, "tried to keep the jewel, but it didn't help your wife get better, it only led you to murder."

"I didn't mean to!"

"You hit him with a vase!"

"You have no proof of that."

"His mother told us everything before she died."

"If Eastfield would have simply shut up, stopped lying, he'd still be alive. Why did he provoke me that way?" Windebank asked beseechingly of his wife.

She blinked at him.

"Then you had the house burned and killed even more people," Julian said with contempt. "How many people have to die for the Scandalous Lady? It can't bring back my father, I know that. Only honest work resurrected my family, and you can't say that about yourself. You use murder and deception to get what you want."

The gun wobbled again. "It all got out of control. I tried so hard to make everything work perfectly . . . each piece fit together . . ."

Here was a man who thought he could take care of everything, without any help. Julian saw himself in that fixation, and he didn't like what he saw.

Lady Florence began to move again, and not in her frantic pacing mode. She was watching Rebecca, her head tilted thoughtfully. Her husband's gaze kept jerking to her. Julian held still, biding his time.

"I was bored with it, you know," Lady Florence said, her voice almost singsong.

Windebank went tense, but Julian spoke before he could. "Bored with what, Aunt Florence?"

"The Scandalous Lady, of course," she said, wearing a dreamy smile. "What a name for a diamond." She giggled.

"Don't, Florence," Windebank whispered.

Julian caught Rebecca's gaze and tried to instill patience in her, so that she did nothing foolish. She gave a small shrug, as if she didn't know what he wanted.

Windebank was focused on his wife now, the gun pointed somewhere between Rebecca and Julian.

"I was bored, bored, bored," Lady Florence said, playing with a strand of her hair that had fallen to her shoulder. "I gave it to Roger when I was done sleeping with him."

Windebank looked appalled, as if it had never occurred to him that Eastfield wasn't lying about the affair. Had he really trusted his unstable wife—or had he only wanted desperately to believe in her after all the crimes he'd committed for her?

Windebank had turned so much of his attention to his wife that even the gun now wavered on her more than on Rebecca and Julian.

And Rebecca had begun to move, taking tiny infrequent steps toward the hearth. Julian barely looked at her, afraid to draw Windebank's attention her way. Julian was beside himself with fury and fear, wondering what foolish risk she might take.

"Florence, be quiet," Windebank said, sounding as if it took everything in him to keep his quivering voice calm. "None of that is true. You know I'd do anything for you. Julian has the Scandalous Lady. I'll have it for you soon. But you must keep quiet, so I can deal with this."

Julian wasn't certain she was listening, for her eyes seemed unfocused, and she wore a faint smile.

"You're a fool, Harold," Lady Florence said.

Windebank gaped at her.

"You couldn't make me happy, and I never loved you anyway."

His grimace full of torment and fury, Windebank took a step toward his wife.

The rest happened so quickly that Julian could barely process it. He saw Rebecca lunge for the fireplace poker.

Windebank caught the movement and whirled around, gun raised. Julian felt too slow as he dived at Windebank. He was too far away, he wouldn't be able to stop him—

And then Lady Florence slammed a heavy vase onto her husband's head. The gun went off as Julian landed hard at Windebank's feet, rolling, looking for Rebecca in fear. Thankfully, she was still standing as the mirror above the fireplace shattered behind her. Windebank crumpled and lay still right in front of Julian.

Julian vaulted to his feet, and then his arms were around Rebecca. They clung to each other for only a brief moment.

She whispered, "Your aunt."

Still keeping an arm about Rebecca, he turned to see Lady Florence standing over her husband's inert form, wringing her hands.

"There's so much blood," she said, giving them a dazed look. "How did this happen?"

Julian went to her. "Sit down with Miss Leland, Aunt Florence, while I see to Uncle Harold."

She nodded and let Rebecca lead her to a sofa on the other side of the room. "Do I know you, Miss Leland?"

"Surely you know my mother, Lady Rosa Leland?"

"Oh, yes, of course!"

Feeling like Lady Florence was sane for the moment, Julian dropped to his knees beside his uncle. Blood flowed from a wound in his head, making a small puddle in the carpet. But he was still breathing. Julian looked about for something to staunch the blood and settled on a silk table runner from a nearby coffee table and wrapped it about Windebank's head.

The door slammed open and several people burst in. Julian grabbed the pistol just in case, but kept it low. Some of his tension eased when he saw that several of the newcomers were women, dressed as servants.

A man came forward. "We heard the gunshot. Who are you, sir? Has Mr. Windebank been shot?"

"I hit him with the vase," Lady Florence volunteered.

And since the broken vase was in pieces all about Windebank, the man seemed to ratchet back his anxiety, although he turned a confused gaze on Julian.

"I am Dudley, the butler. And you are . . ." His voice died away as Julian rose to his feet. "Lord Parkhurst! Forgive me for not recognizing you immediately."

"Send for the physician, Dudley."

The butler turned to speak to one of the footmen hanging back near the door.

"Station several men outside the nearest parlor," Julian continued. "I've imprisoned a man there who will need to be questioned by the authorities. Send for a groomsman from the stable. I'll need him to go for Chief Constable Bulmer in Lincoln."

"We have a local sheriff, my lord."

"This matter is above him. Tell everyone to be wary outside. There were men shooting at me out in the park, and although I believe they've mostly run off, you will find two bodies. Don't let them be moved until the constable gives such an order."

Dudley's eyes widened almost imperceptibly, but he only nodded.

"Is there someone to care for Lady Florence?" Julian asked.

One of the women stepped forward. "I am Lady Florence's nurse, my lord."

"Is there a place where she can be kept under guard, where she won't hurt anyone?"

"Of course, my lord," she said. She looked down wide-eyed at her employer. "Mr. Windebank told all of us to stay away, that he had business colleagues in here. I never would have left her, but he insisted that—"

"This isn't your fault," Julian said firmly. "Take good care of my aunt."

Biting her lip, she nodded. "My lord, keep Mr. Windebank's wound bound tightly until the doctor arrives."

"Thank you."

Then she went to speak softly to Lady Florence. Julian watched his aunt be led away.

Rebecca came to him, and he put an arm around her.

"You're bleeding!" she said, staring at his arm.

"It's of little consequence, although I promise to have the doctor look at it."

"Thank you. Can we speak in private?" she asked softly.

He nodded. "Dudley, stay with your master until the doctor arrives. I will be right back. If you need me, shout. I'll be able to hear."

Several doors down, Julian led Rebecca into a morning room with tall windows that overlooked the park. A feminine desk was placed strategically so that its occupant had a beautiful view. But now the sun had set, and the grounds looked shadowed and menacing.

Rebecca touched the empty desk gently. "Do you think she was ever able to sit here, like a normal woman?"

"Yes, she did. I've seen it myself. Rebecca . . ." To his embarrassment, his voice broke. "When I knew he'd taken you, when I thought of the terrible danger you were in because I hadn't kept you safe—"

"No, Julian, no. Your uncle is a criminal. It wasn't your fault."

She came to him then, folding her arms about him. They clung to each other for several long minutes. He was so grateful for her safety that he was shaking with it.

"When you went for that poker—"

"When you dived at him—"

They broke off, giving each other shaky smiles.

Rebecca took a deep breath. "I'll tell the constable everything, Julian, all about how I came by the diamond."

He frowned. "What are you saying?"

"I want to help clear your father's name, even if it means exposing the painting to the world. I don't care about notoriety." She reached up to cup his face. "I care about you. I want to help heal the terrible things in your past."

Julian simply stared at her, stunned that she would sacrifice herself and her reputation—for him. He gave her a gentle smile, "No, Rebecca, I can't let you do that."

"But—"

"Just listen to me." He rubbed his hands up and down her back as he held her to him. "Remember, Chief Constable Bulmer is a friend of mine. He'll be able to ensure that the official saga of the jewel won't mention your painting. It won't matter, after all, since we can connect the jewel to my uncle, and through my aunt to Eastfield, and eventually to the poor man's death. Promise me you won't mention the painting at all."

When she hesitated, he gave her a little shake.

"Rebecca, you've done so much to help me. Let me protect you in this—let me protect your family."

At last she nodded. "If you're certain it won't harm the case against your uncle."

"I'm certain."

Someone knocked on the door.

"I'll be out in a moment," Julian called. He kissed her, and although he meant it to be swift, they lingered together until at last he lifted his head. "I have to go. The doctor will be arriving soon, and then the constable. But promise me we can speak again later. There's so much to say."

Her eyes widened even as she nodded. "Tonight, then, Julian. I'll be waiting."

After Rebecca bathed and dressed in a nightgown and dressing robe, she felt clean and new. Servants had brought her a tray for a late supper, but she hadn't wanted to eat it alone.

There was a soft knock on her door, and she opened it so that Julian could slip in. He, too, was wearing clean clothing, trousers and a shirt that didn't quite fit his broad shoulders. He was clean-shaven, and when he smiled, he looked more like an earl than the common traveler she'd spent the last days with. She almost missed his rakish, dangerous look.

But then it was back as he looked down her body. She spread her arms and twirled for him.

"Am I presentable?" she asked.

"No, which is how I like it." He sighed. "You know what I want to do to you in that bed, but there are things we must discuss first."

Nodding, she took his hand and led him over to the small table where she'd placed the tray. They sat down and she uncovered it to find selections of cold meats and bread, a pudding and fresh fruit.

But Julian didn't begin to eat, only sat back wearily in his chair and looked at her.

"How is your uncle?" she asked.

He shrugged. "The doctor doesn't think he'll ever do much of anything again, though he doesn't think he's in danger of dying at the moment."

"I don't understand."

"It's as if his mind was damaged from the blow. He'll be bedridden for as long as he lives. The doctor doesn't even know if he's conscious, if he even understands what's going on around him. He can't quite explain how my aunt was able to do such damage."

Rebecca sighed. "It's his own prison, in a sense."

He gave a half-smile. "You have the right of it."

"What about your aunt?"

"She doesn't seem to remember much of it. Now that I know the extent of her illness, she'll be under constant guard in her own wing of the house." He parted the loose collar of his shirt and lifted the Scandalous Lady. "I'll have a paste copy of this made to soothe her. It's a shame my uncle never had the same thought."

He looked so contemplative and sad that Rebecca went to him, sitting in his lap and looping her arms gently about his neck.

"At least everything went as you expected with the constable," she said.

"You answered his questions well. He was impressed.

He agreed to try to keep the details of the crime as quiet as possible to protect my young cousins, but with the newspapers desperate for scandal, there's only so much that can be done."

She nodded, letting her fingers touch the hair at the back of his neck. "Is it my turn to speak now?"

He gave a faint smile. "Always."

"I am so grateful to you."

She saw his gathering frown, and she covered his mouth before he could speak.

"No, listen to me. You cannot blame yourself for the events your uncle set in motion, so you must promise me you'll stop. Promise?"

At last he nodded, and when he began to nibble her fingers, she smiled and pulled her hand away.

"I'm not finished, so you must stop distracting me. I am very grateful to you because you trusted me to help you capture your uncle. You could have sent me home— you would have found the money—but you treated me as a partner. That doesn't happen much between men and women. You've changed, you know."

He rolled his eyes.

"The old Julian would have done everything himself."

"I did try."

"You did, but you compromised. And I appreciate it more than you know."

"Can I speak now?"

He adjusted her so that she faced him from her place on his knees.

She grinned. "Very well."

Solemnly, he said, "I love you, Rebecca."

Her smile faded and she found herself blinking, stunned and suddenly near to tears. "Julian—"

"No, just hear me out." He touched her hair, her arms, then took her hands. "I love your bravery and optimism, your joyful sense of adventure."

She couldn't let this go on. "Oh please, I've been nothing but childish, as if life is one big amusement meant for me. I had no idea how much anger I still had inside me. I'm not owed something special because of what was dealt to me in childhood. So many others have it worse than I did, and yet they bravely go on with their lives."

"And so did you, my darling." He squeezed her hands. "You helped me to see that my own anger was strangling me. I *was* living in the past by not forgiving. You were right about everything. Let me make it right. I love you, Rebecca," he said again, and there was joy in his deep voice. "Would you consider marrying me even though I'll never hunt artifacts in Egypt or explore a jungle?"

She smiled as the first tear rolled down her cheek.

With his thumb, he wiped it away, then spoke softly. "Live for the future with me, darling. You can't live like you might die. You're too strong for that."

She had to sniff then, as even more tears made an appearance. "Oh, Julian, I love you, too."

He took a deep breath and let it out slowly, as if he'd still had doubts.

"I'll marry you," she said. "And I'll even settle for a honeymoon in Italy—for now."

He laughed and hugged her tight, then lifted his head to look into her face. "Even the great paintings of Europe can't hold a candle to you."

She watched him cautiously. "Does that mean you still care about the wager with your friends over the painting?"

He reached beneath his shirt, lifted the Scandalous Lady over his head and draped it about hers. "I've already won the best prize of all, your hand in marriage. Although it will be interesting to hear how Peter and Leo do against such worthy opponents as Elizabeth and Susanna."

"We'll just have to discover the details later," she said, leaning close until her forehead brushed his. "We have far better things to do with our time."

Their eyes met, his grin faded, and his lips met hers. She had her entire life to explore the natural wonder that was Julian Delane.

Epilogue

Lady Rosa Leland did not understand the change that had come over her daughter, Rebecca, since her return from visiting Aunt Rianette. Her cheeks were flushed with too much sun, and she seemed to be humming all the time, kissing her parents at odd times of the day and for no reason at all. She'd come so willingly to the ball this evening, that Lady Rosa almost asked if someone else had replaced her daughter.

Rebecca, who'd taken much care with her toilette for hours during the day, left her mother's side immediately after being announced. She seemed to be looking for someone, and Lady Rosa watched her move through the crowd and nod at friends without stopping to speak.

"Who is she looking for?"

Lady Rosa glanced at her husband, seeing the confusion in the hazel eyes that so matched their daughter's. "I wish I knew."

While they watched, Rebecca came to a stop, her face in profile, her expression full of joy as she lifted a hand in a slight wave.

Gaping, they followed her line of sight, and there stood the Earl of Parkhurst, who seldom came to the London balls. Lady Rosa gasped, expecting him to coolly nod, or perhaps look as confused as she felt. What was Rebecca thinking? Lady Rosa had seen his distant reaction to her matchmaking efforts just a few weeks before.

Instead, the earl paused on catching sight of Rebecca, and the smile that came over his face softened his harsh features.

"Will you look at that," Randolph said in a low voice.

The two young people moved toward each other, ignoring everyone they passed. Rebecca took his arm, he leaned over to say something to her, and then they both crossed the ballroom and went out the terrace door.

"Good lord!" Randolph said.

Lady Rosa could barely find speech. And then she saw Lady Parkhurst, the earl's mother, who'd obviously seen the same thing they had, for her mouth was agape in wonder. The two women looked at each other, and Lady Rosa experienced the first moment of hope.

She turned to Randolph. "Do you think—?"

But he was already striding away, frowning, heading for the terrace.

"Oh dear, Randolph, perhaps we should wait," she called, walking quickly to keep up with him.

"Not after what I saw."

Lady Parkhurst joined them, breathless, just before they left the ballroom. "Professor Leland, please do not look so concerned. My son would never do anything to harm a young woman's reputation."

"There's a first time for everything," Randolph said firmly.

He pushed open the French doors, and the two women followed helplessly in his wake. There in the shadows, not far from the door, they found Rebecca kissing Lord Parkhurst, held tight in his embrace. Lady Rosa gasped.

The young people broke their kiss, but Lord Parkhurst boldly kept his arm around Rebecca. Couldn't he see the way Randolph stared at him?

Rebecca's eyes widened. "You're all here! How perfect!"

At least that made Randolph pause, Lady Rosa thought in relief. Her husband folded his arms across his chest, waiting.

Lord Parkhurst grinned—and never had Lady Rosa seen such a happy expression on such a sober young man.

"Professor Leland," Lord Parkhurst said, "I was planning to speak with you in the morning, but now I won't have to wait."

Lady Rosa took her husband's arm even as Lady Parkhurst began to sniffle happy tears.

Rebecca giggled. "He's asked me to marry him, Mama. And he's given me this as an engagement present."

Around her neck was a heart-shaped diamond that glittered in the torchlight. Lady Rosa felt confused, for she thought the jewel looked familiar. Didn't her daughter already have something like it?

But then Lady Parkhurst cried out. "Julian! Is it really . . . ?" She covered her mouth, as if she could not continue to speak.

Julian nodded. "It is, Mother, and I promise to tell you the story of its recovery. But not now." He looked back at Professor Leland. "I'm in love with your daughter, sir. I would like your permission to marry her."

Lady Rosa felt tears sting her eyes at the way Rebecca looked at the earl with such adoration and love. She'd worried that Rebecca would never find a man she could respect, one who'd love her in return.

"This is rather sudden," Randolph said.

But Lady Rosa knew by his voice that he was already pleased with this turn of events.

The earl cleared his throat. "I didn't know how much I would miss your daughter until we were parted."

Rebecca blushed as she looked up at Lord Parkhurst, still held against his side, her hand resting with a bit too much familiarity on his chest.

Oh dear, Lady Rosa thought, biting her lip, trying not to blush. Lady Parkhurst was already blushing enough for both of them.

Then the two older women looked into each other's eyes and shared the unspoken relief of mothers who know that their work is done, that at last their children have found love.